Spark

T.D. WILSON

authorHOUSE®

AuthorHouse™
1663 Liberty Drive
Bloomington, IN 47403
www.authorhouse.com
Phone: 1 (800) 839-8640

Published by AuthorHouse 07/02/2018

ISBN: 978-1-5462-4870-5 (sc)
ISBN: 978-1-5462-4869-9 (e)

Library of Congress Control Number: 2018907506

Contents

Chapter 1

"Hey, Lucas! Check this out!"

Lucas Tavera looked up from his phone. His friend Ty Bridwell was jogging up to him, beaming with excitement. His other friend, Nate Wissen, had been looking over Lucas' shoulder. Nate was blond and lanky, while Ty was dark-haired and stood barely five feet tall. The boys loitered under a live oak tree outside Fulmore Middle School while Lucas played a game on his phone. Even in the early morning, the temperature hovered around 95 degrees in the September sun.

"What is it?" Lucas asked, barely looking up.

"The *Justice League 3* trailer came out," he said, holding out his phone, and Lucas paused his game to take it. In a rapidly-edited fight scene, Batman and the Flash fought alongside each other against a crew of mooks. The Flash dashed away, too fast to be more than a red blur, with lightning trailing behind him.

"Looks cool, I guess," Lucas shrugged, handing back the phone.

"Ty, look what Lucas is playing," Nate said with a sideways nod.

Ty craned to look at the screen of Lucas' iPhone. It was brand-new, a gift for his twelfth birthday back in June.

"Is that *Limbo*?" Ty asked, frowning.

"Yeah," Lucas nodded, tapping and swiping with his thumbs. A diminutive character ran forward and jumped across a monochromatic background.

"I don't understand that game," Ty said, wrinkling his nose. "And the puzzles are stupid."

"You just have to work at it for a little while," Lucas said without looking up.

"You should have seen how quick he solved the last one," Nate added.

"But there's no explanation," Ty protested. "It doesn't tell you anything about what's going on. Not even the rules."

"It's simple," Lucas shrugged. "Just solve the puzzles till you rescue the girl. This is the new version; it's way better."

Ty rolled his eyes.

"You want to try?"

"No, I told you--it's stupid."

"Hey, watch out," Nate warned, tapping Lucas' shoulder.

Lucas looked in the direction Nate was staring; a few yards up the sidewalk, a group of eighth-graders strolled toward them, talking and hooting loudly. Music boomed loudly from someone's portable speaker. In the front was Val Espinoza, a Hispanic boy whose hair was shaved into a mohawk; to his left walked Darren Jones and Howard Mays, two former football players who were kicked off the team after they were suspended for setting off fireworks in the boy's locker room last year while the PE class was inside changing; to his right was Brick Wallach, the biggest and scariest-looking of the whole group, a full foot taller than the rest. The only reason he wasn't the leader was because Val was smarter and meaner, bullying the others into submission though he was only half their size.

As they swaggered past, Lucas, Nate and Ty fell quiet and lowered their eyes. Lucas kept his hands down, concealing his phone at his side. Any of them - Val, Howard, Darren or Brick - would go out of their way to steal a brand-new phone like his, but they all kept moving without a sideways glance, heading toward the backside of the school.

"That was close," Nate sighed.

"Yeah," Lucas nodded, watching the group walk off.

The first bell rang to allow the students into school. The two main doors opened, and the kids who had been waiting outside began to stream through them while a couple of assistant principals stood by the stairs to mitigate rowdiness. Lucas picked up his backpack and walked with Nate and Ty, following the others through the wide double doors. Inside, a large hallway split into five smaller ones, leading the students past grumpy-looking teachers, display cases of decades-old trophies, and wrinkled posters. Lucas' first period class was located in the 200 wing, the first left, so he wove through the slow-moving crowd, making his way to the left side of the main hallway.

"Text you later, guys," he called over the noise to Nate and Ty, who had classes on the other side. They waved and then went on their way.

Some commotion behind him caused Lucas to look up from the game he was still playing as he walked. He looked back over the heads of the crowd of kids and saw Val, Howard, and Darren now entering the building, jostling and shoving the other students in the midst of the over-crowded hallway. An assistant principal yelled at them to settle down and keep moving, but Val sneered at her over his shoulder. She glared at him, but moved on up the hallway. Lucas kept to the wall, which was already crowded with several other students, as he slowly got closer and closer to his classroom. Music came on over the intercom to signal the last minute of passing period, and Lucas could finally see his classroom door. He came upon two eighth-graders making goo-goo eyes at each other, and his progress slowed as he waited awkwardly for a chance to move around them.

Then something big slammed into him. The two goo-goo-eyed kids yelped and jumped out of the way, and Lucas was pinned helplessly to the wall by something incredibly strong.

"Oops," the thing chuckled. It was Brick. Brick had a thick, jutting forehead, acne scars and red stubble across his chin. His breath stank as his face leaned much too close. He had both of Lucas' wrists locked in a vice-like grip with one hand while the other dug into his pocket. Lucas felt his phone slip away.

"Hey!" he exclaimed angrily but Brick pushed him into the wall harder with all of his one hundred and seventy pounds, his forearm pressed against Lucas' upper back, squeezing the air from his lungs.

"Brick!" a hall monitor called from down the quickly-emptying hall.

Brick immediately released Lucas, but kept one firm hand on his shoulder. He grinned at the hall monitor.

"Hi, Mr. Stevens; we're just playing around," he said, patting Lucas' back. "Right, Lucas?"

Lucas couldn't respond. He was out of breath, and his chest hurt from being crushed against the wall.

"Come on, get to class, or you're both going to be late," Mr. Stevens said dully, ushering them along.

"Yes, sir," Brick nodded, and trotted off. Mr. Stevens walked past Lucas without a second glance, following a group of kids who were just leaving the bathrooms.

Lucas picked up his backpack from the floor, then took several steps toward the classroom before patting the pockets of his jeans. He froze as panic set in.

Where's my phone? He wondered, but he already knew: Brick had stolen it. Of *course* he stole it. Lucas' heart sank and he kicked the wall. What was he supposed to do now?

"Lucas, hurry up!" Mr. Sanchez, his first period teacher, called irritably from the doorway.

Lucas realized he was alone in the hall. He hurried into the classroom and took his seat in the second row from the back. Mr. Sanchez shut the door and instructed everyone to answer the warm-up question in their notebooks. Lucas fished his notebook and a pencil from his backpack, but he was too distracted to write anything. He *needed* to get his phone back. All he could think about were the horrible things Brick might do with it. Was he going to give it to Val? Were they going to sell it? Would he take disgusting pictures with it first? To make matters worse, he knew how furious his mother would be. He would be grounded for life.

Mr. Sanchez called for everyone to put down their pencils, then he walked the aisles, inspecting the students' responses to the writing prompt. He strolled past Lucas' desk and shook his head.

"Disappointing," he sighed. "You need to stop daydreaming, Lucas. You can do better work than this."

Lucas put his head in his hands, drawing a deep breath. He did his best to focus for the rest of class, but Mr Sanchez's lectures on Texas History were anything but interesting. He bit his lip and squirmed impatiently. Finally, the bell rang and he squeezed his way past the other students and shot out the door. His next class was Art with Mrs. Grint, the only class he had with both Nate and Ty together. He jogged through the hallways to her classroom and met them outside. As he arrived, Nate gave him a nod and reached out his hand for their secret handshake, and Lucas quickly complied.

"That was sloppy," Nate chided. "Hey, Lucas, do you have notes for Mrs. Cunningham's class I can borrow? I'm going to fail that quiz today for sure."

"What? Yes, but - guys, listen, I need to tell you something." he said breathlessly. "Brick stole my phone. He pinned me in the hallway and took it."

Both boys winced.

"Damn... that sucks," Nate remarked.

"Yeah, my mom is gonna be pissed," Lucas grumbled. "What am I supposed to do?"

"Pray, I guess," Nate replied with a shrug.

"I'm sorry, man," Ty shook his head. "That phone is gone."

"No, I have to get it back," Lucas said angrily. "I'll just report him to the office. Maybe the police can get it back."

Nate burst out laughing.

"What?" Lucas said. "I'm gonna tell the office that he took it."

Nate and Ty shared an incredulous look.

"Yeah, and maybe the tooth fairy will leave you money for a new phone under your pillow," Ty retorted.

"You know Val once got in a fight with his girlfriend's step-dad and got away with it?" Nate said.

"So?"

"*And* he's in a fight club!"

"That's not true," Lucas said flatly.

"Maybe not, but he can still make you regret you ever snitched on one of his guys," Ty said seriously. "He definitely would, if you reported him. You remember the fireworks in the locker room?"

"Yes, we were all there," Lucas said impatiently.

"Scared the shit out of me," Nate added.

"Remember what happened to Matt after he told the office?" Ty said.

"I heard he changed schools," Nate remarked.

"Yeah, 'cause Val broke his nose," Ty said. "But nobody can prove it."

"Guys, that's exactly what I'm talking about!" Lucas exclaimed. "They pull this shit all the time, and sooner or later, somebody's gotta stand up to them."

"I'd rather it be later," Ty muttered.

"Me too," Nate agreed.

"Either way, I have to get my phone back or I'm gonna be in deep trouble."

"Well, good luck with that," Nate said, shaking his head. "When are you gonna go?"

"Right now," Lucas said with more conviction than he really felt.

The music started over the intercom, signaling one minute remaining in passing period. The hallways were nearly empty now.

"Lucas," Ty said seriously. "He'll come find you once he finds out. And if he doesn't, Brick, Howard, or Darren will. You know what they do to snitches."

"Well, it's either I tell on them, or I tell my mom that I lost the brand-new phone she gave me for my birthday."

"I guess it depends on whether you want to live to see your next birthday or be grounded until then," Nate said dryly.

"Thanks for the moral support, guys," Lucas said, rolling his eyes. With that, he approached the art teacher where she stood outside the classroom door, monitoring the halls.

"Mrs. Grint?"

She turned to him with sharp, inquisitive eyes. "Yes?"

"May I go to the office?" he asked.

"No," she said. "There are no trips to the office allowed during class time. You know that."

"Please," Lucas begged. "It's important."

Mrs. Grint shook her head dismissively. "Go to your seat; class is about to start."

Abashed, he found his desk and hung his backpack on the back of his chair. He sat at the end of the row, with Ty to his right and Nate across the aisle on his left.

"What happened?" Ty asked in a whisper.

"She said I couldn't go," Lucas whispered back.

"What now?"

"Give me a minute," he said. "I'll think of something."

A red-haired girl entered the classroom just as the bell rang, and took her place two seats down from Lucas at the long table. It was Lily Hofstetter, a girl who lived on his street, though he'd never spoken to her. She brushed her long braid aside and glanced over her shoulder, then waved shyly at him. He managed a smile and waved back, but he had to remain focused on the problem at hand.

As Mrs. Grint directed the class to construct their clay models, Lucas tried to pay attention, but was largely unsuccessful. The clay was a shapeless lump in front of him; he was supposed to mold it into anything that came to mind. Beside him, Ty worked fastidiously on his model of a human face. At least, he guessed it was a human face; it had a long nose and wide, eerily detailed eyes. Nate was squishing his clay between his fingers. Lucas knew that he was just trying to look busy, because he had absolutely no inspiration for a sculpture and hated art. Lucas did too, and was dying to leave. He raised his hand and asked to go to the bathroom; to his delight, Mrs Grint said yes. He picked up the orange bathroom pass by the door and then walked quickly up the hall. He kept his eyes forward as he passed a hall monitor, then hooked a left beyond the bathrooms and made for the office, almost jogging now.

The receptionist looked up as he entered, but he kept moving, his eyes down. She called out to him.

"Hey! Whoa, where are you going?" she asked.

"I need to talk to my counselor," he said breathlessly, pausing in his step.

She blinked with hesitation, then said, "Oh, okay. Well, go ahead."

He walked down the corridor to the counselors' offices; there was one for each grade level. Lucas stopped in front of Mrs. Boyd's office. She was the counselor for seventh-graders. Inside, Mrs. Boyd was typing something into her computer, her eyes down. He knocked on the door and she looked up and then, with an expression of surprise, reached over and opened it.

"Lucas, how are you?" she asked with a concerned frown. "Are you okay?"

"Uh, yeah," he said hesitantly. "I need to talk to you."

"Of course," she answered. "Take a seat."

He stepped into the tiny office. Mrs. Boyd's desk took up nearly a third of the limited space with bookshelves, a file cabinet, and an armchair crowding the rest. She pointed to the red-and-gold upholstered chair and Lucas sat down.

"What's going on?"

"Brick Wallach stole my phone," he said.

"When did this happen?" she asked.

"This morning," he replied. "Before first period."

"In school?"

"Yes, in the 200 wing hallway."

"Well, I'll have to get a campus police officer," Mrs. Boyd said. "Do you want to talk to one?"

Lucas nodded, swallowing hard. "Yes, I do."

Mrs. Boyd stepped past him and poked her head out the door. She hailed the police officer standing by the door of the discipline office, and he came over. She spoke quietly to to the officer before he came in.

"What happened?" he asked, taking a small notebook from his front pocket.

Lucas described how Brick had surprised him, pinning him against the wall while he took his money and phone. He gave every possible detail he could remember about his iPhone.

"Anything else?" the officer asked.

"That's all," he answered. His hands were tucked under his legs to hide their quavering.

"Alright, well if you think of anything, just give me a call," the officer said, handing Lucas a card. Lucas nodded again, then placed the card in his pocket.

The officer left, closing the door behind him. Mrs. Boyd returned to her desk, swiveling her chair to face him.

"Well, is there anything else you need?" she asked.

"I don't know," Lucas admitted. "I guess I'm a little afraid that if Brick finds out I ratted on him, he'll beat me up. Everybody says that's what happens."

"They're sending the hall monitors to look for him right now," Mrs. Boyd said. "I can't tell you what will happen, but if he is caught with your phone, it is likely that Brick will end up in A-School, at least for a few days." Either way, he won't be able to bother you again. We will make sure of that."

Lucas nodded, though he didn't feel much better.

"Have you tried talking to them?" Mrs. Boyd asked.

"To them? Val and the rest?" Lucas said incredulously.

"Yes, communication can accomplish more than you think. This isn't the first time you've had issues with them. If they are bothering you, you should express very clearly that you want them to stop."

Lucas raised his eyebrows.

"And that would help?" he asked doubtfully.

"It may keep things from escalating. They're human, too; with some effort, you may get them to listen."

"Okay, well... thanks," he said.

He stood, then opened the door and left the office. Bathroom pass in hand, he walked down the corridor and back to the main hallway where his art classroom was located. Mrs. Grint was not pleased that he had been gone so long, and told him that he couldn't leave class again to go to the bathroom for the rest of the week. Lucas settled back into his seat and returned to his project, pretending to concentrate on it for the remaining ten minutes of class. When the bell rang, he, Nate, and Ty walked out of class together.

"Hey, where did you go?" Nate asked. "You were 'in the bathroom' for a long time."

"I told my counselor what happened," Lucas replied.

Ty shot him a look. "You mean you actually did it?"

"Yes, I *had* to," Lucas replied. "It's not right that Brick and the others get away with stealing from everyone, and beating up anyone they want to."

"You're gonna get it," Ty said ominously.

"Nah, we'll look out for you," Nate said. "We'll fight 'em all if we have to, although we won't last long."

"Thanks," Lucas said with a grin. "But I think it'll be okay. Mrs. Boyd said they were going to call him into the principal's office right away."

"Let's hope they do," Ty said. "It's about time those guys got what they deserved."

They went to Science class together, then split up for fourth period when Lucas had English, Nate had History, and Ty had Spanish. At lunch, Lucas kept a wary eye out for Brick, but there was no sign of him or any of the others. That should have been comforting, but for an inexplicable reason, it wasn't. He chatted and made small talk with Ty, Nate, and some of his other acquaintances, and even made eye contact with Lily from across the cafeteria, but it was hard not to feel a sense of uneasiness. *They're all in the office being questioned right now*, he reassured himself. He tried to picture Brick crying as Principal Guerrero reamed him. When lunch ended and he walked to Spanish, he noted that he hadn't seen Brick, Val, Howard, or Darren again all day. *They're in the office...*he told himself again. *They're going away to A-school.*

He suddenly spotted Darren ahead of him in the hallway, looking straight at him. Howard appeared, walking beside him, and both were making a beeline for him. Lucas turned around, but there was Val and Brick, waiting. Together, they grabbed Lucas by the shoulders and half-carried, half-shoved him into the boy's bathroom nearby.

With lightning speed, Val slammed his fist into Lucas' face, just beneath his eye. Lucas staggered backward, then crumpled to the floor.

"Heard you snitched," Val said. "Maybe now you'll know better."

"How'd you know?" Lucas croaked, his head spinning.

"Ain't hard to find somebody willing to snitch on a snitch."

Brick, Howard and Darren laughed.

"I just want my phone back, Val," Lucas stammered.

"You mean *this* phone?"

Val produced it from his pocket. "Oh, no, this is *my* phone now. You don't deserve something nice like this, 'cause you're nothing. You're a loser and a freak. But I'm not, so I'm gonna keep it."

He tucked it back into his pants pocket.

Lucas raised his head. His cheek stung, and the entire right side of his face throbbed, but he was angry. Suddenly, he wanted nothing more than to send his own fist flying into Val's smug face. He found himself standing, his heart thumping in his chest.

Val expressed a brief look of surprise as Lucas lunged. Brick responded, plowing forward like a linebacker, his shoulders and head down. Lucas sidestepped, avoiding Brick's freight train-like assault, then evaded Howard's tackle with another quick feint. Now, only Darren remained between him and Val, but his luck had run out. Darren grabbed Lucas in a headlock while he kicked and thrashed. Val smirked, raising his fists. A well-aimed kick connected with Val's stomach, and he sank to the ground, gasping for breath. Darren was clearly surprised, and Lucas felt his grip loosen. He quickly wriggled free and sped out of the bathroom, narrowly escaping another tackle by Howard.

He raced up the hallway, which was empty except for one hall monitor who was slowly ambling in the direction of the bathroom. Passing period was over, and he was now late to class. He made a left, then a right, then knocked frantically on the door of his classroom, and Ms. Serna opened it.

"Mr. Tavera, you're three minutes late," she said sharply.

"Yes, I know," he panted. "Can I come in?"

"No, you have to go get a tardy pass," she snapped.

Lucas paled. He was afraid she'd say that. The last thing he wanted to do now was walk back toward the office and risk running into Val or the others again.

"But, Ms. Serna -" he objected.

She shut the door in his face. He watched through the small window in the door as she resumed teaching, pacing down the floor as students recited their vocabulary terms. *What do I do now?* If he went to the office, and Val was there, Val might do something so dastardly as to accuse him of fighting, and then he would be in trouble with the principal and his mom, once they called her. Or, more likely, Val would just attack him again, regardless of the presence of adults; Val didn't care. He was just that evil. Lucas had heard a rumor that he once stabbed a kid through the hand with a pencil in elementary school, right in front of the teacher. Lucas was really beginning to panic now. He wondered if he should call the cops.

With what? Brick has your phone! he reminded himself.

He couldn't go back to class, and he couldn't risk making it back to the office without running into them again. Where could he go? There was only one other option.

He went quietly a short ways down the hall to the 400 wing girls' bathroom; after listening for any commotion, he determined that it was empty and slipped inside. There was a frosted window high in the far wall, above the last sink. This window had no lock on it, and if the latch was jimmied just right, it would open. He himself had never used it, but he had heard rumors of several kids who had skipped class using it as their escape route.

He tested the sink, then climbed carefully onto it, balancing on its edge to reach the window. The window was screwed shut, but the bolts wriggled in their concrete housing and loosened without much effort. He pushed the window open and peered out. It was about eight feet to the ground, with some shrubbery below. He pushed his backpack through first, then scrambled up onto the ledge and lowered himself down, feet-first. He dropped to the grass, scratching himself on the bushes and snagging his shirt. He pulled free, then scooped up his backpack and ran across the schoolyard. He reached the street and kept running, past houses and a small neighborhood park, and didn't stop until he reached the busy intersection with South Congress Avenue. Then he finally slowed to a walk, breathing hard and sweating profusely in the sweltering Texas sun. *Now what?* He thought. He didn't have much of a plan for what to do now that he was outside. He considered going home; he could watch TV and think of something to say to his mother, and would have a little over seven hours of freedom to enjoy before she came home from work and he had to face his punishment. Or he could walk a few more blocks to the lake and swim. *If you're going to skip class, you might as well go big, right?*

He was contemplating this when he realized with dread that he was being followed. Glancing surreptitiously over his shoulder, he spotted four boys tailing him, about fifty yards back. Brick, Val, Darren, and Howard were behind him, all wearing cold, determined expressions.

Lucas felt a chill in his blood. He picked up his pace, striding past several storefronts and restaurants. When he stopped at a corner, where the crossing signal told him to stop, he looked back. The boys were running now. His heart leapt into his mouth. Without waiting for a walk signal, he dashed across the street. A car screeched to a stop and the driver honked the horn. He sprinted down the sidewalk, weaving between afternoon pedestrians and tourists. He could hear footsteps slapping the pavement behind him and knew the boys were in pursuit. His apartment building was still five blocks away - he would run out of steam well before then. He had to find someplace to hide.

Lucas raced as fast as his feet could carry him to a set of industrial buildings located behind a large grocery store. There were six large, metal-sided buildings set on a cross-street, with stacks of pallets and large machinery in the fenced-in yards. He ran to the farthest one on the end, which had grass poking through cracks in the sidewalk and several overgrown trees. He heard Val shouting his name as he ducked under the padlocked chain on the gate, then ditched his backpack beside a large pile of disassembled pallets. The boys were just behind him now - he could hear them breathing as they ran.

Adrenaline coursed through his body; he thought his heart would hammer out of his chest. He scrambled over broken scraps of wood and ran to the front. The large double doors were chained closed with another giant padlock. Looking around quickly, he spotted a gap in the sheet metal siding. He raced to it and slipped through the gap then quickly scanned his surroundings. Crates stacked more than ten feet high towered in front of a wall to his left. To his right were aisles of what looked like heavy power tools and beyond them, a door with a red "Exit" sign. He thought his chances might be better hiding among the shelves of power tools, then he could simply wait for his pursuers to give up, and walk home.

He heard a screech of metal. Val was suddenly right behind him, squeezing through the gap in the siding. He lunged, and Lucas sprinted for the door with the Exit sign above it, only to slam against it uselessly. The door was locked, and no amount of pounding his shoulder against it could make it budge. The other boys' voices echoed through the warehouse. Val was now inside the building, with Darren and Howard close behind him. Lucas left the door and made for the far corner of the building as Darren and Howard split up, each circling around like wolves closing in on their prey. Val stayed locked on his trail, and was gaining ground. Lucas met another locked door, and his feet dragged. He was tired, and Howard and Darren were converging at his right and left. Brick hung back by the gap they all came through. Lucas turned to face Val, hands raised.

"You win," he panted.

"Yeah, I do," Val said with a smile, drawing closer. "I always win. And I'm going to make sure you never forget it."

"I'm sorry for kicking you," Lucas pleaded. A knot formed in his throat, and his eyes burned with tears. "Please, just let me go."

"Listen to him beg," Val chuckled to the others.

Two of the boys laughed, but Brick remained silent. He looked on, stony-faced. Lucas swallowed down his fear and made a break for it; he shoved past Val, knocking him off balance, and ran for the gap in the metal siding as fast as he could. He thought maybe he could fight past Brick alone and make his escape. He sprinted, straight for him, head down, his breath coming in quick gasps.

Something hard hit his legs, and he stumbled. A wrench clattered on the concrete floor as he hit the ground, badly scraping his hands and knees. Brick seized him by the collar and dragged him to his feet as Val pounced.

Val's fists were a blur as he peppered Lucas' ribs with a flurry of punches, then sent two at his face. His head snapped backward and hit a hollow-sounding wall. Brick released his shirt to throw a few punches of his own, then passed him off to Darren, who, with both hands, propelled Lucas backward into the wall of crates. Then all three boys attacked, trading off; Lucas had no clue who was hitting him at any given time, but he felt every one of their jabs. His ribs cracked, and splintering pain made it impossible to take a breath. He raised his hands to protect his face, but they were easily smacked aside as the boys continued to rain down punches. His eyes swelled to the point that he could barely see, and he tasted hot blood in his mouth. Then his nose burst, and mind-numbing pain exploded across his face. His mouth was full of blood; he was blind and suffocating. The darkness spread to his mind, and he felt himself slipping into unconsciousness.

He came to as the wall behind him rocked, and the blows suddenly stopped. Through the fog, Lucas was vaguely aware that his opponents were running away with fearful yells. *Why are they running?* He thought dimly.

With a groan, then a deafening crash, the wall of crates behind him was giving way. Brick, Darren and Val retreated, looking very small through Lucas' nearly-swollen-shut eyes. He tried to run, too, but something heavy struck him very hard on the head, and he went down. Many, *very* heavy things fell on top of him, several all at once, then one after another, like massive hammers pounding. He could no longer move, and he was drowning in pain. His bones felt like they were on fire. Then he wasn't aware of anything at all.

Chapter 2

SOMETHING WAS BEEPING. OVER AND over again. It reverberated inside Lucas' head like crashing cymbals. He hated the sound, and wished somebody would shut it off. There was noise everywhere… people were talking above him, below him, and in the room next to him. And machines. Machines humming… whirring… beeping. *Machines talking…*

He opened his eyes. The light blazed, so he squeezed them tightly shut again.

"Lucas?" a voice asked.

He opened his eyes again, but just barely. A freckled woman with dark hair sat in a chair next to him. She was in her mid-thirties, but several gray hairs showed and she had faint creases around her eyes and mouth. A long scar showed on her wrist, as well as a thin, faint line on her chin near her mouth.

"Mom?" Lucas rasped. His throat felt like sandpaper.

"Oh my goodness," she said, choking back a sob. "I'm so glad you're awake. How are you feeling?"

"Water," he croaked. His head pounded and his skin crawled like he was covered head to toe in thousands of tiny insects.

His mother, whose name was Leah Tavera, reached over to a pitcher sweating with condensation and poured a glass of water, then put a straw in it. Lucas sipped through the straw and let the cool water coat his tongue and the inside of his mouth. Looking down, he saw that he wore a pale yellow hospital gown; an IV needle was stuck into the back of his hand, and a clasp on his index finger connected to an ECG machine next to him.

"How are you feeling, Lucas?" Leah asked again. Her eyes were red.

"My head hurts," he answered with difficulty. "And I itch. All over."

He wanted to scratch, but his arms were too weak to lift.

"I can ask for some Advil," she said. "And if they can give you some different bed sheets if those are too itchy. Do you remember anything that happened to you?"

Lucas scanned the room through half-open eyes. There was a small table and a chair beside his bed, where his mother sat. To his right was a countertop below a wide window, where sunshine pooled in through a gap between two heavy curtains. The countertop bore a few vases of flowers and cards. A bunch of balloons were tied to the foot of his bed; one read *Get Well Soon* with a picture of a monkey. To his left were big sliding glass doors. Through them, he could see a hospital corridor lined with similar doors where nurses busily came and went. Directly beside his bed was a stand with an IV pouch and the ECG that monitored his heart rate, beeping determinedly.

All of this information was paled by the fact that his skin itched.

"Lucas?"

"Yeah?" he said, looking back at his mother. The creeping, prickling sensation was getting worse. He felt like a horde of insects was crawling over his body. He was also disoriented by small spots of light that kept flashing in his eyes, distracting him.

"Lucas!" Leah said again.

"What?"

"I asked you if you remembered anything," Leah said earnestly.

"I, uh, I remember something falling on me," he said, straining to focus. "Boxes or crates."

He thought a while longer. The process hurt. *What is happening to me?* he thought. *Maybe my head injury was just that bad*, he wondered, and the thought frightened him. *Did I get brain damage?*

"Anything else?" Leah asked.

"I remember Val, Darren and Brick. "They chased me into a warehouse and pushed me into the crates, and then the crates fell on me."

"What were you doing at the warehouse?" she asked.

"Fighting," he admitted. "Brick stole my phone."

His mother nodded, tears in her eyes.

"He called the ambulance after the accident," she said.

"What?" Lucas exclaimed, taken aback.

"He pulled you out, too. You had a terrible concussion. When the ambulance arrived, he was talking to you and told them what happened."

"You mean I was awake?"

"You passed out in the ambulance."

Lucas was astounded. *Brick* saved him? After letting Darren and Val nearly kill him?

"I don't remember any of that," he said.

"You were hit in the head. He's really shaken up about the whole thing," Leah added. "He feels terrible."

"Sure he does," Lucas grumbled.

Then he noticed his hands. They were perfectly fine, except for the IV needle stuck in the back of one. There were no scrapes, scars, or even a bruise. Gingerly, he touched his face. It wasn't swollen; in fact, his skin and nose all felt normal, and he could see perfectly clearly now.

"How long was I asleep?" he asked, amazed.

"Nearly a month," his mother answered.

His mouth dropped open; he couldn't breathe. *A month?*

"The doctor said you must have suffered some brain trauma," she continued. "They couldn't figure out why you stayed passed out for so long. He'll want to talk to you now that you're awake."

Lucas nodded, but couldn't find the words to speak. Leah put a sympathetic arm around him, hugging him tightly.

"Are you okay? I know it's a lot to take in, I'm sorry."

"I'm okay," he said weakly, squirming. "It's just... my skin itches. It itches really bad."

As his heart pounded, the sensation grew worse. His nerves were firing uncontrollably, all over his skin.

"Where?"

"Everywhere!" he exclaimed.

"Lucas," Leah said, a frantic edge in her voice. "I'm going to tell the doctor that you're awake. He'll want to talk to you."

Lucas heard her, but he couldn't respond. His body seemed frozen.

The lights began to grow. Circles of light, like halos, formed around several of the objects in the room, as if they all went suddenly nuclear. His mother's phone and the computer monitors all began to glow brightly - not just from their screens but in all directions, like small suns radiating brilliant, kaleidoscopic colors. Then the walls and ceiling of the room began to glow with an eerie, unearthly blue at first, then with all the colors of the rainbow and more.

A bubbling sensation started in the back of his mind. It grew, spreading in a chain reaction. Like acid dissolving everything in its path - crackling, popping, bursting thoughts decaying the instant they were formed.

"Lucas?" his mother's voice came from somewhere, and sounded panicked.

The light was so bright that it drowned out all shadows; nothing had any recognizable shape anymore. It gained intensity with no sign of slowing down as the pain mounted inside his head, and the itching, prickling sensation increased to the point that it was torturous. He was trapped, immobile, unable to make the pain stop. He was sure he would soon reach a breaking point, like his head would explode at any second...

Then everything went black.

He opened his eyes. The room was very dim, lit only by a desk lamp in the corner and the light through the doors to the hallway. His mother was sleeping in the chair beside with him with her head resting in one hand; a book lay open in her lap and her iPhone lay on the table beside her. Darkness showed outside the window. He tried to lift his head, but it felt too heavy. The room was quiet and still.

Something tickled the top of his head, but he couldn't lift his hand to his face to scratch it. His limbs felt sluggish and heavy. With a great deal of focus, he could raise his arm a few inches off the bed before it flopped back down. His heart beat quickly. He felt afraid that he would pass out again or that whatever triggered the light show in his head would come back.

"Mom?" he said, though it came out like a whisper. His voice was still weak.

His mother didn't move, which was understandable. Lucas knew she couldn't have heard him.

He lifted his hand to touch her shoulder, and it quavered; moving it took his full concentration. He brushed her arm with his fingertips, and she jumped, knocking her phone off the table. It clattered on the floor as she faced him.

"Lucas!" she exclaimed, leaping up from the chair. She touched his face with both her hands.

"What happened?" he coughed.

She kissed his forehead. Lucas saw that her eyes were red from crying.

"You had a seizure after you woke up, and you've had a few more since then."

"How long ago was that?" he asked, dreading the answer.

"Um, it's been a few days," she answered slowly. "I'm going to let the nurse know that you're awake, okay?"

Leah leaned over and hit a button that read, "Nurse's Station." Seconds later, a nurse entered the room. She was an older woman with gray hair tied into a ponytail.

"How long has he been awake?" she asked Leah promptly.

"He just woke up about a minute ago," his mother answered, her voice husky.

"Can you hear me, Lucas?" the nurse asked.

"Yes," he answered.

"How are you feeling?"

"It's hard to move," he said. "My arms and legs feel weird."

"Okay," the nurse nodded. "Anything else?"

He hesitated.

"Like what?"

"Are you thirsty, tired, feeling fuzzy or lightheaded, or hearing anything strange?"

"I'm thirsty. And - "

He paused. The lights were back: glowing, rainbow-colored lights so bright that he had to squint. They appeared suddenly and brightly. The sources of the halos - there was more than one - were somewhere behind his mother's head. He could barely see her face now, but it was evident that both she and the nurse were looking at him. Lucas was afraid that his brain would shut down again, but this time was different. At least he could still speak.

"What else?" the nurse prompted.

Neither of them seemed to notice the strange lights, which meant they were only in his mind, he realized. *That can't be good...* he thought.

"I - I keep seeing lights," he stammered. "Is that normal?"

"Like spots?" the nurse asked.

"No, they're like... halos," he said.

The nurse frowned, wearing a concerned expression, then glanced at something over Lucas' head. He craned his neck, and saw a computer monitor above his bed, slightly to the left. He couldn't see what was on it from this angle, but the nurse studied the screen intently for several seconds.

"Are you seeing them right now?"

"Yes."

"Where?"

"I don't know - all over the place,"

The nurse was still looking at the monitor. She pointed at it with her finger and motioned to Leah to look.

"You see that there?" the nurse said. "That spike in activity?"

Lucas didn't understand what the nurse was talking about. Then the halos of light suddenly vanished.

"Now they're gone," he began to say with relief. For a fraction of a second, everything in his vision was normal, until the computer monitor over his head gained its own halo. It was the only object in the room with one; rays of light emanated from it in all directions in a wide spectrum of colors.

"There it is again," Lucas breathed with astonishment.

The nurse and his mother glanced up at the monitor simultaneously.

If Lucas wasn't so frightened, he would have thought it was beautiful; he had never seen such a variety of color. The light ebbed and flowed in a cascade of rainbows like the *Aurora borealis*. There were tints and shades that he didn't have names for. The light also varied in degrees of intensity: some rays burst out in glaring flashes, while others flickered like a candle, like the whole thing was alive.

"Its coming from this?" she asked, pointing at the monitor.

"Yeah," Lucas nodded, his eyes wide.

Besides the bright glow, he felt a warmth coming from the halo of light. It wasn't like the heat of the campfire, it was... electrical. He raised his hand, suddenly drawn to it. Immediately, he felt a tickle across his fingertips, so he retreated, and the sensation disappeared. Carefully, he moved his hand near the light again and a strange, static buzz crawled over his skin, like thousands of tiny needles all pricking him at once. It was a low, energetic humming that he could feel in his skin and the muscles of his hand. He was in awe. He was *touching* light.

The nurse leaned close, staring into his eyes, and he stopped gaping. The bright halo of light vanished, and the rush that Lucas felt went with it.

"Lucas, are you feeling any dizziness or headaches?" she asked.

"No, I feel fine..." he said. He raised his hand to his face. "It's easier to move now. But I'm still thirsty."

The nurse nodded. "I'll get you some water. Are you still seeing those lights?"

"No, not anymore," he answered.

She handed him a small Dixie cup with some cold water in it. It was barely a mouthful.

"Okay, good. I'm going to call the doctor," she told both of them. "I'll be right back."

Leah came over and sat in the chair beside him. She placed the back of her hand against his forehead.

"Sweetie, are you sure you're okay?" she asked.

"Yeah, I'm fine," he said, but he wasn't sure. Seeing things that weren't there was never a good sign. He sipped the water tentatively.

Outside in the hall, the nurse tapped the screen of her phone. For a brief second, while he was looking at her, an image appeared in his head. It looked like a phone's screen. Specifically, it looked like an iPhone's interface. He saw words, maybe a name, before the image disappeared. The nurse put the phone to her ear, and a buzzing began in Lucas' ears. The sound was tangible; a prickle began on the back of his neck as the buzz continued. He shook his head, trying to clear it. It was loud, like bees were hovering beside his ears. The nurse put the phone to her ear and spoke; words then began to mingle with the crackling, static-like sound. The glow from her screen had enveloped her entire head in an electrified halo.

He marveled, then noticed, through the corner of his eye, that his mother was watching him with a concerned expression on her face. A minute later, a tall man in powder-blue scrubs entered the room. He had neatly combed, salt-and-pepper hair and an amicable smile.

"Hello, Lucas," he said cordially. "I'm Dr. Campbell. How are you feeling?"

"Fine," he answered hoarsely.

The doctor took a penlight from his shirt pocket and shone it into each of Lucas' eyes, causing him briefly to see black, floating spots.

"Do you have a headache or feeling any nausea?" he asked.

"No," Lucas answered, blinking the spots away.

"Any dizziness?"

"No."

"Are you still seeing those lights?"

Lucas hesitated.

"Yes," he said.

"They're like halos?" the doctor asked. He sat in the chair beside the bed and leaned forward.

"Yes. They're made up of different colors, like rainbows."

The doctor nodded.

"What's that computer for?" Lucas asked.

The doctor looked up at the screen, then back at Lucas.

"It's a map of your brain activity," the doctor answered vaguely. "We attached electrodes to your scalp to monitor how your brain behaves, and to make sure there aren't any problems."

Lucas raised his hand to the top of his head. To his surprise, his hair had been shaved off, and his scalp felt rough like sandpaper. He also found wires attached to small metal disks that were stuck to his skin with adhesive.

"Why do you need to monitor my brain?" he asked.

"Because you've had several seizures, and it's important to check for any brain damage. You're on some medicine now to keep the seizures from coming back. Do you see those rainbows all the time, or only sometimes?"

"Only sometimes. They disappear and then reappear again."

The doctor nodded. He spoke to Leah now.

"If the lights keep coming back, I can refer him to an ophthalmologist to see if any damage was done to his cornea," he told her. "But I want to run another MRI to see if there's any swelling that we may have missed. Or maybe some other problems."

"Okay," Leah nodded, her face tight.

"We'll get him prepped and have him ready to go in a few minutes."

The doctor left the room, and Lucas and his mother were alone. Slowly, it dawned on him that they all must have thought he was hallucinating.

Well, he thought, *of course I am. I was hit in the head then spent a month in a coma...*

"I'm going to call your grandmother; she'll want to be here for this," Leah said.

She unlocked her phone and stood up, pacing away from the bed. The halo-like glow appeared again, enveloping her hand. Lucas' breath quickened. He concentrated and felt something in his brain - like a muscle - shift, and the glow disappeared. He shifted it again, and the glow reappeared. So there was something different about his brain after all, he realized, but it was clearly something that he could control. He was evidently able to turn it on and off again. He practiced flexing this muscle, making the glow vanish and then immediately return once more. He began to feel a mixture of relief and confusion. *Why* could he do this, and more importantly... *what* exactly was he doing?

Then the strange image appeared again, and lingered in his mind's eye. It was definitely an iPhone's interface. He saw his mother's iPhone screen inside his head, as clearly as if it were in front of his face. He could see the time (1:24 am), the date (October 19th) and the background setting (a photo of himself blowing out the candles on his twelfth birthday). Lucas was stunned. His mother was a full six feet away her phone facing away from him, yet he could see clearly what was on the screen. In fact, the view from his brain was *better* than any phone screen. The graphics were crystal-clear, and the backlight shimmered with energy and ocean-like depth.

Then the screen he saw inside his head began to change in real time. His mother opened her call history and scrolled upward, and he read each of the names clearly as they went by. She had made several calls within the past 24 hours to only two names, besides his grandmother's: his mother's boss - a man named Danny Clark who owned the corner store where she worked - and the insurance company. His mother selected his grandmother's name, and her picture appeared in Lucas' mind's eye with exceptional clarity. She hit "Call," and then put the phone to her ear. Once more, a buzzing sensation spread across his skin. The glow from the phone spread over Leah's entire head, with tiny jets of multicolored light leaping out. He heard a soft ringing tone. The sound was close, almost as if the source was directly in his ear. It rang twice, and then his grandmother answered.

Hello?

He heard her kind, warm voice as clearly as if she were standing in the room.

"Mom," Leah said. "He woke up again, about twenty minutes ago."

How is he? The relief in his grandmother's voice was unmistakable.

Leah glanced at him over her shoulder before stepping outside the room. Though she stood out in the hall, her lips close to the phone's receiver as she spoke in low tones, her voice remained perfectly audible.

"He seems okay," she said, her voice tight. "He's talkative, and seems to understand what's going on, but… I don't know, something's different. I think the seizures must have done a real number on him. He keeps spacing out, and he says he's seeing lights, like everything is glowing…he seems really out of it, and it worries me. It's like he's not all there anymore…"

Leah faded off, and rubbed her eyes. Lucas felt an ache in his chest, despite the thrill of what was happening. There was silence on the other end for a moment, then his grandmother spoke.

What does the doctor say?

"He wants to do another MRI, to see if something's changed, or maybe the first one missed something. They keep telling me that his brain looks fine, and that as far as the tests show, there's nothing wrong with him."

What about the blood tests? His grandmother asked in a low, solemn voice.

"They're still running those," Leah said with exasperation. "Nobody can tell me anything. I'm… I'm terrified, Mom."

Try to be calm. You've got to keep yourself together. You need to be strong for him. I'll come straight over so you can get some sleep, alright? I can be there in an hour.

"Alright," Leah answered with a slight sniffle.

She hung up, and the glow and the buzzing noise vanished at once. Lucas' head was suddenly clear. She straightened up and appeared to take a deep breath before sliding open the door and returning inside, and her expression brightened the moment she stepped across the threshold.

"How are you feeling?" she asked cheerfully.

"Fine," Lucas answered. "What did Grandma say?"

"She's excited that you're awake," his mother replied. "And she can't wait to come see you. She's coming tonight, just to give you a hug."

Lucas studied his mother's face.

"I can't wait, either," he said. "What else did she say?"

"She asked what kind of cookies you want her to bring."

He felt a chill. He knew her answer was false. Leah sat down in the chair beside him with a soft smile, but Lucas was reeling. Why would she lie?

"Is that okay?" he asked in a quiet voice. "Will the doctor let me have cookies?"

She seemed to think for a moment.

"I don't know. Maybe not before your MRI."

The deep ache returned to his chest.

"I'm scared, Mom," he said, and she covered his hand with hers.

"It'll be okay," she told him. "You have nothing to worry about. It's only a test to make sure they didn't miss anything."

"Is there something wrong with my brain?"

She looked at him, her expression soft, but he could see the fear in her eyes.

"They're not sure," she admitted. "Something might have hurt it in the accident."

"I'm sorry," he said thickly.

"About what?"

"About the accident."

"Don't be, sweetheart," she said. "I'm just relieved that you're here, and you're alive. It wasn't your fault."

"But if I hadn't left school, it might not have ever happened at all. Val and the others wouldn't have followed me, they wouldn't have beat me up, and I wouldn't be here."

"Maybe, but it doesn't matter right now," she replied, shaking her head. "Let's just focus on getting you better, so we can go home."

The gray-haired nurse slid open the door and entered, a syringe in hand.

"Alright, we're ready for you," she said.

She used a cotton ball to swab the inside of his arm, then raised the syringe and tapped the side of it. She slid the needle into his skin, and he felt the sharp sting of pain.

"What's that?" he asked nervously.

"It's a contrast fluid," she answered robotically. "It's to help us see the picture of your brain better."

"Oh," Lucas replied, watching the liquid disappear into his vein.

He heard a whisper close to his ear, and he turned his head to look at his mother. She was standing at the foot of the bed, watching the nurse work with a serious look. Her lips were tight, but the whisper continued. *Where is it coming from?* He wondered. Then a cacophony erupted, like a stadium filled for a concert. Thousands upon thousands of voices, music, a loud applause, and a deep-throated roar all echoed in his ears, building and building until the noise filled his head with one long, piercing shriek.

Then silence.

"Lucas?"

A muffled voice reached him through the thick blanket of nothingness.

"Lucas!"

"What?" he found himself saying.

His mother was standing in front of him with the nurse, both looking concerned.

"Are you okay?" she asked.

"Yes."

"What happened?" the nurse asked.

"It got really loud all of a sudden," he answered, shaken. "And now it's quiet."

Lucas put both his hands over his ears. Aside from the repetitive, insistent beeping of the ECG machine, all was relatively quiet. He felt dazed from the sudden onslaught, then absence, of noise.

The nurse placed the back of her hand against his forehead. Her brow furrowed.

"It's gone now?" she asked.

"Yeah, I'm fine," he lied. "I'm okay."

"Alright," the nurse said. "Let's get going, then."

Lucas felt nothing but indescribable terror.

Chapter 3

THE NURSE UNHOOKED HIM FROM the ECG machine, and a couple of strong-looking men in pale blue scrubs entered the room. They raised the side rails, then began to wheel Lucas' bed away from the wall, out the door, and down the corridor. The nurse pushed the IV stand along beside him, and his mother walked briskly on his other side, her hand on the gurney's railing. They took an elevator down to the first floor, and then traveled to another wing of the hospital.

Lucas attempted to distract himself by watching the various doctors, nurses and other adults that passed by. If they had a phone on their person, and nearly all of them did, his brain alerted him with the appearance of a bright halo and a tickling sensation along his spine. The halos were visible around the owner's hand if they were holding the phone, or around the pocket where the phone was located. Those that were talking on their phone carried a halo that wrapped around their entire head, or sometimes around their whole upper body. He practiced turning the halos on and off, with great success. When he wanted them to, they disappeared entirely, and when he focused, and willed it so, they reappeared again. He also found that, when he focused on a person's phone, he saw everything that the user did. He could read their texts or emails, see the name of the person they were talking on the phone with, or, in the case of one individual, be spectator to a game of Solitaire.

This isn't a hallucination, he thought. *This is me; my brain is doing this.*

He was fascinated, and all his other senses felt electrified. His excitement was short-lived, however, because he and his entourage had arrived at a tall room with wide windows on the left side from the door, and a long, narrow tube in the center, dominating the room with its presence. There was a low hum filling the air. From the moment he was rolled into the room, he felt a strong tingling cover him from head to toe. He had an enormous urge to scratch all over.

"Alright, we're going to lift you onto the table now," one of the orderlies said.

"I want to go back," Lucas told them, fighting panic.

"It'll be okay," the nurse said. "This won't take long."

She unhooked him from the IV stand, then the two men lifted him from the bed together and laid him on the table that stuck out from the long tube. The hum grew louder.

"I don't want to go in there," he insisted.

"We can sedate him if he's claustrophobic," the nurse said to Leah.

"He's not claustrophobic," she said, watching Lucas.

"Mom, I don't need to go in there," he pleaded. "I'm fine, I can control it now. It's okay."

The hum was so loud that he barely heard his mother's response.

"It's okay, sweetie," Leah said gently. "It will be quick."

"Your mom can talk to you the whole time," the nurse said. "And there's a microphone in there, so you can talk to her, too."

Lucas didn't respond. The itchy, crawly feeling subsided, but only for a moment. The nurse, his mother and the orderlies all left the room, then his mother reappeared on the other side of the window with a couple of men who sat on computer screens. Leah stopped directly behind one of them, her arms crossed and her forehead creased with worry.

The machine came to life. A nebula of colors burst from the machine and spun with hurricane speed. The hum rose to a deafening roar, coupled with searing pain that reached deep into his bones. He screamed and thrashed as if he was on fire. Blisters rose across his skin as the heat swelled, then he was blinded by the maelstrom of swirling, spinning light.

Then darkness swallowed him.

Lucas awoke back in his quiet, dimly lit hospital room. The ECG machine beeped, and liquid dripped from the IV bag on the bed beside him. His mother stood to his right, talking to someone. Lucas recognized his grandmother, seated in the large chair. She was a small woman with the same dark hair worn in a long braid as Leah, his mother, though her face bore many more wrinkles and her hair was heavily streaked with silver. An immigrant from Mexico, she spoke English with a thick Spanish accent. Her name was Maria, and when she smiled, the wrinkles bunched at the corners of her eyes. She wasn't smiling now; she and Leah were speaking in low, serious tones. Neither of them had noticed that he was awake.

"His body is full of metal," his mother said in Spanish. Her voice was low, and sounded constricted.

Lucas closed his eyes and pretended to be asleep. He listened intently, barely daring to breath.

"They said that the mass is surrounding his spinal cord," Leah continued quietly. "Somehow they missed it in the first MRI. If it was a tumor, he wouldn't be able to walk, or even move. This is… something different."

"Do they have any idea what the stuff is?" Maria asked.

"Not a clue. They don't even have tests for this kind of thing. They know it's some kind of metal because of his reaction to the MRI this time around. It's spread everywhere, and they have no clue how it could have gotten there, or how they missed it the first time."

"Oh, *mi Dios*," Maria breathed.

"It's just one thing after another," Leah said, her voice catching. "First head trauma, then a coma and seizures, now metal in his blood and a mass in his spinal cord. I mean, what's going on?

"Calm down, Leah," Maria whispered warningly.

"I'm trying, but I'm at my wit's end. This is exactly what I spent his entire life dreading, and now it's happening. It's my worst nightmare."

"Stay calm," Maria said again. "You don't know that."

Leah's voice broke.

"Look at him; you can't tell me it's not happening right now… that this isn't what we were most afraid of."

Maria said nothing.

Lucas could barely contain himself. His heart began to race, and the ECG's beeping sped up. He sensed Leah moving closer, so he opened his eyes. He pretended to be dazed, and yawned as if he had just woken up.

"Hey," he said sleepily. He rolled his head. "Hi, Grandma."

She smiled, and stood to hug him as best as she could reach. She was very small in stature and Lucas was lying in a tall bed.

"How are you feeling?" she said gently.

He quickly ran a test. He focused on his mother's phone, which rested on the side table. A glow appeared, floating above the phone's surface, and he could see the image of her lock screen floating in his mind. Everything seemed the same, much to his dismay.

"I'm okay," he said slowly. "What happened?"

"You had a reaction, so they had to stop the MRI scan," Leah answered.

"Oh," he said. "Did they find anything in my brain?"

She shook her head. Her face was completely unreadable.

"The doctor said they'll just have to try something else. But everything is fine."

Why is she lying? Lucas wondered silently, bewildered and angry. Was it really *that* bad?

"What about the lights?" he asked, doing his best to contain his feelings. "Do they know anything about that?"

"Not yet," she said, stroking his hair. "But they do know that everything is going to be fine. They're working hard to make sure that you can go home soon."

Lucas nodded, his jaw set. His mother obviously knew something more about what was happening to him than she was saying. What did she mean, that this is what she had been dreading? Did she know that something like this could happen? Lucas was bursting with questions that he was too bewildered to ask. Why wouldn't she just tell him the truth?

"I'm hungry," he said. "Can I eat anything?"

"I'll ask," Leah said, straightening up. She left the room and disappeared up the hall.

Maria quietly sat back in the chair. He thought about asking her what she knew, but had a feeling he wouldn't get very far. She simply stood there saying nothing the entire conversation.

"Your hair is growing back," she remarked sweetly.

Lucas ran his hand over his scalp. The sticky leads that had monitored his brain were no longer there, and the top of his head was covered in thick, short bristles.

"How long have I been here?" he asked.

"All told? Since September 21st, and it's October 27th now. So about five weeks."

He let out a breath. He had been unconscious for another eight days. His fingers traveled down to the base of his skull, where Leah said the mass, or tumor, was. He didn't feel anything unusual. Then something else occurred to him.

"If I was hit in the head during the accident, why don't I have a scar?" he asked.

Maria looked up from her phone and pursed her lips.

"The doctor thinks it was only blunt force," she said. "It knocked you out, but didn't break the skin."

That didn't seem right. He rubbed the back of his head pensively, feeling the contours of his skull. His mother returned, accompanied by a young nurse. He saw that she brought a tray with food on it. There was a bowl with some broth, and crackers in a little plastic wrapper.

"Let's take those leads off," the nurse said. "You don't need them right now."

The nurse set the tray on the countertop, then approached the bed. She removed the ECG lead from his index finger, and pressed a few buttons to stop the alarming beep that resulted. Then she took his hand and a cotton ball and gently slid the long needle from where it was inserted in the back of his hand. All three watched as she applied the cotton ball.

"Hold that there," she instructed. He obeyed, and the nurse then placed a Band-Aid over it, securing the cotton ball in place.

"All set," she said.

"Great. Can I go use the bathroom?"

"Of course," she replied. "Let me help you up."

Leah stepped forward to assist; she took on arm while the nurse held the other, supporting Lucas as he cautiously slid off the bed and stood up. He was surprised by how much his legs shook. He felt frail and unsteady as he put one foot in front of the other, leaning heavily on his mother and the nurse. They helped him to the single-toilet bathroom that adjoined his room.

"I got it from here," he told them, staggering inside by himself. He shut the door, and held onto the corners of the sink as he stared into the mirror.

He saw the same coffee-brown face and long, thin nose. He looked strange with his hair so much shorter; besides that, something wasn't right. He looked healthy, if a bit puffy-eyed, and that was exactly what perturbed him. Val had broken his nose and several other bones, and opened up many cuts in his face, yet there was no sign of any scars or even the smallest bruise. He put a hand to his side and felt along his ribs. There was no pain there either, though he was certain that several ribs had broken, nor were there any cuts or breaks in his arms. Could all of that have healed so completely in a month?

He leaned closer, looking into his own eyes. Everything looked the same from the outside, but he knew that inside, what he couldn't see, things were drastically different. His brain was different and something else about him, something both his mother and grandmother were keeping from him, was different. He had changed.

"Lucas?" the nurse called. "Are you okay?"

"Yeah," he called back, his voice quavering.

He completed his business and opened the door. The young nurse helped him back to the bed, then set the food tray across his lap. He tasted the soup. It was very bland, so he crumbled some crackers into it.

"Remember to go easy," Leah warned.

"I'll make some cookies for you as soon as we get home," Maria offered sweetly. "Chocolate chip, your favorite, and all you want to eat."

"I can't wait," he said.

"I'm going to get some coffee," Leah said to him. "Are you gonna be alright?"

"Yes, I'm okay," he replied without looking up.

"I'll watch him, he'll be fine," Maria said.

"Are you sure?"

"Yeah, Mom," Lucas insisted.

"Okay," she said.

She slid the door closed behind her, leaving him alone with his grandmother. She picked up the remote, which had been sitting on the window sill.

"Want to watch some TV?"

Lucas shrugged. "Sure."

She clicked on the television. Spongebob Squarepants began tiptoeing across the screen wearing a ski mask, making his way to Patrick's rock.

"You like this?" Maria asked.

"Yeah, this is good," he said.

Then he paused, the spoon halfway to his mouth. Much like with the phones, an image of the TV screen appeared in his head, and with better quality. The episode played in his mind's eye, in perfect time with the one playing outside his head. He heard it, too; the audio was coming from the TV that sat in the upper corner of the room, but it also came from somewhere closer, like when he listened in on his mother's phone call. It came from somewhere *inside* his head.

He looked at his grandmother. She was reading something on her phone, paying no attention to him; instantly when he switched his focus to her phone, he saw the news article that she was reading from *The New York Times* online - something political that he had little interest in. He directed his attention back to the TV, and the episode jumped back inside his head.

He knew that televisions and cell phones alike worked by receiving signals from a tower, satellite, or cable network of some sort. So, he wondered whether or not his brain somehow received the same signals.

My brain gets wifi now?

His grandmother glanced his way, so he continued eating to prevent any unwanted attention, but his mind was not on his food. Somehow, he reasoned, everything that was happening to him had to be connected, and - whatever it was- it was growing stronger. Since he had woken up from his coma, he was seeing strange lights that came only from electronic devices specifically phones, televisions and computers; he could intercept phone calls, watch TV in his head, and see emails, texts, and whatever else other people saw on their phones. Thankfully, though, he no longer got seizures or dizziness from it.

How could this be happening? The doctor had said that he had metal in his blood, and that there was a mass around his spinal cord, and they were clearly very concerned about his brain. Maybe the metal was the cause of all this; maybe it did something so that his brain could capture the same signals that those devices could get. He had seen an old movie once about a man who got a brain tumor that caused him to become hyper-intelligent, and could move things with his mind. He wondered if, maybe, the mass around his spinal cord did something similar? The spinal cord attached to the brain, right? But, he recalled, the man in the movie *died* from his tumor. Lucas hoped he wouldn't share the same fate.

He shut out the *Spongebob* episode and looked again at Maria, who was scrolling through the day's headlines on her phone. A multi-colored halo surrounded the phone and Maria's hand up to her elbow. His brain mirrored her phone's screen, showing him the website she accessed to read the news. As she clicked, a new window opened up in his head and a video began playing. It was an interview with someone the video title identified as a White House spokesperson. A gray-haired man in a suit began talking while standing at a podium.

Ugh, Lucas thought. *This is gonna be boring....go back!*

He began to shut it out of his mind, but to his surprise, the video stopped, cutting the man off mid-sentence. Then it disappeared, returning to the main page.

Maria blinked at her phone. She tapped the link to video again and it expanded to fill the screen, then tapped *play* determinedly.

Lucas felt a prickle of uncertainty. *Go back*, he thought.

The video closed. He thought it once more, exiting the website.

Now he felt a thrill of excitement. The back of his neck continued to tingle like something electric was plugged into his brain.

Open contacts.

Maria's contacts opened. Lucas told the phone to scroll, and the list of names zoomed by straight to the *L's*. He selected his mother's name, then *Call*, then quickly hung up.

"This damn thing is broken," Maria grumbled, mashing the power button.

Lucas closed his eyes and laid his head back against the pillow, breathing slowly and deeply. *No way*, he thought. An electric feeling, like static, coursed through his veins. He opened his eyes and focused his mind. The halos surrounding the computer monitor, his grandmother's phone and the television all seemed alive with the same energy that pumped through his body. He was now familiar with that tickle that seemed to constantly crawl across his skin. Every cell was aware of the energy that pulsed through the cables and hovered in the air; his body felt... *connected* to it. And his mind had power over it.

Outside in the hall, Dr. Campbell was speaking to the burly, gray-haired nurse. Lucas sensed Dr. Campbell's phone in the pocket of his scrubs. In his mind, he could see the lock screen.

Open, he thought.

Bold red letters appeared, requesting a password.

Lucas hesitated, then began to think of something to guess, but at that moment a *ding!* sounded in his brain, surprising him. Dr. Campbell immediately took his phone and typed *0-3-1-5,* unlocking the phone, then opened his email where an unread message waited in the inbox. Lucas saw it all inside his head.

Wow... I'm like the NSA, he thought.

He wasn't interested in reading any of Dr. Campbell's emails; instead, he located his phone's music files. A rapid scroll through his saved titles showed that Dr. Campbell downloaded nothing but NPR podcasts with boring titles.

"What the hell?" Dr. Campbell said, shaking his phone.

Grinning to himself, Lucas opened the internet browser, then YouTube. A second later, a music video of "Boogie Wonderland" by Earth, Wind and Fire played at loud volume. Dr. Campbell angrily fiddled with the *Home* button and the volume rocker, trying to shut off the tunes.

Lucas felt immense satisfaction. *This* was power.

Chapter 4

HE SPENT THREE MORE WEEKS in the hospital. His mother or grandmother were nearly always with him, so he was rarely alone. With his grandmother, he played board games like *Clue* or *Monopoly*, or listened to her stories about Mexico or her first years in the United States and the many jobs she'd held. He practiced walking several times a day, assisted by his mother and a nurse. Within three days, he was walking without any assistance. His hair grew back slowly, and the nurse had long since removed his lead attachments to the ECG machine and computer that monitored his brain. He was told that he had recovered well enough that there was no longer any need to watch his vitals so closely, and there was next to no risk of another seizure. Soon, he would be allowed to go home.

Lucas still felt very angry and tense with his mother, grandmother and the doctor. He was well aware that none of them were being forthcoming to him about the metal in his blood, or anything specific regarding the cause of his seizures. His mother often held hushed discussions with the doctor or Maria outside the room, while they believed Lucas was asleep. As often as possible, Lucas listened in on these secret conversations. Whenever Leah and Dr. Campbell talked outside, out of earshot, he listened in on their conversations through their phones. He instructed one phone to call the other, then set it to speakerphone. It wasn't perfect, but if he closed his eyes and concentrated, he could pick up their voices and filter out most of the background noise. By this method, he quickly learned that they all believed he should be doing much worse than he actually was. Dr. Campbell informed Leah that they had no way to remove the metal in his blood, nor the mass around his spinal cord. However, the metal did not seem to be harming him in any way; despite all odds, his condition was improving. Dr. Campbell couldn't explain why.

At first, Lucas considered telling them all about his new abilities. He practiced every day in the privacy of his own mind, using his brain to access the technology around him. The inner software of phones and computers became like a new neighborhood that he quickly grew familiar with. He imagined that he was a burglar, and each device was like a house that he had to quietly get in and out of without the owner noticing that he was ever there. He learned that each phone felt subtly different to his mind, and that he could navigate some more quickly than others (he attributed this to processing speed). When his mind immersed itself in the device, each of his thoughts could trigger a different function. He could turn the device on and off, open apps, browse the internet, operate the camera, and even type out texts - all with his own thought commands. He became adept at breaking into a phone and feeling out its contents, and even learned to keep the screen dark to prevent his activities from alerting the owner, whenever the phone wasn't in use. He practiced this on the occasions that his mother left her phone on the chair-side table.

He was certainly getting stronger every day, and his focus was sharper. He was alert, and it had been weeks since his last blackout. When it became clear that his health was improving, he decided against revealing his powers to Leah, Maria, and the doctor. He told himself that it was because he didn't want to worry his mother and grandmother unnecessarily, because they had already been through enough. But if he was being honest with himself, he would admit that he simply didn't trust them. Their hushed conversations held late into the night told him that they knew, or at least believed, much more about his condition than they were willing to tell him, and the last thing he wanted to do was give them was more reasons to keep him here and run more tests, or put him in a lab to be sliced open, like in the movies. So, instead, he kept exploring his new gifts to gain better control over them on his own. During the last few weeks of his stay, they were his main source of entertainment. Right now, he rationalized, staying quiet and appearing as normal as possible was the quickest way out of this hospital, back home, and back to his life.

Two weeks before Thanksgiving, he was finally released. His mother gave him his backpack and some clothes that she had packed for him. He changed in the bathroom, putting on the pair of jeans and t-shirt, and left the hospital gown on the floor. He was relieved to finally be out of it. When he returned to his room, Maria was folding clothes and organizing them in the duffel bag, and his mother was nowhere to be seen.

"Where's Mom?" he asked.

"She went to bring the car around," she answered. "Get your cards and balloons together, if you want to bring them home."

Lucas went to the window sill. There were four *Get Well* cards lined up, and he opened each of them to read the message. One was from Ty Bridwell and his family with short notes from each of them inside, like *Get well soon!* and *Thoughts and prayers with you!* There was another from Nate Wissen which made him chuckle. It had a picture of a flattened cat with tire marks across his back. It read *Get well meow!* There were others from various classmates, and a bunch of balloons. Lucas glanced over the tag; it had no name or message.

"Did anyone visit me while I was here, Grandma?" he asked.

"Your friend, the Bridwell boy, and that other one," she answered. "The blond one."

"Nate," Lucas said.

"Yes. They did once at the beginning."

"Only once?" he asked. "They didn't come back?"

Maria came over and squeezed his shoulder tightly.

"Well, you have to understand, *mijo*, that you and your friends are so young. It must have been very difficult for them to see you that way."

Lucas couldn't deny that he felt disappointed, and couldn't really help it. He packed up the cards and tied the balloons to the strap of his backpack. When his mother returned, they all followed her down the corridor to the elevator, then down to the first floor. There, they walked past the emergency room reception area, through a pair of sliding doors to the sidewalk outside.

The sun was shining, but the air felt cool. A crisp breeze was blowing through the dull green and pale brown leaves on the trees. When Lucas went into the hospital, summer had just ended, but the blazing heat still remained; now, fall was well underway and the leaves were already changing. Clouds hurried across the sky and a great flock of birds settled on the powerlines.

"Come on," Leah said, her hand on his back.

His mother's 1995 Honda Civic was idling in the loading area. She took his backpack and put it in the back seat, the balloons bumping lazily against the roof of the car, then led him around to the other side.

"I got it, Mom," he said, brushing her hand away. He climbed into the back seat on the driver's side. Maria got into the passenger's seat, and Leah pulled the car away from the curb. They were going home.

Lucas watched the trees and the buildings creep as the car rolled slowly down the highway. Traffic in Austin was always backed up. The interstate was four endless rows of cars, clouded with haze, inching along through the middle of downtown. After they passed over the interstate, skyscrapers, glittering in the sun, towered overhead. Underneath were the storefronts of shops, boutiques, cafes and restaurants that Austin was known for, each trying to outdo the other for attention. Some were painted bright, gaudy colors; others bore flashing neon signs or a mural across its front. Lucas and his mother lived in South Congress, a neighborhood south of downtown where the skyscrapers gave way to a popular shopping district. There were outfitters for boots, sports clothing, and river gear, as well as tattoo parlors, bars, and adult video stores. It was late afternoon, and pedestrians filled the sidewalks and bicycles zipped past in the narrow, parallel lanes.

After several more shops and a gas station, they made two right turns and arrived at their apartment complex. It was a relatively small building - only eight units - with virginia creeper growing thickly over its red brick in the front, and a few small oaks in the parking lot. It stood directly behind the gas station corner store where Leah worked. From Lucas' bedroom window, he had a full view of the busy street of South Congress Avenue. They pulled into the parking lot and began to unload their bags.

"Home at last," Leah said tiredly.

Lucas took his backpack and balloons and headed up the front walk to Unit 4. He unzipped a side pocket of his backpack and found his key, then opened the door and stepped inside. The apartment was dark, so he clicked on the standing lamp beside the couch. His bedroom was off to his left, and his mother's was beyond that, with a bathroom in between. The kitchen was straight ahead, on the other side of the living room. The apartment was cramped, but impeccably clean, with minimal furniture, books and pictures, and no knickknacks whatsoever. He hadn't even known what those were until the first time he visited the Bridwell house. Mrs. Bridwell kept doilies and decorative plates, and countless porcelain figurines covering every shelf and side table, and there was a glass-fronted hutch completely full of them. His mother, on the other hand, always said that simplicity was best. She kept all of her keepsakes in her room on a low bookshelf: Lucas' baby book, a small clay bowl, and a turtle carved from pine wood.

He went into his room and dropped his backpack on the carpeted floor. He released the balloons, and they drifted to the ceiling. He lay down on his bed, feeling suddenly very tired. He had longed to be in his own room, in his own bed, for months, but now that he was finally here, he didn't know what to do next, and he felt exhausted. It was late morning, which meant that Ty and Nate were at school. Outside his door, he heard Leah and Maria unpacking and moving about the apartment, getting re-settled.

Now what? he thought.

His brain didn't seem to be tired at all. He felt it connect to the wifi and an electric tingle spread across his skin. He could feel his mother's phone, his grandmother's phone, and dozens of other devices - downstairs in the neighbor's apartment, across the breezeway and, if he really reached, he could feel hundreds if not thousands more in the neighborhood beyond. He closed his eyes and spent a few minutes snooping: scanning emails, listening to snippets of phone conversations, and reading texts. He didn't really try to learn anything; he just enjoyed the thrill of *doing* it. It was exciting, having that kind of power. There was a whole new world open to him through the power of his mind. He watched some TV inside his head, and about an hour later Maria knocked on the door.

"Are you hungry for lunch?" she said, poking her head in.

"Yeah, what are we having?"

"I made some curry," she answered. "I found the recipe online, from this very nice woman in Iowa."

"That sounds good," he said with a chuckle.

He got up and followed her to the kitchen, then took a seat at the table. Leah brought him a glass of milk, then sat down next to him. In the center of the table was a large bowl of steaming red curry, made with beef, vegetables and potatoes. The spicy aroma filled the air, and Lucas' stomach growled. Maria ladled a large helping onto everyone's plate, pouring the thick sauce generously over a mound of rice. He dug in; every few bites he had to take a sip of milk to cool the fire inside his mouth.

"Do you like the curry?" Maria asked after everyone had eaten quietly for several minutes.

"Yes, it's delicious," Lucas replied.

"That woman in Iowa posts so many recipes," Maria reported. "I wrote many of them down. Pastas, meatloafs, pot pies..."

Lucas listened, nodding patiently as she rattled them off.

"What do you want to do today?" Leah asked, changing the subject.

"I want to go to Ty's house, after he gets home from school," Lucas replied.

"That's in about two hours," she said. "Do you want to walk with me to the store? I need to check my work schedule."

"No thanks," he answered, shaking his head. "I'm pretty tired. I think I just want to sleep."

"Okay," Leah nodded. "I think that's a good idea. You don't want to overdo it."

After they had finished eating, Maria gathered the dishes and began washing up, and Lucas went back to his room. He laid down in his bed, with his clothes on, and closed his eyes as if he was going to sleep. He thought that he might, but his mind was racing with questions. He knew he could control wireless devices with his thoughts, but what else? And how exactly did it work? He sat up in his bed and looked around the room. He had no phone, no laptop, and no TV. So what could he try to control? His skin tingled with energy, and that energy had to come from somewhere. There was a tall lamp beside his bed, and from it emanated that same humming, living, rainbow colored halo that he had seen around the computers in the hospital. His mind and his body felt connected to it. He extended his mind toward the halo, and his hand reached up. A prickle crawled up the back of his neck, and the hairs rose on his arms. Something in his brain responded, and the light flickered. It dimmed, then, with a loud hum, flashed bright again. Lucas looked at the lamp hard, its bulb burning bright and yellow. He extended a hand toward it once more, something inside him twinged, and the light flickered again. Then a spark jumped from it, zapping his hand. He jerked his hand back, startled and shaking from excitement. He couldn't help but smile.

So energy was the key to his power, he realized. Electricity *was* energy, so if he could manipulate energy, electricity was included. Wireless devices ran on energy, too, even though they weren't plugged in, and energy drove both hardware and software. Something clicked in his brain, and words appeared in his mind's eye.

Energy [en-er-gy]: power derived from the utilization of physical or chemical resources, especially to provide light or to work machines.

He felt a strange rush, and was suddenly slightly dizzy. *Where did that come from?* he wondered.

Wireless devices communicate through the use of transmitters and receivers. Transmitters and receivers sit at each end of the wireless system, using an aerial antenna at each end. At the receiving end, electromagnetic waves induce small, electrical signals in the antenna, which are then picked up by an electrical circuit...

Lucas had a sensation similar to leaving a 3D movie: disoriented, and a bit nauseous. His head was spinning, but that was because his mind was still sorting through millions of words and pictures at a rapid rate - so fast that he could not possibly read or process them all. It was like one part of his brain was the human part, and the other was a supercomputer racing forward without any regard for whether or not its human counterpart could keep up. There was something there, something alien inside his head, working the controls without him, and Lucas was quickly growing dizzier and more disoriented.

Stop, please stop, he thought.

The words and images halted, then disappeared. Lucas knew by now that he had just visited the internet with his mind; he was familiar enough with the feeling, but this time he had done it without first connecting to somebody else's phone. He had made the journey on his own, independent of another device. Slowly, it dawned on him just how powerful his mind really was, and what it was capable of doing without his own conscious thought. It was like his brain - the strange, supercomputer part - was learning faster than he was. On the other hand...*he had the internet inside his brain!* In his excitement, he got up and paced the room, shivers covering his body. He couldn't wait to tell Nate and Ty. He *had* to tell them; unlike his mother and that doctor, he had no doubts that they could be trusted.

His internal clock told him that it was 2:45; they would be out of school in one hour. Lucas was too excited to keep sitting in his room, so he wanted to leave now to walk over to meet them, but the school was only a few blocks from his apartment. He would still have a lot of time to wait around after he got there. Still, he could think of a few things to do while he waited.

He sat down on his bed and put on his shoes, then got up and opened the door. Maria was sitting in the reclining chair, watching the news. The news anchor was interviewing some health expert about a viral outbreak in Florida, which had spread from some countries in South America. Lucas felt his skin tingle, then text popped up inside his head:

South America is a continent located in the southern hemisphere, with a small portion located in the northern hemisphere. Countries include Brazil, Argentina, Chile -

He shook his head to clear it, and quickly turned to leave.

"Where are you going, Lucas?" Maria asked, sitting up.

"I'm gonna meet Nate and Ty at school," he said.

"You should wait for your mother to take you," Maria said. "She should be back any minute."

Lucas immediately located her phone. His GPS told him that she was still at the store.

"Then I'll wait for her downstairs," he said.

Before Maria could say anything else, he opened the front door and stepped outside, then closed the door behind him. The wind swept across the breezeway, dead leaves making a hard, scraping sound as they danced across the concrete. Tree branches creaked and swayed, and the sky was clear blue. Lucas descended the stairs to the ground floor and marched down the sidewalk to the street, making his way to the busy avenue. He could hear the noises of traffic, and smell the mixed odors of restaurants and smog. When he reached South Congress, he turned right - away from his mother's store

He walked two blocks up before crossing the main avenue and doubling back toward the school. As he went, he let his mind wander the internet. He skimmed through the website of a restaurant he passed, including Yelp reviews. Inside the restaurant, a woman snapped a photo of her meal, then posted it to Twitter, Facebook, Foursquare, and Instagram. Lucas saw the photo in his head and watched in real time as she added filters and the caption *Yummy!!! #cheatday* followed by a half-dozen different emojis. A couple seated outside on the patio were both staring their phones: the man was scrolling through his Facebook feed while the girl was texting someone named Beau about how bored she was. He kept walking, his head filling with information and his senses alive with stimulation. Every one of the electromagnetic signals around him provoked a prickly response in his skin. A man on the corner posted a snarky comment to Twitter, and Lucas' brain immediately took him to the page where he could freely peruse the man's feed. Farther on, he could hear the soulful music of a band performing live inside a bar. He looked up the band's name and within seconds went to their web page, then YouTube channel and enjoyed a few more songs.

After five minutes, he became dizzy and had to sit down. The vertigo was so bad that he forced his head to clear itself so he could re-center himself in reality. He watched the cars pass, and watched some birds chase each other through the branches of a tree. He breathed deeply through his nose, while at the same time trying to look normal to the people passing by.

After a few more minutes, he checked the time. School would be letting out in ten minutes, so he turned the corner and headed south. He stopped on the sidewalk beside the park across the street from the school and waited. Buses lined the street to his right, but he knew that both Nate and Ty had to pass this way to get to their respective houses. The bell rang and students began to flood out. Kids passed by without paying attention to him. He scanned the crowd, searching for Nate and Ty. Far off, he spotted Val, Darren and Howard meandering away in the opposite direction from the buses. He felt a chill as a mixture of anger and fear filled him as he remembered the terror and pain that they had made him feel. His fists clenched at his sides as his heart raced.

"Lucas?"

He turned. Nate was less than ten yards away, frozen and gaping. Ty was close behind him, and dropped his backpack in shock. Lucas felt suddenly nervous.

"What are you doing here?" Ty asked with disbelief.

"I came to see you guys," he answered.

"When did you get out?" Nate asked.

"This morning," Lucas said.

"What?" Ty exclaimed. "You were in a *coma*. We saw you."

"I got better," Lucas said, his hands in his pockets. "And there's a lot I want to talk about."

"I should think so," Nate said, shaking his head.

"Can we go to your house?" Lucas asked Ty.

"Yeah, I guess," Ty nodded with exasperation. "When did you wake up?"

"About three weeks ago."

"What the heck, man?" Nate asked as they continued up the sidewalk. "And you didn't call us?"

"I had... a lot going on."

"What does *that* mean?" Nate said angrily. "We thought you were gone, like you were gonna be a vegetable forever. You couldn't just let us know you were okay?"

"I was a little busy, alright?" Lucas retorted. "I had to learn to walk again, and eat, and recover from a bunch of seizures... I mean, it's not like I was on vacation!"

"Hey, let's all calm down, okay?" Ty interjected.

Nate looked at the ground.

"It was hard seeing you like that."

"And I was disappointed that you guys didn't come see me while I was in there," Lucas said.

"We did," Ty said.

"I meant while I was awake."

They exchanged uncomfortable glances.

"Lucas... it was really hard," Ty said solemnly. "You were unconscious, and nobody knew when you were going to wake up, or if you were ever going to. I'm sorry, but being there was just... really scary."

Lucas said nothing more. Presently, they arrived at the Bridwell house. The front yard was heavily decorated with pumpkins, turkeys, cornucopias and smiling pilgrims. A wreath made of fall leaves hung on the door. Lucas knew already, by tracking their phones, that Mrs Bridwell was at the elementary school three miles away and that Mr. Bridwell was across town. Ty unlocked the front door, and Nate and Lucas followed him inside. Ty went to the fridge in the enormous kitchen and came back with sodas for each of them, then they all moved to the entertainment room. A massive TV hung on the wall, and the room was filled with giant leather couches and bean bags on the floor.

"So, tell us what happened," Ty said, sitting down on a couch. "We heard you were in some kind of an accident after you snuck into a steelmakers' warehouse."

"Did you hear about Val and his gang being there?" Lucas asked.

"Only Brick," Nate said. "They said on the news that Brick rescued you after he heard some noise, or something like that."

"There was a news story about it?" Lucas asked, surprised. His brain then did a rapid internet search and recovered several short reports by a few local news stations, dated the day of the accident. All were calling Brick a hero.

"Yeah, everybody wanted to interview Brick. They wanted to talk to your mom, too but she wouldn't do any interviews, or let them see you."

"Well, everything Brick said is bullshit," Lucas spat. "He made all that up."

"We thought so too," Ty remarked. "But nobody knew what happened, and your mom didn't tell us anything."

"What really happened?" Nate asked.

"I'll tell you, but first I need to show you something," Lucas said. "After the accident, the doctor found some metal in my blood, and in a mass around my spinal cord. They said I was going to be fine, that it wasn't doing anything harmful to me, but I think it did something else. Cause after I woke up, I could do this..."

Lucas pointed at the giant, flat-screen television that hung on the wall behind him. Without saying anything out loud, he gave it a command, and it turned on. The screen lit up to show a football game, then, at his instruction, flipped through several other channels including a game show, a few reality shows, and, finally, the cooking channel. Then he took control of their phones. Both phones began to play Eminem's "The Real Slim Shady" simultaneously and at high volume, and the boys jumped in surprise.

"Take your phones out of your pockets," Lucas said.

Nate and Ty looked at him with confusion, but complied. Once they had them out, Lucas typed out a text message in his head and sent it to them.

"What the hell?" Ty said. "Is this a trick?"

"Read it," Lucas said.

"*I can control technology with my brain,*" Ty read, then lowered his eyebrows. "Did you get somebody to send this? What kind of number is that?"

"No, it's really me," Lucas insisted.

"That's creepy," Nate said with a chuckle. "You really had me going there."

Lucas took a deep breath and closed his eyes. Both phones began to vibrate as they received a call at the same time, but he didn't wait for Nate or Ty to answer it. He accepted the call himself, then put them both on speakerphone.

I am doing it, his voice came through the phone, but Lucas didn't move his lips. *When I woke up in the hospital, something in my brain was different. Then I found out I could do this… plus a lot more.*

He opened his eyes. Nate and Ty were both white as sheets, staring at their phones in horror. Lucas hung up the call, then turned off the TV. He let out his breath slowly, and his heart pounded.

Chapter 5

T Y RECOVERED HIS VOICE FIRST.

"What the hell!?" he cried. "What just happened?"

"I told you, something changed in my brain," Lucas said.

"Obviously!" Nate said, still looking very pale.

"It can communicate somehow with electrical signals. I think it, and it happens. I can basically make your phone do whatever I want."

"Can you turn it into a fighting robot?" Nate asked sardonically.

Lucas rolled his eyes.

He suddenly felt a prickle down the back of his neck.

"Look, I want to tell you everything," he said. "I can't deal with this by myself. But, Ty, your mom is about to come in here, and you both need to act natural until I can explain it all to you."

They both stared at him. Without waiting for an answer, he turned on the TV to a rerun of *Samurai Jack*, then dropped onto the couch between them. The front door opened, and Ty's little sister, Emma, entered, followed closely by Mrs. Bridwell. Emma dashed past the entertainment room and then up the stairs, while Mrs. Bridwell stopped in the doorway, her purse on her shoulder.

"Lucas! How are you?" she said with a smile.

"Fine, thank you," Lucas answered.

"You're looking very well," she said. "When did you get out of the hospital?"

"Today."

"Wow! I'm so glad to see that you're doing so much better. Please, let me know if you need anything. Oh, and I'm making pasta for dinner. It'll be ready in an hour."

"Okay, thanks," he said.

Mrs. Bridwell left, and the boys were quiet. Then Ty shoved Lucas off the couch.

"How did you do that!?" he exclaimed.

Lucas closed the door to the entertainment room.

"I told you," he said again. "I did it with my mind."

"Bullshit," Nate spat.

"How did you know my mom was about to come in the door?" Ty asked.

"GPS. I'd been tracing her phone since we got here, because I wanted privacy."

"You have GPS?" Ty said skeptically. "In your head?"

"Yeah. Wifi, too."

"What else can you do?"

"Access the internet," Lucas said. "Anything that's not password-protected. Read people's texts and emails, listen in on phone calls."

"So, you're like the NSA now?" Ty said.

Lucas grinned. "I thought that, too."

"How is that even possible?" Nate said, scratching his head.

"I don't know... I really don't," Lucas said. "I just woke up and I was seeing weird lights everywhere, and then gradually those lights started to make sense. I was hearing voices, too, and realized that those voices were in radio signals and cell phone conversations. Then, with practice, I figured everything else out."

"Start from the beginning," Ty said.

Lucas did. He sat down and told them the whole story, starting with his fight with Val, Howard, Darren and Brick in the bathroom at school; he told them about being followed to the warehouse and the fight that occurred there, then waking up in the hospital and the painful discovery of his powers. He described his experience as thoroughly as he could, and they listened quietly and intently.

"Why not tell the doctor about what was happening to you?" Ty asked when he had finished.

"What could he do about it?" Lucas replied. "I told him I was seeing lights at the beginning and he assumed there was something wrong with my brain, which got me put in the MRI machine. The last thing I wanted was more of *that*."

"Yeah, Ty, they'd just cut his head open," Nate added.

"The whole time I was there, Dr. Campbell and my mom just seemed bent on coming up with reasons why I *shouldn't* be getting better," Lucas said. "Like they believed there must be something wrong. All they did was hide everything from me."

"Lucas, it's pretty reasonable for them to be concerned," Ty said. "You were in a coma for over a month."

"But - "

"Now the shoe's on the other foot, and you're keeping a secret," Ty continued. "Two wrongs don't make a right."

"So what am I supposed to do?" Lucas asked with frustration.

"Tell her," Ty said simply.

Lucas said nothing, and looked at the ground.

"You don't trust her," Nate remarked.

"She was probably just trying to protect you," Ty said. "You know?"

"No, it's not that," Lucas shook his head. "Something just doesn't feel right. I've caught her lying about even the simplest things. She lies all the time. Why would she do that?"

Ty frowned sympathetically. "I don't know; I'm sorry."

"Let's go to your room, Ty," Nate said, after a moment's silence. "Can we play some XBox?"

"Yeah, let's do that," Ty nodded.

The other boys got up and began to head upstairs, but Lucas didn't move.

"Wait, that's *it*?" he said, confused. "I tell you all that and we're just going to go play Xbox now like everything's normal?"

Nate and Ty shrugged.

"What do you want to do, Lucas?" Nate asked.

"I don't know," Lucas answered despondently. "I want to figure all this out, like what I am or what I'm supposed to do now. Everything's different and confusing."

Nate and Ty looked at each other.

"Well, we don't really know how to help you," Ty said uncomfortably. "But if you want to come play with us, you can."

A tingle ran up the back of Lucas' head.

"Hold on," he said, then, to Ty: "My mom is calling your mom."

Ty raised his eyebrows. In the kitchen, Mrs. Bridwell's phone rang. Lucas heard her answer:

"Hello?"

Then, inside his head, came his mother's voice: *Sonia, hi. Is Lucas over there?*

"Yes, he is," Mrs. Bridwell said. "He's watching a movie with the boys. Is something wrong?"

Well, the thing is, he didn't tell me where he was going... and it's really important that he take it easy for the next few days...

"What's going on?" Ty whispered, elbowing Lucas. "Are you okay?"

Lucas shushed him, trying to listen.

"Oh, of course," Mrs. Bridwell said, lowering her voice. "I am so sorry, I didn't know he didn't ask. Would you like me to drive him home?"

No, thank you, I'll come get him. Be there in a few minutes.

She hung up, and he turned to Nate and Ty.

"My mom's coming to get me," he told them.

"Why?" Nate asked.

"I didn't exactly tell her where I was going," Lucas admitted. "And I'm supposed to be at home."

"You snuck out?" Ty asked.

Lucas shrugged.

"Wow, man," Nate said, shaking his head. "You really *are* different."

Mrs. Bridwell walked up the hallway toward them, dish towel in hand.

"Your mom's coming to pick you up, Lucas," she said. "She'll be here in a few minutes."

"Okay, thanks," he said politely.

She departed back to the kitchen. Lucas motioned for the others to follow him back to the entertainment room, and he shut the door again, and the boys dropped onto the couches.

"You heard all that in your head?" Nate asked Lucas.

"Yeah," he nodded.

"Whoa," Nate breathed. "And you think this is because of that metal that got in you?"

"Look," Ty said, shaking his head. "I don't like this. It's all just a little bit too weird for me."

"It is weird," Nate agreed. "Isn't there a way to fix you? Didn't they try to take that metal out of you?"

"Yes, but they have no idea what it is. They couldn't figure a way to get it out of me either."

"If the doctors couldn't figure it out, there's probably no way to get it out," Ty remarked.

"It must be something smarter," Nate mused. "Some kind of alien technology."

"Could he get other people sick with it?" Ty asked, wearing a grimace. "Like if his blood got on them, or something?"

They both looked at him uncomfortably, and Lucas' face reddened.

"Guys, I'm not an alien," he assured them. "I mean, things aren't that different… I'm still me."

"Then why don't you want to play with us?" Ty asked.

"I guess because I still have a lot to think about," he said sullenly.

"We get that," Nate said, nodding. "Why don't you just forget about it for a while and come relax? You probably need it."

A knock sounded on the front door, making Nate and Ty jump.

"It's my mom," Lucas said, and began to head toward the door.

Nate and Ty looked sympathetic, and Nate suddenly grabbed Lucas' wrist.

"Oh, and be careful," he said. "You know how it happens in the movies, if the government finds out. They might take you and try to use you to spy on foreign governments or something."

Lucas swallowed hard. He felt weak.

"I'll be careful," he promised.

"Are you going to tell you mom?" Ty asked.

"Don't know," Lucas answered with a hint of frustration.

Ty nodded, then got up and opened the door. Leah was outside, and leaned through the doorway.

"Come on," she said sharply to Lucas. "Get in the car. Thanks for having him over, Sonia."

Mrs. Bridwell had come up the hallway and stood behind Ty.

"Of course, he's welcome back anytime," she said cheerfully.

Leah put her hand on Lucas' shoulder and led him down the front walk to the waiting car. Lucas climbed into the passenger's seat and they pulled away. The Bridwell's house grew smaller behind them, and then disappeared as the car passed by the neighborhood's other massive houses and sprawling oak trees. The wind blew, and pedestrians on the street shivered and hunched their shoulders as they walked.

"Lucas, what were you thinking?" Leah said, her eyes on the road.

"I wanted to see my friends," he answered.

"Yes, but you can't just go wandering around town by yourself," she said sternly. "It's not safe, and besides, you just got out of the hospital."

"I get it," he said. "I'm sorry."

"You have to take it easy, do you understand? I want you to stay home and rest."

"What about school?" he asked.

"After winter break, we'll talk about going back."

"What about my friends?" Lucas said with disbelief. "When will I see them?"

"Will you just slow down?" she snapped loudly.

Lucas fell silent. Leah stared at the road, her lips tight. They were on the main avenue now, with cyclists and buses joining the traffic. Ahead, the sun was setting over the city skyline. They arrived at the apartment and Lucas climbed the stairs and went inside. Maria was in the kitchen, and warm smells floated through the apartment. He could see in his head that she had a recipe for English pot pie open on her phone. Lucas went to his room without a word and closed the door.

He spent the next few days mostly alone in his room. Within his mind, he surfed the internet and lost himself in information about electromagnetic waves, the effects of various metals on the human body, and computer hacking. Much of what he learned was beyond his understanding, so he spent additional time learning basics about computer coding. He decided to take a step backwards and focus on how computers worked the way they did, studying how interrupting the flow of electricity could be translated as commands. He found a lot of information about bits, transistors, arithmetic and logic units, registers, and circuits - all of which he had to sift through and re-read over and over again to make any sense of it. By the following week, he had a small grasp on how his abilities *might* work, but still no understanding of *why*. He couldn't understand the stuff, the mysterious metal, that was hidden away inside him and out of his reach. Mostly, he felt overwhelmed and brain-fried. He gave up completely on several occasions, and spent hours playing online video games in his head. He downloaded a few different games, then competed against himself for the high score.

One night, a week later, he awoke hearing his mother's voice in the next room. His grandmother had long before gone home; he and his mother had been alone in the house for the past several hours. He waited and listened, but heard no other voices in the apartment. Was she on the phone?

Lucas focused, shifting that new muscle in his brain, and now he heard a second voice inside his head. His mother was definitely on the phone with someone.

"Do you have anyone who can look at him?" Leah asked.

We have some experts, a man said. His voice was gruff, deep, and familiar, but he couldn't place it. *I've given them your son's hospital records, but it doesn't give them a lot to go on.*

"Believe me, once they've seen him, they'll know what to look for," Leah said. "But it won't be like anything they've ever seen before."

God, I hope you're wrong about all this. For everyone's sake.

Lucas' breath quickened, but he lay perfectly still. His focus was razor-sharp. He traced the call, but all he learned was that the man was located at an apartment downtown on 1st street. He saw the name Danny Clark in his mind, and became more confused than ever. Why was his mother talking about him with her boss in the middle of the night?

"Me too, but I don't have any doubts," Leah continued. "He's getting worse. He sleeps all the time, and he's stayed shut up in his room all day, every day for a week. He hasn't been himself, not since the accident."

Have you taken him back to the hospital?

"There's no point; they don't know how to deal with this. Nobody does."

Good. I would have advised against it. What are you going to do?

"I'm going to enjoy the holidays with my son while I still can. When can I bring him to you?"

Let me finish getting my people together. I'll need a couple more days. Can you hang in there until then?

"I'll do my best. There's no telling how much time he has left."

Lucas felt a chill. What could she mean by that? What was going to happen to him? And now it was glaringly obvious that there was something going on behind his back that concerned him. He had to find out. He felt terrified, but got up from his bed opened the door. The apartment was dark except for a yellow glow of light from beneath his mother's bedroom door. His heart hammered in his chest as he walked toward it. Then suddenly, the door opened, and his mother emerged wearing an oversized shirt and cotton pajama pants, holding a water glass in one hand and her phone in the other. If she was surprised to see him, she did not show it.

"Sweetheart, what are you doing up?" she said.

"Who were you talking to?" he asked softly.

"Oh, it was just a work thing," she said dismissively. "Do you need anything?"

"Don't lie to me," Lucas snapped, his voice rising as his anger flared.

Leah startled, because at that moment the apartment became fully illuminated as every light came on at once. There was a great hum and a pop, and Leah let out a shriek of surprise as as several bulbs, including the one in the lamp behind her, burst. Just as quickly, the apartment was plunged in darkness, and there was no sound except Leah's panicked breathing.

"I need you to tell me the truth," he said slowly through gritted teeth. "Something happened to me, Mom. I'm different, and I think you know that. You need to tell me what's really going on."

He willed the kitchen light to turn back on; it was the only one still functioning. With his mind, he granted power to return to it and it flickered to life. In the dim light, he could see Leah's face. She was very pale and visibly shaken. Lucas worried that she might faint, but she took a deep breath and composed herself.

"What did you do?" she gasped.

"I have powers now," he answered. "Something's changed inside me since the accident."

Her eyes widened.

"How long have you been able to do this?" she stammered.

"Since waking up in the hospital."

Her brows lowered as she looked at him, as if she was trying to make sense of the information.

"Come here," she said suddenly, and walked to the dining room table. Lucas followed. She turned on a standing lamp, set the half-empty glass and her phone down on the table, then pulled out a chair and sat. She pointed to the chair across from her. "Sit down, Lucas. I'll tell you everything that I've kept from you."

He obeyed. Leah looked steadily into his eyes.

"Some of this is going to be very hard to hear," she told him. "And I wish that you never had to hear it, or at least not until you were much older. But things are clearly different now, so here it is. First of all, I have known about your condition since this began. In fact, I was discussing it with the CIA."

"But I saw Mr. Clark's name in your phone," Lucas interrupted.

"Mr. Clark is an agent assigned to protect me," Leah said. "His real name is Seth Kowalski, and my job at the store is all a disguise. It's just to keep me safe. Now, to be clear, I didn't know about these things that you can do, but I knew that something was different--something beyond what the doctors could see."

"A long time ago," she said with a deep breath. "Before you were born, I was a very different kind of person. When I was young, I ran away from my family. I had no job, and got involved in some very bad and irresponsible things. Ultimately, I and four other girls were kidnapped and taken to a facility in California. We were given lots of drugs... so, thankfully, I don't remember all the things that were done to us there. I do know that they did many terrible experiments on us, and we were kept in isolation from one another. The FBI found us three weeks later, and two weeks after that, I learned that I was pregnant with you. I was afraid for so long that whatever was done to me had hurt you in some way, but the doctors found nothing wrong. After you were born, I began to believe that maybe my fears were unfounded. You were healthy and seemed perfectly normal in every way. Then your accident happened and the doctors told me all of those terrible things... and I became afraid again. The people who kidnapped us were never caught, and the case hasn't been closed. The FBI moved us to Austin while you were still a baby and found me a job, a place to live, and a new identity so that we would be safe, and my case was turned over to the CIA. They even moved your grandmother here. But I never stopped worrying that they would come back for me."

Leah's voice broke at the end.

Lucas was horrified. He sat in stunned silence while she wiped her eyes.

"After your accident, when the doctors told me what they found inside your body, I thought that my worst nightmares had come true. They found - "

"Metal, in my blood and in a mass around my spinal cord," Lucas said. Leah blinked at him, confused.

"I heard what Dr. Campbell told you," he explained.

"Lucas, three of the girls died in that facility. The medical examiners said that they died from some sort of neurological disease; they were all found with metal embedded in their spinal cords, their brains deteriorated. One of the other girls made it out with me, but she died a few days later from the same thing. I am the only one left, and I was clean. Then your accident revealed the same metal inside you, so I was afraid…"

Her voice trailed off, and Lucas felt like a vice was squeezing his chest.

"Afraid of what?" he asked.

"That they found me, and they're trying to get to me through you. They're punishing me for escaping… for surviving."

"The metal wasn't in me before the accident, was it?"

She shook her head. "No, it couldn't have been. I had you checked the day you were born. They did every test I could think of."

Their tests failed before, Lucas thought grimly. *Still, I'm not dead yet. Maybe it happened at the warehouse. Maybe there was something in those crates.*

"I was so terrified of losing you," she continued. "My only hope is that maybe we might find a cure."

"Have the experts at the CIA found one?" he asked.

Leah shook her head. "Not yet," she said thickly.

"But this isn't like what happened back then," he insisted. "This has to be different. Did those girls have the same abilities that I do?"

"I don't know. Maybe they did, and maybe they didn't. We were kept separate from each other, and they died soon after."

"Who are they?" Lucas asked. "Who took you?"

"I don't know. No one does."

He was reeling. A tight knot formed in his throat.

"You can't tell anyone about this," she continued. "This is a federal investigation; you can't tell anyone about the case or your condition."

"I'm not dying, Mom," he said in a firm voice. "This isn't like what happened to those girls."

Tears were streaming down her face now.

"I've told you the truth, everything that I know, and, honestly, I don't know what will happen now. I'm sorry… I'm sorry that I lied, and I'm sorry that I can't give you more."

Lucas got up and hugged his mother tightly. He hugged her for a long time, and they both cried. Finally, when the pale light of morning began to glow over the city skyline, Leah went to bed. Exhausted and unable to cry anymore, he went to his room, but he didn't go to sleep. His mind was racing, and he was burning with fury.

There was work to be done.

Chapter 6

THE FIRST THING LUCAS DID was find the location of the warehouse where his accident occurred. He searched through the news reports of the incident until he found an address. Then he delved through the depths of the internet until he found the reports about his mother's rescue. He found a few short articles describing the rescue of several young women - all unnamed in the article - from a human trafficking ring The women were scarred, nearly starved, and heavily drugged. He remembered his mother's scars, and his anger rose. The news reports claimed their salvation as a human rights victory, but there was no mention anywhere of the four deaths, or of the ongoing CIA investigation. It seemed that the story was simply buried and forgotten.

Lucas had to believe that his mother was wrong. He felt fine - stronger than he was when he came home. He didn't *feel* like someone on the brink of death, but then again, maybe he was a time bomb just waiting to go off. Regardless of how he got his powers or where they came from, they were *his* now and he would use them to find the people that did these horrible things to his mother and make sure that they got what they deserved, whatever it cost him. He continued looking, his mind working at inhuman speeds.

When morning came, he still had no other leads except the warehouse. The only progress he had made was the realization that his brain must produce an electronic signal of its own, as if it contained its own cellular device. He could sense phone calls and texts made by others, but what if he could generate his own? To test this theory, he washed his face and changed his clothes, then put on a jacket and left his room. The apartment was still quiet, and he knew his mother was sleeping. He focused on the clear signal made by her phone, then typed out a message in his head, saying that he was going to visit Nate and Ty. He visualized a pathway between his mind and her phone, and thought *send*, but not before making sure that her text alert volume was off so the message wouldn't wake her up. An image of her screen came to life in his mind's eye, displaying a message received from an unknown number. Lucas felt the warmth of confidence blossom in his chest, then crept to the front door and stepped outside. The air was chilly, and he turned his collar up against the wind. The sun was shining now through the trees, and the morning traffic was bustling. He walked down the sidewalk, and typed out another text in his head as he went:

Coming over. Meet me outside. URGENT.

He sent this to both Nate and Ty. Nate responded first. The words hovered, a floating ribbon of letters.

Okay, Techboy, what's up?

He winced. His answer was typed out and sent with only a flick of his thoughts.

That's a terrible name. Tell you when I get there.

This was fun. He made his way to Nate's house, walking purposefully. He felt confident that he made the right decision, telling them about his powers. They might as well know about the investigation too, he reasoned. Besides, he might need some help… if he could convince them to help him.

Nate lived two streets down from his apartment in an aging two-story house with overgrown trees and neglected landscape. A 70s-era Buick squatted in the driveway with leaves gathered on its hood, and Nate sat on its trunk eating a Poptart. He hopped down as Lucas approached and jogged to meet him.

"Hey," he said. He pulled another shiny, silver package from his sweater pocket and handed it to Lucas.

"Thanks," Lucas said. He unwrapped the Pop-Tart and ate it as they began walked together toward Ty's house.

"So what's so urgent?" Nate asked.

"I need to go to the warehouse where the accident happened," he told him.

"Why?"

"Because I think there might be some clues there. We're going to solve a mystery."

"What kind of mystery?" Nate asked.

"I'll explain when we get to Ty's, 'cause I don't want to say it more than once," Lucas said. "He hasn't responded to my text yet. By the way, what's my number?"

"What do you mean?"

"What number comes up when I text you?"

"There isn't one," Nate replied. "Why? Did you forget it? Did you get amnesia when you got hit on the head?"

"Stop asking so many questions."

Nate opened his contacts and showed Lucas the screen. Where the contact number should have been was only a row of ten empty boxes.

"I thought my phone was messed up, but I think the problem is with yours. How did you finally get your phone back from Brick?"

Before Lucas could answer that he didn't, a message from Ty popped up on the screen.

Just woke up, but I'm ready. What's going on?

Lucas replied effortlessly. He typed out the text in his mind and thought, *Send.* The message appeared on Nate's screen.

Be there in a sec.

Nate stared at his phone. Since it was a group text, he received Lucas' reply, too. He glanced at Lucas, then back down to his phone, then back again, eyes widening.

"Wait, how did you do that?"

"With my thoughts," Lucas answered.

"Oh, is that all?" Nate exclaimed. "Are you telling me you're texting now, with your *brain*?"

"Yeah, I can do that. I just figured it out this morning."

Nate ran a hand through his hair. He took a deep breath, puffing out his cheeks.

"You know this is all really weird," he said.

Lucas nodded.

"I'm not completely used to it yet, either," he admitted.

"What does it look like, in your head?" Nate asked.

"Like a lot of lights and colors, kind of hovering around. The longer you look, the more they start to make sense and form patterns. You know how the stars look like a whole lot of meaningless dots in the sky? Until you know where the constellations are, and then it's like they were there all along? Only in this case, you can move the constellations around to where you want them to be."

"That doesn't make a lot of sense."

"Think of it this way," Lucas explained. "Everything runs on electricity, right? Electrons moving around in a computer's hardware are turned into language, codes and programs that a human being can understand, and vice-versa. When you tell a computer to do something, with some keystrokes and mouse-clicks, you're basically controlling the flow of those electrons. I do the same thing, just without the mouse or keyboard. I can see those electrons flowing, and even feel it in my skin, and my brain can push them around to make a computer do what I want it to."

"Wow," Nate said with a low whistle. "That's amazing. Really weird, but amazing."

They arrived at Ty's house just past eight o'clock. Ty's front door opened and he came running out. His dark hair was wet and combed flat, and he carried his backpack. He stopped in his tracks, looking confused.

"What's going on?" he asked. "We're not going to school?"

Nate gave Ty a quizzical look. "What part of 'urgent' says 'we're going to school'?"

"So, we're skipping?" Ty gasped.

"This is a matter of life and death," Lucas said. "We're going to the warehouse where I had my accident."

"Why?"

"Come on, I'll tell you while we walk," Lucas answered.

He turned and began walking. They quickly caught up to him, heading in the direction of South Congress. Lucas was following the GPS in his head, which he hoped would lead him to the place where it all happened. He didn't know what he would find there, if anything, but maybe it would give him answers.

"Okay," he said, clearing his throat. "This whole time, even since before I was born, there's been an CIA investigation into some people who kidnapped and experimented on some prostitutes. My mom was one of them. She's been weird since the accident because she thinks that something that happened to her then caused my powers to happen. She's the only one who survived; all the other girls died from the experiments, and now I've got the same metal in my body that killed them."

Nate and Ty both gasped in shock. Lucas stopped walking to face them.

"But I think this is different," he said. "I didn't have the stuff in me when I was born, or I would have died a long time ago, based on how quickly it killed those girls. I don't think it was passed on. I think it got in me later, maybe during the accident. Either way, I have to find out for sure."

"So, this stuff that's inside of you, giving you your powers, might be killing you?" Nate asked.

"My mom thinks it is," Lucas answered. "But I think there's something else going on here, and that's what I want to find out. And, maybe, we'll find something that will lead us to the bad guys who started all of this. Maybe I can catch them."

"This is really heavy," Nate said. "Shouldn't we tell the police?"

"The police are already investigating it," Lucas said. "They have been for over twelve years, but it's not enough. I can do things that they can't, and if I can help, then I should, right?"

Nate nodded at once. Ty, looking solemn, nodded as well.

"Alright, then," Lucas said. "Let's go."

He led the way. After some time, Lucas recognized some of the buildings that he had passed months ago, on that day. They crossed busy South Congress and continued going east for nearly an hour, following Lucas' satellite-guided sense of direction. Eventually, they came to a cluster of six warehouses. They were all steel-sided, and some were busy with yellow-vested workers in the concrete yard outside. Lifts moved pallets and crates to a row of trucks that lined the street. Lucas, Nate and Ty stopped on the sidewalk, gazing through the chain-link fence.

"Is this it?" Ty asked.

"It's one of these," Lucas said, pointing at the group of buildings. "I only have the location of the block, not a specific address."

"You don't remember which one?" Nate said, raising an eyebrow.

"I was running for my life from Val's gang," Lucas replied flatly. "Pardon me if I don't remember the details."

"But you've got the whole internet in your head!" Nate said.

"Guys, watch out," Ty spoke up suddenly, and the two stopped bickering. He nodded over his shoulder at a lone figure approaching from across the street. It looked big enough to be a man, with flaming red hair and thick, jutting forehead. He strode casually with his long arms swinging free, clearly heading straight for them.

"Brick," Lucas growled. Ty tugged anxiously at his sleeve.

"Let's run," he squeaked.

"No," Lucas said. "I'll take care of this."

Brick was now only ten yards away, looking directly at him.

"What're you guys doing here?" Brick asked.

"It's none of your business!" Nate said loudly.

Brick's beady eyes fixed on Lucas.

"What are *you* doing here?" Lucas spat.

"I followed you," he replied. "I was going to school when I saw you walking this way. When did you get out?"

"Why do you care?" Lucas shot back. "You put me there."

"No, I didn't," Brick said simply. "I saved you."

"Bullshit," Lucas snapped. His face felt hot with rage. "It's because of you that I was in a coma for a month. I could have died, and it was all your fault!"

"I could have left you there, but I didn't. You should be grateful."

"*SHUT UP!*"

There was a series of loud, popping sounds, like wood cracking. Intense heat filled Lucas' body and crackled across his skin. Nate and Ty jumped back, and Brick took a step backward with surprise, his hands raised. Lucas was startled, too, and brought his hands up to his face, but they looked ordinary. *What just happened?*

"Look, I know you probably came here for answers," Brick said. "I can help. I was there, and I saw it happen. I want to help you."

He reached very slowly into his pocket and brought out a phone. An iPhone that Lucas recognized immediately. Brick held it out to him.

"This belongs to you, and you can have it back if you want it," he said. "I'm sorry I stole it. That was wrong."

Lucas was taken aback. Brick slowly closed the distance between them and stopped directly in front of Lucas, offering him the phone.

"Keep it," he said. "I don't need it anymore. Tell me the truth; how did you know I would be looking for answers?"

"I would, if I were in your shoes," Brick answered.

"What do you mean? What do you know?"

Brick gave him a quizzical look.

"You don't remember anything, do you?"

"No, so start from the beginning."

Brick dropped down and sat down cross-legged on the sidewalk. Lucas sat down across from him, and signalled to Nate and Ty to do the same.

"Well, Val, Darren, Howard and me chased you all the way here, and they beat you up, and then these crates that were stacked up real high against the wall fell down. Val and the others got out of the way, but you didn't, so some of them fell on you. You got buried under all this broken wood, and I wasn't sure you were even alive anymore. The others ran off, but I didn't. I thought, 'Maybe he's dead, but maybe he's not, and he shouldn't be left here alone. That wouldn't be right.' I'm not a killer, you know. I dug through all the wood and busted crates til I found you and - man almighty - you looked bad. I think just about every bone had to be broken, and there were a lot of cuts that bled everywhere. One of your arms was bent the wrong way, and your head was busted open, too, so I thought your brain was going to fall out if I moved you anywhere. I remembered that I had your phone, so I called 911, and figured I would just stay there til the ambulance arrived. My dad would have said that was stupid, but it seemed like the right thing to do. Like I said, I'm not a killer, and I sure couldn't leave somebody to die like that all by themselves. I don't know CPR or anything so I didn't do that. It didn't seem like it would have helped much anyway, since you were probably dead already. But then, all of a sudden, you opened up your eyes and started looking around. Scared the living daylights out of me, and even more when I realized what was happening. All those cuts started closing up, and that broken arm straightened out. You were healing up right before my eyes."

He paused to take a breath. He was speaking so earnestly that Lucas hung on every word.

"Then you started talking," Brick continued. "Most of it was complete gibberish that didn't make any sense, but I asked some questions and got a few answers, like what your favorite movie was, things like that. I heard somewhere that you should keep a hurt person talking to make sure they stay conscious, so I kept the conversation going best I could. Then the ambulance showed up, and I told them we were goofing around, snuck in here, accidentally knocked over the crates and you got hit in the head. By the time they loaded you up, you passed out again."

He stopped talking, and gave Lucas a look that said he was finished.

"And that's it?" Lucas asked.

"That's what happened," Brick said solemnly.

"You stayed with me, through all that?"

"It seemed like the right thing to do; any decent person would do it."

"You're not a decent person," Lucas said acidly. "Why didn't you run away?"

Brick shrugged. "Guess I'm a better person than you thought."

Lucas rolled his eyes.

"So you know which warehouse all this happened in?" he asked.

"I know exactly which warehouse," he replied confidently.

"Where are Val and the others now? Why are you here by yourself?"

"I don't hang with them anymore, and they haven't even been back to school since all that happened."

"Alright," Lucas sighed, getting to his feet. "Then you can show us. I need to see it."

Brick stood up, grinning.

"Follow me," he said.

He set off up the sidewalk. Lucas followed, with Nate and Ty at his heels, and he sensed their apprehension. He had some qualms about trusting Brick, too, but those were overshadowed by his amazement at the story, and desire to see the place where it all happened. Brick led them up the cross-street, past a long line of delivery trucks. Workers on forklifts loaded the trucks up with crates and pallets; some were moving large scraps of metal. Brick took them half a block down to a warehouse that appeared unused. The yard was overgrown with grass, and trees crept up to the sides. The front doors were locked with chains and a padlock, and a sign that read *Closed*.

"I got in through a gap in the siding," Lucas said, looking around. He pointed to the right. "Over on that side I think."

"Yeah they closed that up," Brick said. "And added electronic locks and alarms to the side doors in the back, near the delivery bay."

"How do you know?" Nate said skeptically.

"I've been back here a couple of times," Brick replied. "So what?"

"Who's 'they'?" Lucas asked.

"People who own the building, I guess."

Lucas looked the building up and down. What could be in there that needed protecting so badly? He remembered the shelves of power tools, but everything looked so old and neglected. Why bother installing new locks and alarms now?

"Well, how do we get in?" Ty asked.

"I have an idea," Lucas said, and set off walking.

"Oh, this should be interesting," Nate said.

"What are you talking about?" Brick asked, looking from Lucas to Nate. "What's he going to do?"

"You'll see," Nate replied with a grin.

Lucas walked around the side of the building. His shoes crunched over the gravel, and the wind whistled through the metal eaves. He kept walking, the other three trailing behind him, until he came to a wide gravel driveway leading up to an elevated door. The door was well over twenty feet tall and just as wide. A few yards just to the right of it was a smaller door, partially hidden by a young elm tree. As Lucas approached the door, he spotted the digital keypad beside it. It was small, square, and had a blinking red light and a small screen. He didn't know what to do, but as he focused, his senses came alive. A glowing halo surrounded the keypad. Something in his brain knew what to do, and he tried to let that part of his mind come out. His hand rose toward it, and an electrified buzz spread across his skin. The prickle grew stronger, and the buzz grew louder, and that strange new muscle flexed. Then, suddenly, the light turned green and with a click, the lock slid open. Lucas let out a sigh of relief.

"Wow, that was awesome!" Ty said.

Nate smiled, and Brick's mouth was open in awe.

"What did you just do?" he asked.

"I opened the door, obviously," Lucas said with a smile.

He pushed it open, and no alarms sounded.

"Follow me, guys," he said.

He stepped inside the warehouse. The room was dim and dusty; some daylight streamed through the skylights in the roof. Even so, Lucas turned on the lights. With a hum, yellow light burst from dozens of hanging bulbs. There was some empty space in front of them before the rows of shelves started. To their left stood a wooden desk with nothing on it, and a telephone hung on the wall. Slowly, Lucas began to walk forward. He strode down the long aisle between the shelves, which were still weighed down with power tools, just as before. Everything was covered in dust and cobwebs. He walked for some time before he came to a second clearing, which felt familiar. There were no more crates against the wall, but he could tell where they had been. The walls and the floor there were completely bare, even of dust.

"This is where it happened," he said quietly.

"So what do we look for?" Ty said.

"I don't know," Lucas said. "Anything weird."

Nate and Ty looked at each other with a shrug, then split off. Nate walked slowly back up one of the aisles, looking down at the ground, while Ty got down on his knees to look under some of the shelves near the empty wall. Brick stayed.

"What are you, exactly?" he asked.

"What do you mean?" Lucas replied.

"I think you know what I mean," Brick said. "What else can you do?"

"I'm still figuring it out."

"But you do have other powers?"

"Yes," Lucas answered. He didn't like Brick's tone.

"Stuff you couldn't do before all this?"

"No."

Brick nodded.

"I thought that was the case," he said with a smirk. "You wouldn't have been so afraid of getting beat up if you had powers to fight back."

Lucas said nothing, but walked to the empty wall. He had no clue what he was supposed to be finding. He looked down at the ground. The concrete was smooth and clean. There was heavy dust on the floor only a few yards farther, but everything surrounding the spot where he stood was polished and dust-free. A few feet away, near the center, he found a dark stain on the floor, and walked over to examine it. Suddenly, a strange feeling came over him. A prickle spread down his spine, combined with a sharp tug inside his chest. He wobbled, suddenly dizzy. *What's happening?*

"Lucas!" Ty's voice pierced the quiet, making him jump.

He spotted Ty standing at the end of a row of shelves, arm raised.

He was pointing at Brick, in a corner. A weird blue glow illuminated his grinning face.

"Brick, what are you doing?" Lucas shouted.

Brick looked up as if it was the first time he noticed Lucas standing there. His face looked sickly pale, and his eyes were so wide that the whites were visible all around. He held out his hand to reveal a thin tube, about six inches long, that seemed to contain nothing but brilliant blue light. Footsteps sounded across the pavement as Nate came running, but he stopped short when he saw the tube in Brick's hand.

"This is it, isn't it?" Brick asked, his voice almost in a whisper. "This is what gave you those powers?"

"Brick, you shouldn't touch that," Lucas warned. "We don't know what it is!"

"*I* know what it is," Brick said earnestly. "It's the stuff that changed you. It is, isn't it?"

The tug in Lucas' chest was sharp; like a magnetic pull, it was drawing him forward. The tube, or whatever was in it, was calling to something inside him, and every one of his cells was responding. He stumbled a few steps, then dropped to one knee, his body shaking. Nate and Ty saw this and their expressions changed from apprehension to outright horror.

"It also might have killed four people," Nate said quickly to Brick. "And it might be killing Lucas right now. Put it down!"

"I could have powers like you," Brick mumbled. "And never be hurt by anything."

"Does he look powerful right now?" Nate challenged.

Lucas was down on all fours and felt like he was about to vomit. *What the hell is that stuff?* he thought, terrified. That stuff couldn't be what gave him his powers; maybe, Brick had just found his kryptonite, like Superman had. Powers came with weaknesses, right? He felt the urge to crawl until he was face down on the ground, and he couldn't move any further. The pull in his chest was unbearable. A pain started in the back of his head like his skull was being split open, back to front.

Brick held the tube up to his eyes, peering into it. Then, without warning, he raised his hand over his head and smashed it on the ground at his feet.

"No!" Lucas cried.

Shattered glass flew across the pavement, and blue liquid splattered across Brick's shoes and up the legs of his pants. Nate and Ty scrambled away and retreated to the far corner of the room. Lucas could barely breathe; his muscles tightened, his bones ached, and he felt like his ribs were going to burst open as Brick bent down and touched the pool of glowing liquid on the ground. The light began to dwindle, Brick's smile widened, and the pool slowly dried up. Lucas couldn't believe what he was seeing. He watched, stunned, as the liquid seemed to disappear *into* Brick like it was alive; it was drawing itself into his skin until not a single drop remained. His veins glowed a faint greenish-blue as the light was absorbed into his limbs, then traveled up to his neck.

Then his face drooped. His eyes went blank, and he dropped with a heavy thud to the ground as his legs went limp. He lay on his back, head lolling to the side. Nobody moved. The whole of the building was silent.

Something's wrong, Lucas thought. His breath came in quick gasps as his heart pounded. Slowly, he rose to his hands and knees once more.

"Is that supposed to happen?" Ty asked in a frightened voice.

Lucas didn't answer. Then Brick's arms and legs suddenly began to flap around, slapping against the concrete with such force that his bones would surely break.

"What's happening?" Ty cried.

"It's killing him!" Lucas gasped, staggering to his feet.

He forced his feet forward, running to Brick's side. The whites of Brick's eyes showed as his eyes rolled back in his head, and the veins in his neck bulged a dark blue color. Lucas skipped out of the way of one of his flailing arms and stuffed his jacket under Brick's head. The tug in his chest grew stronger as he neared Brick, and the prickle across his skin intensified, like being stuck with thousands of needles at once. He could feel the presence of the blue liquid, and some form of consciousness hidden there. It recognized him, and - more frightening still - it *wanted* him.

"It wants me, not him," he said.

"What?" Nate said, stepping up beside him.

"The blue stuff... I don't know, it's alive somehow," he said quickly. "It's calling to me."

"What does *that* mean?" Nate asked.

"I can feel it; it knows me. It'll kill him if I don't get it out."

Lucas didn't know what to do, but knew he had to do something or Brick would die. He commanded part of his brain to call 911, then placed his hand on Brick's head. The stuff was alive, but also felt mechanical. There was definitely an electrical signal there and Lucas' senses responded, latching on. That gave him confidence.

Leave him alone, he thought, extending his will to whatever the alien substance was. *Get out now!*

That terrible pull grew until it was like a knife was being twisted in his chest. Suddenly, glowing blue liquid began to pour from Brick's eyes, nose and mouth. It seeped from his pores, gathering in globules the size of quarters that began to climb toward Lucas' hand. Brick continued to thrash; an arm flew up and struck Lucas' face, breaking his nose. He cried out in pain, and Nate and Ty grabbed hold of his shirt to pull him away.

"Wait!" he yelled, shaking them off. "It's working!"

Blood dripped down his chin and tears welled up his eyes, but he held on. The thick, blue globules crept up his fingers and over the back of his hand, then shrank as they were absorbed through Lucas' own skin. He gasped, and very nearly let go then, but the clinging ache, the tug in his chest, began to abate. More and more of the blue liquid left Brick's body and was sucked into him, drawn in through his pores. Brick stopped thrashing, and his limbs lay still on the pavement. Minutes crawled by until there was nothing left inside him and the blue light faded completely.

Lucas let go and collapsed, panting. He waited, expecting to blackout or fall into a seizure, but nothing happened. He felt nothing but the hammering of his heart inside his chest. Tasting blood, he remembered his broken nose. He reached up and touched it, but felt no pain. He pinched the bridge, and found that his nose had reformed itself. It was whole. He looked down. Beside him, Brick looked as if he was sleeping; his huge chest rose and fell in a steady rhythm.

Sirens sounded in the distance, and Lucas looked at Nate and Ty. Nate had his hands on his head, his face pale; he looked like he had just thrown up. Ty was on the ground, shivering and hugging his knees. Lucas slowly got to his feet; his legs shook at first, but held. He walked over to them. The sirens outside were getting louder.

"I think everything's okay," he said to Nate. "It's over."

71

Nate dropped his hands and gave a short nod. His cheeks were wet with tears.

"Help me get Ty up," Lucas told him.

Lucas stepped over to Ty, who shrank away from him, then got to his feet and walked off without a word, heading toward the warehouse door. Nate looked apologetically at Lucas, then followed Ty. Lucas was left alone with an unconscious Brick as tires crunched over the gravel outside.

Chapter 7

MEN WEARING WHITE PROTECTIVE SUITS and masks came in the building with orange duffel bags and a stretcher. They attended to Brick, and Lucas watched as they fitted an oxygen mask over his face, then moved him onto the stretcher. Brick no longer looked so peaceful; his face was gray beneath the mask. They wheeled him outside, then one of the EMTs looked over Lucas. They made him sit down, and shone lights in his eyes, listened to his pulse, made him breathe with a stethoscope against his ribs, but in the end there was nothing to be done except help him clean the blood off of his face. He felt sick, but knew that was only because of his sudden loneliness and fear. Physically, he was perfectly fine.

His fear grew exponentially when three police officers entered the warehouse, flashlights in hand. Lucas wished dearly that he could sink through the floor and disappear. When they spotted him, one of the officers - a balding, burly-looking man - strode directly to him. He was also wearing a mask and gloves. The other two began to walk around the room, shining their flashlights everywhere.

"Is he hurt?" the cop said to the EMT who was placing the blood-covered wipes into a plastic bag.

"No, he's fine," the medic replied. She held out the bag. "You're going to need this."

"Save it for the feds," the cop said. "They're pulling up now."

He looked hard at Lucas.

"You stay right there," he said sternly. "Don't move."

Lucas was reminded of when he was small and had to be put in time-out, except that now he was completely terrified.

A moment later, someone walked slowly in, gazing around at the floor, walls and ceiling of the room. He was very tall and looked like an astronaut, because he was wearing a bulkier protective suit than the others, with a helmet and full face shield. He seemed to meander in circles, stepping carefully with a flashlight aimed at the ground just in front of his feet. Then, as if noticing them for the first time, he came to the spot where the cop and the EMT stood on either side of Lucas. Through the plastic of the face shield, Lucas could see a man in his forties, with blue eyes and an oddly familiar face.

"What's wrong with him?" the man said to the EMT. His voice was slightly muffled, but that did nothing to detract from the sharpness of his tone.

"Nothing; he's not hurt," she answered. "Just a little shaken up."

"I'll say," the cop said.

"Are you Lucas Tavera?" the man asked.

"Yes," Lucas said. His voice sounded so small.

The medic handed the bag to the man.

"He had some blood on his face," she said.

"Alright, you can go," he said to her, taking the bag. He turned to the cop. "Go wait over there while I talk to him."

The medic went outside, while the officer walked a few yards away and stood with his thumbs in his belt. The man squatted down in front of Lucas so that their eyes were level. His eyes were bluish-gray, like steel, and just as cold. Lucas felt like they were looking straight through him.

"Hello," the man said. His voice had become surprisingly gentle, now that he was talking to Lucas. "You don't need to be afraid; we're not going to hurt you. Will you tell me what happened here?"

Lucas opened his mouth. His jaw trembled, and he could see his frightened reflection in the man's helmet.

"Well, I came here with my friends to look for something. There was an accident here about a month ago and… w-w-we were trying to find out what happened…"

"What accident?" the man asked. His voice was still low and soft.

Lucas saw no point in lying.

"I was here a month ago and I got in a fight with three guys from my school and some crates fell and I got hurt, but then I wasn't hurt anymore but I still went to the hospital because something happened to my brain. There was something in the crates, and it - whatever it was - got in me and… it changed me. Everything's different now. I came here to find out what it was, and Brick found a container of the stuff and touched it and it started to kill him but I saved him by… well, it just went from him to me. It's all inside me now, but it's alright, because I think that's what it wanted."

"What do you mean, 'that's what it wanted'?"

"I could hear it, and I felt it. It called to me."

"What did this stuff look like?" the man asked.

"It was blue and glowed."

"Who else touched it?"

"Just me and Brick."

The man nodded, still scrutinizing Lucas. His expression was pensive, and Lucas wondered if the man thought he was crazy. Then his tone changed again.

"My name is Agent Kowalski," he said sharply. "I'm part of a special task force with the CIA. I have been investigating this blue stuff for quite a while now, and I know a little bit about it. I want you to come with me and help me learn more. I will have some experts look at you, and I'll ask you some more questions."

Lucas' heart beat faster.

"Seth Kowalski?" he said.

The man blinked. "Yes. How did you know that?"

"My mom told me," he said. "You're pretending to be her boss, Danny Clark."

Agent Kowalski's face was cold and stony.

"Don't say anything else," he said. "We'll talk more when we get where we're going."

"Where are we going?" he asked.

"Somewhere safer."

"Can my mom come?"

"Yes," the man answered shortly. "She has to."

Lucas suddenly felt like he had made a huge mistake as he nodded slowly. The man rose.

"Let's go."

Lucas stood, and Kowalski guided him to the door with a firm hand on his shoulder. The cop followed them out, keeping about ten feet back. Outside, three cop cars sat with lights flashing beside a black, unmarked sedan. The ambulance rolled away over the gravel drive, presumably with Brick inside, while two others remained. Radios squawked, and people in white protective suits wandered all over the grounds, carrying different pieces of equipment. Nate and Ty sat in the back of the second ambulance, wrapped in blankets, while another white-suited person spoke to them. They looked up as Lucas came past; their faces looked drawn and pale, like victims of a car crash or war zone. They stared in silence and Lucas looked away, keeping his eyes forward as Kowalski led him to the third ambulance, then opened the back door and told him to get in.

Lucas stepped up into the back of the ambulance. There was a stretcher secured on the floor, and benches on either side against the walls. Lots of medical equipment hung in various places. Lucas took a seat on one of the benches. Through a small window, Lucas could see into the cab of the ambulance. One man in an EMT uniform sat in the driver's seat, while a man in a white suit rode in the passenger's seat. Kowalski said to wait a moment, then he walked off and called to the person talking to Nate and Ty. The person came over, and Lucas now saw through the face shield that it was a woman. The two spoke in low tones, then the man returned and climbed up into the ambulance. He took the bench across from Lucas.

"We'll be going in just a few minutes," he said.

"Why are we going in an ambulance?" Lucas asked. "I'm not hurt."

"We like to be prepared." Kowalski replied.

Lucas said nothing. *What does that mean?* he thought. *Prepared for what?* He kept his hands in his lap, and his eyes lowered.

"Are you hungry?" Kowalski asked.

He shook his head.

"You're safe, Lucas," Kowalski said. "You're not in trouble."

"What about my mom?"

"Depends," he replied. "Why did she tell you my name?"

"She thought I was dying, because of the blue stuff. I have it inside me."

"And you're not dying?"

"No. It's different with me."

"Why?"

"I don't know," Lucas said. "Do you?"

Kowalski tilted his head. "No, I don't but that's what I hope to find out."

The woman returned, and climbed up beside Kowalski.

"Hello," she said in a smooth, clear voice. Lucas could see dark skin and dark eyes through her face shield.

"This is my partner, Shelley Iweala," Kowalski said.

Someone closed the door and the ambulance was put in gear. The next thing Lucas knew was that they were pulling away from the warehouse and bumping and jostling down the drive to the street. Lucas looked through the small window to see out the front. They were passed on the left by two more police vehicles heading toward the complex of warehouses. He felt a sharp prickle and knew, through his extra senses, that Mrs. Bridwell - and her phone - were inside the car in front. Lucas realized that the police must have picked up Nate and Ty's parents.

"Are we going to pick up my mom?" he asked Kowalski.

"Another agent is fetching her now," he replied.

They made several turns and eventually made it to South Congress. As they approached Lucas' apartment, he spotted a black sedan parked beside the curb. They continued by it without slowing. Lucas typed out a quick text to his mother's phone, which he felt was in the car now tailing them:

It's Lucas. I'm okay. I am sorry for all of this.

He waited for a reply, but the minutes crawled by and still none came. He wondered if they might have confiscated her phone. The caravan entered the highway and continued south and slightly southeast, away from downtown. The towering skyscrapers and glittering hotels shrank in the distance.

"Where are we going?" he asked warily.

"To the office," Kowalski said.

Lucas monitored their location on GPS as they left the city entirely. Through the window, he spotted suburban neighborhoods sat nestled in the hills that rolled by. Then these gave way to pastures of grazing cattle, and the hills gradually leveled out to become acres and acres of flat grassland. Lucas could see all the way to the horizon; there was nothing but open fields, and still, they drove on. Occasionally the road took them over rivers and through copses of trees. He spotted some small country homes with long driveways, ponds, and vast plots of land surrounding them. He saw cattle grazing in some pastures, while others had horses, sheep, goats, or even what looked to him like small deer with unusual horns; his brain told him that these were gazelle. He even spotted an ostrich walking amidst some cattle and donkeys in one pasture.

They continued moving south, and the further they went from Austin's bustling noise, the quieter his mind became. His skin no longer crawled, and the voices that had been a constant racket in the back of his mind now faded. It was more difficult to reach the stream of the internet, and when he summoned it into his mind, it came more slowly. Eventually, he gave up trying, but he didn't feel loss; he felt relief. He was finally alone inside his head. As the open, empty country sped by outside, he leaned his head back and fell asleep.

He was awakened by his skin crawling once more. He dug his fingers into the sleeves of his jacket; it felt like ants were crawling underneath. Opening his eyes, he saw an enormous building looming ahead of them. It appeared to be three stories tall and spread north for two hundred feet, with a parking lot in front. The building continued east for an indeterminable distance. Inside the building, Lucas sensed a hum of electrical activity. The building sat alone; no other residences or commercial buildings could be felt for miles. Power lines fed directly into it, and it drew tremendous amounts of energy. Within it, countless computers and phones were abuzz. Lucas' internal clock informed him that it was 8:35 PM, while his GPS told him that they were located thirteen miles outside of Goliad. Men with guns, wearing tactical suits and carrying radios, stood along the driveway and crouched beneath trees. All had their eyes on the sky or the horizon, and all wore protective masks. The car parked directly in front of the building, beside a door guarded by two men, standing on either side, and Agent Iweala got out.

"We're here," Kowalski said as he opened the door and stepped out.

Iweala held out a hand to help Lucas down, and as he got out, put her hand firmly on his shoulder and began guiding him toward the front door of the building. The doors of the car behind them shut, and he saw his mother being led from the car by two other agents. He stopped in his tracks. Kowalski and Iweala both waited until Leah was close behind them. She was wearing jeans and a sweater over her brown work smock, and her eyes were full of worry. She and Kowalski exchanged a glance, and before Lucas could say anything, Kowalski motioned for them to hurry along.

The two men that guarded the door barely looked at Lucas. Once inside, he was taken through a long hallway where more men with guns stood guard every few feet. He could hear a great deal of chatter, like an entire stadium of voices was contained inside this building. Lucas' senses were flooded with the noise, and he felt momentarily dazed. He took some comfort that his mother was with him, though she was kept about twenty feet behind him as he was led deeper and deeper inside by the CIA agents' strong hands on his shoulders. The place looked like a giant warehouse; there were steel rafters overhead with powerful incandescent bulbs hanging from the exposed ceiling. The walls looked like they had been added as an afterthought; they didn't reach all the way to the ceiling, and Lucas could smell paint and the dust of sheetrock. They were more like partitions, and there were many doors leading off of a long, narrow hallway. He counted seven before he was ordered through one of them, into a second hallway, where the floor changed. It was coated in plastic, and felt hollow underneath. Then he came to another door. This door was made of metal, and was vacuum-sealed. The room it led to had a low ceiling, a large mirror, and blindingly-white walls. The floor was concrete, with a drain in the middle of it and a small examination table off to one side. Lucas went in, followed by Kowalski.

"Sit down," Kowalski said, pointing at the table.

Lucas climbed up onto it, then sat facing Kowalski. He was growing more terrified by the second.

"I'm going to explain very quickly what's going to happen here," Kowalski said gently. "We are part of a very special task force put together by the president himself to investigate the origin and purpose of the blue liquid. Some of our experts are on the way here now to draw some blood, and they are going to determine whether you really have it inside you or not. If you do, then we'll have some other tests to do. You're going to have to stay in here until those tests are done, so somebody will be by with some food. I'm sorry, but we can't move forward without those tests. There's nothing for you to worry about; just stay calm and cooperate until this is over. Do you understand?"

This is just like the hospital all over again, Lucas thought.

"I guess so," he muttered.

"You've been a real trooper so far," Kowalski said with a grin. "I knew I could count on you."

Lucas did not smile back. He found Kowalski's attitude patronizing. At that moment, the door opened again. Lucas spotted two armed guards just outside. Then a dozen other people in white suits came in, with a variety of medical equipment. He was made to take off his clothes, and was hosed down with something that smelled like chlorinated pool water. Then he was given a white hospital gown to put on, and had to change in front of the white-suited people. One of them left carrying his clothes, while another set a small tray on the table beside Lucas. There were four clear vials on the tray. Without saying anything, a woman took his arm and tied a rubber band around it, just above the elbow. She wiped the inside of his elbow with a wet cotton ball, and inserted a needle with some kind of valve on it. Lucas watched with a tight jaw as each of those vials was pushed onto the valve and filled with dark blood. When she finished, she removed the rubber band and the needle and pressed a Band-Aid over the wound, and then she left, taking the tray with her. In the next twenty minutes, someone checked his heart rate and listened to his lungs, someone else shone a penlight into his eyes, and the skin on his neck, back, and arms was closely examined. Last, and most horribly of all, he was told to lie on his side, and was given two painful injections into his back. Then a very long, thick needle was inserted into his spine, and some fluid was drawn out. After all this was done, everyone left - including Kowalski. Lucas lay on the table, alone in the white room.

He tried not to cry, but the minutes crawled by and still he was alone. All he could think about was how tired he was, and how badly he wanted to be back in his own bed. He regretted deeply ever going back to that warehouse. His head throbbed, and his eyes were heavy, but he didn't dare sleep now. With his mind, he sought out where everyone might have gone. He knew that Kowalski carried a phone on his person, and tracked it to a room three doors down. He also located his own phone, the one that Brick had taken, somewhere on the other side of the warehouse. Someone was opening up his contacts and scrolling through them. Outraged, Lucas entered the phone with his mind and forced it to shut itself off. Whoever the invader was tried several times to turn it back on, and each time Lucas turned it off again.

After ten minutes, another woman in a white suit did indeed bring some food; she set a tray with crackers and a pint of milk on the table next to him. Suddenly, the door opened with a hiss, and Kowalski returned. There was also movement on the other side of the mirror, which Lucas realized was actually a window with one-way glass, leading to another room. He sensed a laptop, owned by Iweala, and a great deal of other electrical equipment on the other side.

Kowalski approached the table where Lucas lay. The room was very quiet, except for Agent Kowalski's breath through the mask.

"Can you sit up?" he asked.

He did, with some difficulty.

"Lucas, you told me that the blue liquid changed you. Will you explain, please?"

Lucas swallowed, his heart hammering in his chest.

"It… gave me powers."

Kowalski raised an eyebrow.

"I'm not lying," Lucas said quickly. "I can control technology with my mind."

"What kind of technology?"

"Well, so far I've done phones, computers, an alarm system and lightbulbs."

"Lightbulbs?"

"Yeah, like, I turned the lights on and off."

"With your mind?"

Lucas couldn't tell if the man was teasing him or not; his face was completely expressionless, and his eyes were flat. Lucas wondered if that was one of his skills as a CIA agent or just his personality.

"Yes," Lucas answered him. "I can also see what people are doing on their phones, computers, and other things. I see it in my mind, and I can feel it, too. Like, I know that there are people in the next room recording us talking. There are three people, or three phones anyway. And I can see everything that Iweala is typing right now, word for word, in my head."

"Can you demonstrate?"

"She just wrote, *S5 makes claims of supernatural powers. Agent K asks him to demonstrate.* I know that *S5* means "Subject 5" because she wrote it earlier at the top of the page. I also know that somebody a few rooms over at … computer station 19… is looking up porn."

Kowalski just stared coldly, studying him.

"Someone verify that," he said finally, but not to Lucas.

A minute later, a voice crackled over Kowalski's radio.

"He's right about the phones," it said. "And… and the porn guy."

"You could see all that inside your head?" Kowalski asked him.

"Yes," Lucas replied.

"That's very impressive. What else can you do?"

"If you get me a phone, I'll show you," Lucas told him. "It needs to be unlocked, please. And Agent Iweala's laptop, too, if she doesn't mind."

Kowalski got up and left, then returned with another agent's phone and the laptop. He sat down with the computer on his lap, and held the phone in his hand.

"Look at the phone's screen," Lucas said.

As he spoke, Lucas opened the internet browser and searched around until he found a video of a cat playing piano, then let it play for a bit. Then he called the phone, answered it, and put himself on speakerphone so that his own voice rang through the phone's speakers.

I can access anything that's unprotected and do whatever I want with it. I could read your emails and your texts, call your friends, view your social media profile… all with only my brain.

The same words appeared in type across the word document open on Agent Iweala's laptop.

"You're doing this?" Kowalski asked.

Yes. My mind can control any technology and access anything wireless or online.

"Amazing," he said.

Lucas hung up the call.

"Anything else?" Kowalski asked.

"I have GPS and wifi," Lucas said. "I can track people's phones and trace calls."

"Can you access things that are password-protected? Or private servers?"

"Maybe I could… if I had time. I don't know much about hacking."

"Can you track people on social media?"

"I don't know."

"Can you see who is accessing particular sites?"

"I don't know..."

It dawned on Lucas that he may have gone too far in showing off. Kowalski nodded, then got up and left without a reply while Lucas sat, bewildered. He could still see Iweala's computer in his mind, and saw that she received an email which contained a great deal of jargon followed by the words, *Contamination confirmed.* Then, suddenly, he was locked out. The computer was shut down.

The door opened again and Kowalski returned.

"Does the rising mean anything to you?" he asked with that cold, flat voice.

"Rising what?"

"Are you an enemy of the United States?"

"What? No! I'm *twelve*."

"You've also shown us that you have considerable powers," Kowalski replied. "We have to take precautions. So, *are* you?"

"No."

"Do you know anyone by the name of Ari Lytton?"

"No," Lucas answered, getting angry. "Why are you asking me this?"

Kowalski paced the floor. "He is a biotechnologist who developed some microscopic devices called nanomachines. They are basically very tiny robots, so small that you couldn't see them without a microscope. He made them for a company that was researching cures for Parkinson's, Alzheimer's - diseases like that. Fifteen years ago, he disappeared from his research facility in San Diego without any note or indication of where he may have gone. Three years later, we raided a human smuggling operation and found vials containing his patented nanomachines. The operation was run by the Rising, an international terrorist organization. They were experimenting on young women with the nanomachines, studying how long it took them to die. I think you know *that* story."

He paused, and his eyes seemed to bore straight through Lucas, who felt like he might throw up.

"We think they either stole or copied Dr. Lytton's work, or they have him stowed away somewhere and are forcing him to make the weapons," Kowalski continued. "We learned from the corpses that when the nanomachines infect a person, they travel through the bloodstream and attack the brain and spinal cord, killing him within minutes. The Rising has turned the nanomachines into a biotechnological weapon, and we believe that they are planning to use it on a massive scale. It is unstoppable and incurable; with it, they would be capable of wiping out entire cities."

"What does this have to do with me?" Lucas asked.

"Because you are contaminated with these same nanomachines, and have been for weeks now, but you're still alive. You're not even sick. How is that possible?"

"How should I know? I didn't even know those things existed until just now."

"It seems we have an opportunity now that could completely change the game for us."

A feeling of dread came over Lucas. Kowalski paced back and forth, his arms crossed, staring at him.

"What are you going to do?" Lucas asked.

"I'm very sorry, Lucas," Kowalski said quietly. "I'm sure you don't deserve this."

A commotion sounded in the next room. Lucas heard the scuffling of feet and his mother's voice crying, "No! No!"

He was on his feet in an instant. His mother had been there the whole time, watching.

"Mom!?" he shouted in panic. Adrenaline shot through his veins like fire.

Kowalski immediately assumed a defensive stance, his hand at his gun, the other palm-out toward Lucas. The other two men suddenly had guns out and cocked. Lucas felt his stomach drop, and the voices in his head began to swell. They sounded like radio chatter, but he couldn't follow any of the conversations. His temples throbbed.

"Stop! He's just a child!" Leah screamed.

"Put those away!" Kowalski yelled at the men. They lowered their weapons.

"What's going on?" Lucas stammered. "Where's my mom?"

"We are not going to hurt you," Kowalski replied in a low, steady voice. His other hand was still extended toward Lucas. "Everyone just needs to calm down."

"Where's my mom?" he demanded again.

"She's perfectly fine. She's in the next room. Now, why don't you take a seat and we'll keep talking?"

"I want to see her," Lucas demanded.

"Of course," Kowalski said calmly. "And all we want is your cooperation. I think we can work together so that we're both happy."

One of the men paced around to Lucas' left, watching him warily. He was suddenly reminded of that day, months ago, when Val, Howard and Darren cornered him back at the other warehouse, like a bunch of jackals eyeing their prey. But these men didn't look at him like that.

Leah continued to scream, "Seth, please!" until her cries were muffled, then cut off. Lucas couldn't take it anymore. He flew at Kowalski, screaming with his fists clenched in rage. One of the bigger men lunged in, catching Lucas around the waist and pulling him backward. He hurled a punch at the man's mask and heard more than a few bones break with a grinding *crunch*, but Lucas didn't care; he continued to thrash and kick, even as another man caught his hands and attempted to secure them with cuffs. Heat filled his body, and there came a loud popping sound, seemingly out of nowhere. It sounded like distant gunfire. With a thunderous crash, the two men holding him were suddenly jerked back and thrown off their feet, as if bungee lines had been hooked to their belts. One slammed into the concrete wall, the other flattened the table. The room was plunged into darkness. Lucas found himself lying on his back, on the floor, as showers of sparks rained from the ceiling. Smoke stung his eyes, and everything hurt. His heart hammered in his ears.

His mother's voice, far away now, grew smaller and smaller.

Chapter 8

LUCAS OPENED HIS EYES. HE had no clue how much time had passed, but he felt groggy, like he had slept for hours. He was in another, very white room, in a bed with glaring light overhead that made him wince. He quickly recognized the sounds of hospital equipment, and his adrenaline spiked. He was dizzy, and everything he saw was blurry. To his right, a dark silhouette leaned close, only a few feet away.

"Who's there?" he croaked.

"It's me, Seth Kowalski," the figure said.

"You!" Lucas snarled, struggling to sit up. He found that he couldn't move, even to lift his head, and his arms and legs wouldn't respond.

"Try to stay calm," Kowalski said. He came slowly into view, seated in a chair. He was no longer wearing a protective suit, and Lucas could now see his blond hair, neatly combed. "And don't shoot me with any lightning, please."

"Don't give me any ideas," Lucas snapped. "Where am I? Where's my mom?"

"Yeah, about that," Kowalski replied with a smile. "If I were you, I would listen to what I have to say very, very carefully... if you ever want to see her again."

Lucas glared at the man who continued to smile very calmly. He sat with his legs crossed and hands folded. He had a thick neck and strong, broad shoulders.

"What makes you think I won't escape?" Lucas said angrily.

"It would take quite a while for those sedatives to wear off enough for you to stand, let alone walk out of here. We are well aware now that you pack quite a punch, so we're not going to let that happen."

"How about I just destroy all of your computers then? I'll tear down your entire network, fry everything you've got and send you back to the dark ages without even lifting a finger."

"Go ahead," Kowalski said coolly. "But remember that I recommended you listen to me first. Think about where you are, Lucas. There would be nowhere for you to go."

Lucas glared at him, but his fury wavered. His brain felt clouded, like it was padded with cotton balls. As hard as he tried, he couldn't pick up any electrical signals, inside the room or outside. His internal GPS, clock and calendar were all gone.

Kowalski smirked.

"Why aren't you wearing that suit?" Lucas asked.

"It's no longer necessary. You're not contagious."

"I'm better?"

He inclined his head. "No, just not contagious."

Lucas was reeling. For a moment, he had felt almost relieved, but now that was gone, too.

"What day is it?" he asked.

"June 30th. You've been sedated for seven months."

"What? What did you do to me?" Lucas whispered.

"We didn't hurt you; don't worry. We only studied you, and boy, have we learned a lot. One of the most important things was how to contain you. As it turns out, the right combination of tranquilizers will slow down your brain enough to immobilize you and shut off your powers completely. This room is seven stories underground, far beyond the reach of any wireless signal. Even if you had your powers right now, you'd never be able to reach our equipment. We could bury you down here indefinitely, if we wanted to."

He paused dramatically to let that sink it. Lucas only glowered.

"The second-most important piece of information is that you're not really human. Did you know that? More than half your genes are completely artificial. That really threw your mom for a loop."

"What?" Lucas gasped.

Kowalski leaned forward, his elbows on his knees and his hands folded. He spoke very slowly.

T.D. Wilson

"Best we can determine, you were *made*. Pieced together like a jigsaw puzzle. It really is incredible…but it brings so many questions to mind. Is this what the Rising wanted with Dr. Lytton's research? Do they know you exist? And are you the only one?"

"Are you saying that they… they…?" Lucas stammered. He couldn't bring himself to say it.

"She wasn't pregnant when they took her, and you don't share her DNA. Our lab technicians have analyzed your genes backwards and forwards, and compared them to every gene sequence we've got on record. They concluded that you were one hundred percent engineered from scratch."

Lucas couldn't breathe. He would have curled up and hugged his knees, or hidden his face from Kowalski, but he couldn't move. He was helpless, and felt like his entire world was crashing down on him.

All the while, the agent watched him with a cold, impassive expression. Lucas wanted to scream at him, but instead he took a long, deep breath.

"Why are you telling me this?" he asked.

"Because, Lucas, I want you to understand your situation. You are special in more ways than one. You are not only immune to the nanobots' destructive effects, but the *only* one who's immune. Every other natural human being out there would die within minutes if they came into contact with those things. So, like it or not, we need you."

"What do you mean?"

"They are planning another attack, Lucas. And we want you to find them and help us stop them before it happens."

"How?"

"You'll use your powers to help us track the Rising's movements. And where we find any trace of the nanomachines, you'll help us destroy them."

Lucas' mouth dropped open. He couldn't believe what he was hearing.

"Why would I help *you*?" he cried.

Agent Kowalski sat back and crossed his legs.

"For two reasons. First: by helping us, you could save not just the United States, but the entire world. The Rising has kept us chasing our tails for years now; they are well-coordinated and can act like ghosts when they want to. We simply don't have the resources or the manpower to keep up anymore. But you, with your abilities, could help us find and end them once and for all. The second reason is this: the higher-ups see you as dangerous, uncontrollable, and a threat to national security. You put two people in the hospital with that little tantrum of yours. To the government, you're a dangerous, unpredictable liability. They wanted to keep you asleep for the rest of your life - however long that may be - but that proved to be too expensive, so they opted to kill you instead. But, I proposed that if we have a supercomputer at our disposal, we might as well use it, with me as your handler. However, if you say no, killing you is still on the table."

"So, I don't have a choice," Lucas concluded.

"No, I'm afraid not," Agent Kowalski replied. "You belong to the United States government now."

Lucas was quiet for several minutes, mulling all of this over. Kowalski let him think, simply folding his hands over his knee.

"What about my mom?" Lucas asked finally.

"What about her?"

"If they killed me, what would happen to her?"

"She will continue to get her protection, regardless. We keep our word."

Lucas sighed. If he could move, he would have rubbed his eyes in exasperation. They stung with the tears he was fighting back. He would not allow himself to cry in front of the agent.

"Besides," Kowalski continued. "You would help bring justice to your mother's captors."

Lucas set his jaw, feeling his anger boil once more. How dare this man use his mother against him? Still, he was right.

"When do I start?" he said hoarsely.

Kowalski grinned. The door opened and a woman, dressed in scrubs, entered. She cautiously approached the side of the bed. Lucas noticed now that he had the ordinary ECG leads and an IV drip attached to him, but there was also a second bag hanging beside his head that fed clear liquid through a tube that led up his chest and then disappeared from view. The woman put on a pair of gloves, then placed her hands near his throat.

"Hold very still, please," she said.

Lucas realized with horror that the needle was embedded in his neck. He hadn't noticed it before because much of his body was quite numb. He didn't dare breathe as the woman peeled off a piece of tape, then carefully removed the needle. All Lucas could feel was slight pressure. The woman rolled up the tubing and left the room, taking the bag and stand with her.

It took nearly twenty minutes for movement to return to his limbs, but it felt like hours. He waited, feeling helpless and miserable as the weird, prickling sensations slowly returned - first to his hands, feet, and legs, then to the rest of his body. Eventually, he could wiggle his fingers and toes, and then flex his fingers. Kowalski removed the cuffs, and, after a few more minutes, Lucas finally pulled himself up to a sitting position in the bed. When he could stand, he was given a white cotton shirt and sweatpants to wear instead of the hospital gown, and slip-on shoes. Kowalski got up and faced the wall so that Lucas could have some privacy while he changed. He noticed as he dressed that he had lost weight during his sleep. His wrists and knees were bony, and his ribs showed. He gritted his teeth, swallowing down the anger, and threw on the shirt and pants.

Fortunately, food was soon brought for him. Some men entered, bringing a tray with a white paper sack and a drink in a Styrofoam cup; a small table, and a second chair. Lucas sat down and opened the bag to find a cheeseburger, fries, and a large chocolate chip cookie. The cup contained a thick chocolate shake. He dug in as Kowalski came back to the table and sat across from him.

"How is it?" he asked.

"Tastes like heaven," Lucas replied, his mouth full of fries.

"I can't imagine what food must taste like after seven months of not having any," Kowalski remarked.

As Lucas downed the food, the cloudiness he had felt in his brain faded. He could think more clearly, and the prickly sensation returned to his skin. He felt a hum in the back of his mind, but when he went searching for its source, he came up empty. There was nothing out there - no cell phone signals, no wifi, not even a desktop computer. He tried to venture farther, but it was like swimming through mud. As far as he could tell, the CIA had removed all electronics far from his reach.

He caught Kowalski looking at him with a bemused expression. Lucas finished the food, then balled up the paper wrapper. He pushed back from the table, sipping the milkshake.

"You know what I just realized?" he said finally. "I missed my birthday. It was June 14th. I'm thirteen now."

"Happy belated birthday," Kowalski said drily. "Now let's talk about the mission. The Rising has been targeting cities in the U.S., as I told you before. Their M.O. so far has been to post a warning on social media, from a fake account, two days before they attack. Then, the bomb goes off. It only takes one person to start it, but they create dozens of fake profiles and have all of them post the same thing. Then, it goes viral, and our guys are scrambling to trace it back to the source. Meanwhile, our boys on the ground are on high alert, looking for a bomb, but have no idea where to start. Every city is at risk."

"How many times has this happened?" Lucas asked.

"Three," Agent Kowalski said. "The first time was last February, the second time around mid-July, and the third this past Christmas Eve, while you were sleeping. The bomb used in the last attack contained capsules of nanomachines. Four people died from contamination."

Lucas shuddered, knowing how unpleasant their deaths must have been.

"Another warning was sent six hours ago," he replied. "Which means you have eighteen hours left to find out where the Rising is, and where the bomb will be."

Lucas swallowed. It was 11:24 AM now.

"I already told you, I don't know anything about hacking."

"I don't need hackers; I have plenty of those already. I need something new, what you bring to the table."

"Which is what?"

"I don't know, but we're running out of time, and frankly, we're desperate. I think you'll figure it out. If you're ready, I'll take you up to the base of our operations."

Without waiting for an answer, Kowalski stood up, and Lucas followed suit. The agent led him to the door, which he tapped on twice, and then Lucas heard a click. Kowalski opened the door to an antechamber. A second door opened with a hiss; there were three armed guards standing just outside, and half a dozen people in white lab coats. These men and women all stared at Lucas as he came through the doorway, some wearing weird smiles.

Kowalski pointed at the three guards.

"This is your security team," he explained. "Brad, Tim, and Kenny. They are well-trained, and will be with you at all times."

All three were hulking men dressed in black, with visible side arms.

Brad was blond with an impressive scar on his neck; Tim was dark-skinned and enormous in build, and Kenny was a redhead with sleeve tattoos. Each gave Lucas stern looks. Kowalski moved on and introduced a young man who stepped forward from the group. He had olive skin, a dark goatee, thick glasses, and was positively beaming.

"Lucas, this is a very important man for you to know," Kowalski said. "This is the doctor-in-charge, Dr. Benjamin Gill. He's been watching over you for the past seven months, and is responsible for your care and research into your condition."

Dr. Gill reached out his hand for Lucas to shake it. He did, and the young doctor grinned ecstatically. For half a second, he wondered if the man was going to hug him.

"It's truly a pleasure to finally meet you, Lucas," he said. "If you ever need anything, please let me know right away. How are you feeling?"

"Fine, I guess," Lucas replied, eyeing the man warily.

"That's great. It's my job to take care of you and make sure you stay healthy, so you'll be seeing a lot of me. I hope we can be good friends."

Lucas gave him a skeptical look, but Kowalski put a hand gently on his shoulder.

"Come on, you guys can visit later," he said. "We've got somewhere to be."

He led him away, but to Lucas' dismay, Dr. Gill followed. The three guards kept close behind them, marching with expressionless faces. They traveled up a hallway with many doors that led to what appeared to be offices. Lucas saw many computers and stacks of paper, and caught a glimpse of a secondary passage through one office into a laboratory. Inside were rows and rows of filing cabinets and a table in the center strewn with paper.

At the end of the hall was an elevator. They boarded, and Kowalski pressed the button for the ground floor. As they rose upward, Lucas' head gradually began to fill with voices and images. They came slowly at first, but as they neared the ground floor, his senses were flooded with lights, sounds, and deep crawling sensations across his skin. Inside the elevator itself, all was quiet; nobody spoke. The racket came from all the signals Lucas had been missing while he lay seven hundred feet below. He pressed his fingertips to his temples, praying for his brain to hurry up and sort out the noise so that he could think.

"Is he all right?" one of the guards said.

Lucas felt a hand on his shoulder.

"Lucas?" Dr. Gill said.

"I'm okay," Lucas said, taking a deep breath. Everyone was looking at him. He lowered his eyes, wishing for all of this to be over soon.

With a ding, the elevator came to a stop and the doors opened. Dozens of people hurried back and forth, carrying folders and talking on phones. Aside from a few sideways glances, nobody paid much attention to the group. He was brought to a line of golf carts, and Kowalski told him to get on. Brad joined them on the first one, while Tim and Kenny took the one behind. They drove for half a mile, weaving through the crowd until they came to an enclosed area, where Lucas sensed the largest collection of computers in the entire building.

"This is the bullpen," Kowalski told him as he stepped off the golf cart. "The center of the action."

Kowalski led them through a set of doors, and there Lucas saw thirteen desktop computers arranged in a horseshoe, with a man or a woman seated at each computer. They were all busily typing away without looking up as Kowalski brought Lucas closer.

"This is the Gamma team," he said. "There is also a Beta team back in Austin headquarters, and an Alpha Team in Langley. I want you to follow their work and catch anything they may have missed, or report any patterns you find. We've been working round the clock to track these terrorists for a year, but there's clearly something we're missing. You're allowed to ask any question you may have concerning the case. You may not ask them about hacking tools, because many of the ones they are using and the software are classified."

"I'll be able to see everything they do," Lucas pointed out. "It'll all be in my head as soon as I start looking."

Kowalski shrugged.

"I can't prevent that," he said. "Those were the rules we had to agree to in order for the higher-ups to let you be involved."

Then he turned and addressed the whole group.

"Everyone, this is Lucas Tavera. He is here to help us catch anything that may have slipped through the cracks. So, as discussed before, please continue your work, but give him any information he asks for concerning the case."

Some of the hackers rolled their eyes and turned back to their screens, but most gave Lucas looks of skepticism and scrutiny. Lucas wanted to run away.

"I can't do this," he said under his breath. "I'm just a kid."

"Yes, you can, and you are certainly not *only* a kid," Kowalski hissed back. "Now, what do you need?"

Lucas gave a resigned shrug.

"I guess a chair, to start with."

Dr. Gill brought a chair for him. He felt all the eyes watching him as he sat down, and he took a deep breath. He closed his eyes and tried to center himself. The crackling energy washed over him, prickling his skin. He focused, blocking out the apprehensive expressions of the hackers. He could see the open programs that some of them were in the middle of working on; these looked like complex webs of color and light, though some were simple chains of glowing orbs. A few of the hackers appeared to have been doing research on the social media accounts. He decided to explore that first, to catch himself up on the case. Two of the women had been gathering details on each of the fake accounts including photos, addresses, and lists of people who were "friends" with the account. Another was in the process of using a program to search the geographical location that each of the photos was taken, getting precise latitude and longitude.

Lucas quickly found these locations on his GPS, getting back random addresses from all over the country. Finding no pattern, he returned to the lists of "friends" of each of the accounts, and cross-referenced them for overlap. He found thirteen, and put them in their own list. Then he found all the details that he possibly could about these people, searching deep into their history on social media. He uncovered how many other accounts they had, and when they joined, and how many interactions they had with each other and the fake accounts. When he had exhausted that, he began to fish through their posts for anything affiliated with the Rising.

"Kowalski," he said a few minutes later, opening his eyes.

The agent appeared from Lucas' left, and knelt down so that he was at eye-level.

"Did you find something?"

"I think so," Lucas answered. "But I need a screen to show you. Your phone will work."

Kowalski pulled it from his pocket.

"Okay, hang on," Lucas said.

It took nearly a minute, but by the end of it, Kowalski had a list of names, addresses, phone numbers, and dates filling a spreadsheet on his phone.

"What is this?" he asked.

"It's a list of real people who are following your fake accounts," Lucas explained. "They only interact with each fake account once: within an hour after it gets created. And they're always the first ones to share the warning once the fake account posts it. It's been these same thirteen people each time, going back to the first bombing last February."

"That's very impressive," Kowalski said, with wide eyes. "Where did you get this?"

"Just looking through the information they've got so far and making some connections," Lucas answered. "Can you use it?"

"Depends on whether or not those addresses are real."

"How would we know that?"

"Besides visiting them in person, which would be expensive and probably a waste of time, we could find the IP addresses of their computers and see if they match. Put this up on the projector, and we'll share it with the group."

He pointed over their heads, and Lucas looked. There was a large projector suspended from the ceiling, pointed at a blank portion of the back wall of the room. As Lucas focused his attention on it, the machine powered up and the white wall was illuminated with bright blue light. A second later, the spreadsheet list was blown up big enough for the whole group of hackers to see. Kowalski strode to the back of the room and called for everyone's attention.

"Listen up!" he barked. "These are thirteen affiliates that all of our mystery accounts have in common, and have been helping to spread the Rising's bomb warnings. I need to know where these people are, because they may lead us to the head of this snake. Does anyone have any locations for me?"

There was a few seconds of silence as a few glanced furtively backward at Lucas, causing his face to redden. Kowalski folded his arms.

"Then get me something I can use," he ordered. "These are your targets; find them for me."

As he strode back to Lucas, his expression changed. It became the softer, more casual look that Lucas had seen at the beginning, when they first met. He leaned close to Lucas' ear.

"Watch closely what they do, and learn as much as you can," he whispered.

Lucas was baffled, but immediately immersed himself in the computers once more. In his mind, it was like watching a really slow game of *Battleship*; the hackers constructed programs, then launched them into the world of the internet like missiles. After some time, the programs came back, usually with nothing. Then, the hacker set to work on a new one, and sent it out. Other hackers began more research, scrutinizing every detail of each of the targets' accounts, then punching names into a browser to see what came up. It was difficult to keep up with all of it, but Lucas was determined not to miss a thing. He monitored everything that they did closely, committing it all to memory.

It seemed like only minutes later that he felt a hand shake his shoulder gently. They had been at this for hours.

"Lucas," a voice said.

He opened his eyes. Dr. Gill was standing over him.

"It's time to take a break," he said. "You need to rest."

Lucas felt dizzy, and his mouth was dry.

"No," he said, shaking his head. "I just need some water and then I'll be fine."

"Kowalski's orders," Dr. Gill told him. "You're done for now."

A few yards away, Kowalski was pacing the floor with a phone to his ear. Lucas was tired, and realized that he was also immensely hungry. He took Dr. Gill's offered hand and stood up, shakily at first, then walked with him to the golf cart. Brad, Tim, and Kenny escorted them back to the elevator, which they rode back down to Lucas' cell. Two of the guards remained outside, while Tim followed them in, then took up a position by the door. On Lucas' bed, he found a clean set of the same white cotton shirt and sweatpants, along with a small bottle of soap.

"There's a bathroom down the hall," Dr. Gill told him. "I'll walk you down there so you can shower, and then you should eat. How are you feeling?"

"Fine," Lucas muttered.

"I'm your doctor, Lucas," Dr. Gill said gently. "It's important for you to be honest with me and tell me if anything's wrong."

"I feel fine," he said more sharply. "Just tired and hungry."

Dr. Gill gave him a long look, but nodded. Lucas picked up the clothes and the soap and followed him out into the hall then down to the bathroom. It was large, pristinely clean, and smelled like bleach and some kind of air freshener. There was a set of towels on the edge of the sink.

"Just call if you need anything," Dr. Gill said, then closed the door.

Privacy is only for humans, Lucas thought dismally. He looked at himself in the mirror. His cheeks looked sunken, his eyes large and hollow, and his hair was long and hung in his face. His mother had always cut it for him, but he supposed he could learn to do it himself. With a sigh, he pushed it back from his face and turned on the water. He took his time and enjoyed the hot water that blasted at high pressure from the showerhead. It felt delicious, and he could forget, at least momentarily, his imprisonment, the prospect of the government growing tired of him and killing him, and the probability of never seeing his mother again. His life may never again be normal, he might not be human, and he may have been created for some unknown, maybe nefarious purpose, but for now at least, he could relax and use as much of the government's hot water as possible.

Chapter 9

HE WAS DRYING OFF WHEN he checked the time on his internal clock. 6:47PM.

When Kowalski woke him, he said they had eighteen hours until the bomb would go off. Now they had less than eleven hours. Lucas wondered absently how the hackers upstairs were fairing. He dressed, then stepped outside.

Dr. Gill was seated in a chair, reading a book. He looked up with a smile.

"You certainly took your time," he said. "Feel better?"

"Yes," Lucas replied. "What are you reading?"

"*Lord of the Rings.*"

"Which one?"

He showed Lucas the cover. "*The Return of the King.* I've had a lot of spare time down here, and opted to catch up on my reading."

They walked together back to the cell. A tray of food sat waiting on the small table, and its smell made Lucas' mouth water. As he got closer, he saw that it was a meatloaf, mashed potatoes, steamed broccoli, and two piping-hot rolls. There was also a large plastic bottle of water. He sat down and immediately began to eat in large fork-fulls; he had never liked meatloaf before, but in his hunger, it tasted like the most delicious food on the planet. Dr. Gill sat across from him, his book resting on the table. He fidgeted, and Lucas suspected that he was waiting to say something.

"What?"

Dr. Gill hesitated, then said, "Would you mind telling me your story?

I've heard bits of it from Kowalski, but it would be a privilege to hear it from you."

"What do you want to know?"

"How you got your gifts, for one," he said. "He said it was an accident."

Gifts, he scoffed. *So much for that.*

"That's part of it. I snuck into a warehouse because I was running away from some guys at school, and they found me and… well, in the fight, some crates got busted open. There were nanomachines were inside and I got infected with them. The other part is that apparently my genes are different, or made up, I guess… so instead of killing me, the nanomachines give me these abilities."

He paused. He still found it hard to believe the words that were coming out of his own mouth.

"I found that out this morning," he finished, sitting back.

"Yes, I'm sure that was difficult to hear," Dr. Gill said solemnly. "I've seen your DNA, and frankly, it's amazing."

"Does it mean I'm not human?" Lucas asked.

"You appear human, but since most of your genes are artificial, I wouldn't know how to classify you. They simply aren't the same. Some parts are, obviously, but there are other parts of your genetic code that are completely foreign. A category for you just doesn't exist yet. *Android* is the closest description I can come up with."

What? Lucas thought, taken aback.

"Like a robot?" he said aloud.

"Artificial human."

"I don't *feel* artificial."

"No, I don't suppose you would. But how would you know the difference?"

Lucas didn't have an answer for this. He looked down at the table and fiddled with the edge of his plate.

"Then what happened?" Dr. Gill prompted.

"After what?"

"After the warehouse."

"Well, um, I was in the hospital for a long time, in a coma. After I woke up, I spent a lot of time just learning what I could do, practicing as I went. By the time I got out, I was pretty good at getting into phones and computers. I could make them do what I wanted, surf the internet, and all that. Then my mom told me about what happened to her, so I went back to the warehouse to see if any of it was connected. That's when the other incident happened, with Brick. He touched the nanomachines, and they started attacking him, and I stopped it. I was sure then that they wouldn't kill me, and figured they were alive somehow. Like, they're their own separate thing, apart from me."

"You use them," Dr. Gill said. "They do the work, but your mind gives the commands, even if you're not consciously thinking it. They receive a lot of instruction from your cerebellum, where your subconsciousness lies."

"How do you know that?"

"I was recruited from MIT to look after you, but mostly to conduct research and learn what I could about how your gifts worked. My area of expertise is biotechnology."

"Like Dr. Lytton."

"Yes, I'd been a big fan of his work since high school. I'm especially amazed at how you redirect electricity; the nanomachines conduct the energy through your body and even separate the positive and negative charge, allowing you to generate your own current. I call it fulgurkinesis."

"Cool," Lucas said. "I didn't know all that. I didn't even know how to do it; it just happened."

"And then there's your rapid healing," Dr. Gill continued excitedly. "You healed a broken hand in less than an hour. I studied the process and learned that the nanomachines speed up the rate at which your cells divide and respond to injury. They can even draw energy from your surroundings so your body doesn't - "

"Look, I know you're just geeking out and all that," Lucas interrupted. "And sure, what I can do is cool, but honestly, I'd rather not have any of it."

"But Lucas, you're one-of-a-kind. There has never, *ever* been anyone like you in all of human history. If Dr. Lytton was around right now he would surely get a Nobel prize - "

"I don't care!" Lucas snapped, his voice suddenly rising. "I've had nothing but trouble since all this happened. I lost my friends, the government wants me dead, and I'm carrying a nuclear bomb around inside me. If I had the chance, I'd give it all back in a second."

Dr. Gill gave no reply, and Lucas pushed his plate away. He felt bad about yelling at him.

"I'm tired," he said. "I'd like to sleep."

"Alright," Dr. Gill said, standing. "I think that's a good idea. I'll be right outside, if you need anything."

He walked outside, and Tim followed. Lucas heard a hiss as the door was sealed behind them. He took off his shoes and lay down on the bed, eyes closed. Upstairs and nearly a mile away, the team was likely still struggling to uncover the location of the Rising's cyber-terrorists. He decided he didn't care. Why should he? He was a prisoner here, forced to help them. If he didn't do what the CIA said, he would be killed.

He rolled over, hating the prickly, needle-like sensation across his skin. He scratched his arms and his chest through his shirt. With his eyes closed and no more distractions, he was painfully aware of the the electrical current running through the walls and ceiling, powering the lights and the reinforced door to his room.

He sat up and stared at the door, having a sudden revelation. The door drew a lot of power, which he could control. He could turn it all off. But then what? Lucas knew well that he was seven hundred feet underground, with scores of agents between him and the surface.

Still, he got up and walked to the door. He went slowly, because his legs were still weak. He had practically no muscle at all anymore. When he reached the door, he sensed a keypad on the other side; he could see it in his mind's eye. He probed it, feeling for any hint of a weakness. Finding none, he shut off the power. The room went completely dark, and the hum of the AC died. At the same moment, to Lucas' surprise, a loud click sounded as a second, heavier deadbolt slid home. Dread filled him with ice. He was still locked in, only now without light or air conditioning. Surely he had set off some kind of alarm, and somebody would come running. And what would happen to him when they did come? He had no clue. He waited, his anxious breath the only sound in the darkness. A minute crawled by, and nothing happened. He retreated from the door, feeling along the wall, moving ponderously. When he reached a corner, he crouched down. Another minute, and still nothing. Where were his guards? Didn't they care that they were standing in the dark out there?

After ten minutes, Lucas was still alone. He couldn't see his hand in front of his face. Small relief came from the fact that the prickly feeling was gone from his skin, but that was overshadowed by a growing sense of worry. What if they knew all along that he would try this? And what if they simply didn't care? Kowalski had seemed unconcerned when Lucas made his threats. He said there would be nowhere to go if he tried to escape. He had also said that they could bury him underground and leave him there indefinitely. Lucas imagined Brad, Tim, Kenny, and Dr. Gill simply moving upstairs, while he remained here to starve in darkness.

With a breath, Lucas willed the power to return. He climbed into bed once more as tears stung his eyes. He was trapped, in every sense of the word. He curled up in the bed, pulling the thin blanket close.

It seemed only a few minutes later that the door hissed open and his sleep was interrupted. Dr. Gill entered, followed by Tim. The other two guards remained outside. Lucas sat up as Dr. Gill walked directly up to his bed.

"What's going on?" Lucas asked quickly, fear shooting through him.

"Agent Kowalski wants you," Dr. Gill replied. "Hurry up."

"I don't want to go," Lucas replied.

"What you want doesn't matter," Tim replied gruffly. "You have a job here."

It was 3:10AM. The four escorted him upstairs. During the golf cart ride to the Bullpen, he picked up several phone calls being made to Los Angeles. It seemed that everyone was on high alert, and the entire building was abuzz with activity. Everywhere he looked, he saw people walking with purpose, wearing grim expressions. The air was especially charged, and his skin felt the difference.

Kowalski walked up to meet them before the golf-cart had even slowed down. As Lucas disembarked, he grabbed hold of his arm and jerked him along.

"We've narrowed it down," he said. "The target is L.A. We have a Spec Ops team on the ground searching for the bomb, and we've got only three hours left."

"What do you want me to do?" Lucas asked meekly.

Kowalski dragged him past the Bullpen to one corner of the room. Lucas could see the bank of computers clearly, and it appeared to be the center of the action. There were a lot of additional people besides the team of hackers.

"Listen to me very carefully," he said in a low, serious voice.

Lucas nodded, but it was difficult to focus. Everything was so bright

Lucas shook his head, then shoveled large forkfuls of pancake into his mouth. A small carton of orange juice sat to his right.

"When you've finished," Dr. Gill said after a moment. "There's someone I want you to see."

"Who?"

"Your friend, Brick."

Lucas nearly choked on his food.

"Brick is *here?*" he gasped. "Why?"

"We brought him to the Bunker for observation. He is the only human to have survived an infection from the nanomachines."

"Yeah, because I saved him. I took them out of him. And he's *not* my friend."

"Well, he's very lucky all the same. However… he suffered a lot of damage, even during the short time they were in his body. And I think he will still be very grateful to see you."

"I doubt that," Lucas replied drily. There was no way that Brick would be glad to see him after what happened. He had nearly died, and Lucas knew *exactly* how that felt.

"Will you come see him?" Dr. Gill asked.

Lucas sighed, then nodded and pushed back from the table. Dr. Gill knocked on the door, and it opened. He turned left, and Lucas followed him down a wide hallway. They walked past a security guards' station to a door with a small window in it. Lucas wasn't tall enough to see anything through it. Dr. Gill swiped a keycard through a slot by the door; a beep sounded and Lucas heard a lock turn. The door slid open, and through it he saw a room that looked very much like his own. The walls were white, and in the middle of the floor was a small table and chair. A hospital bed was off to one side, and in it was a long-limbed boy with flaming red hair and a thick, jutting forehead. His hair was matted to his head, his cheeks were sunken, and his blue eyes had dark circles underneath. Dr. Gill was right: Brick was… different.

Lucas had a hollow feeling in his chest as he followed Dr. Gill to the side of Brick's bed. The entire way, he avoided meeting Brick's eyes. He noticed shelves of books against the wall. They were large chapter books, which surprised him. Then he began to feel sick in his stomach when he saw an electric wheelchair beside the bed.

"How are you doing today, Brick?" Dr. Gill asked. "I've brought someone to see you."

Brick lay propped up against some pillows, reading a book he held with one hand. He lowered it as Dr. Gill took his pale, bony left hand that had been resting at his side. Lucas noticed with a start that his sunken eyes were open wide and fixed on him. He looked like he was seeing a ghost.

"Uh... hi, Brick," Lucas said weakly.

Brick continued to stare as Dr. Gill felt along his arm, from his hand up to his shoulder. Lucas watched with morbid curiosity as he seemed to massage it deep between the knuckles, then extended each of the fingers. Brick had no reaction, as if his hand wasn't even part of him. When he finished, he placed Brick's arm back down at his side.

"How are you feeling today, Brick?" Dr. Gill asked once more, in that high, cheerful tone that Lucas despised.

"Fine," Brick said. His voice was soft, like a whisper, and reedy, like he didn't have enough breath.

"Is it alright with you if Lucas visits for a while? I'm sure you boys have a lot to catch up on."

Brick nodded slowly, his eyes still locked on Lucas, who felt his stomach turning somersaults. He watched Dr. Gill leave, and as the door slid closed, he turned back to face Brick. He looked very similar to a vampire from one of those old movies. Or a cadaver.

"You've been here this whole time, haven't you?" Brick said, his voice suddenly stronger. Lucas jumped.

"Y-yes," he answered. "My room is down the hall."

Brick furrowed his brow, his face twisted in confusion.

"W-well... I was kept asleep until yesterday," Lucas offered. "And I didn't even know you were here until just a few minutes ago."

"What are you talking about? You were, what, in a coma?"

"They kept me sedated, because they were worried I might break out."

"Could you?"

"No... I've tried," Lucas admitted. "How long have you been here?"

"Seven... maybe eight months, I think. I don't really know - I don't have a clock in here, and I stopped asking because it's depressing."

Brick sighed. He dropped his head back and looked at the ceiling. He was silent for a long time, and Lucas wanted so badly to leave.

"You must hate me," he said.

"Why?"

"Because this is my fault. I wanted to go to the warehouse."

Brick smirked, seemingly amused. He turned his head to look at Lucas. His blue eyes were a sharp as steel. Lucas was taken aback; he'd never seen anything more than dull stupidity in Brick's eyes before.

"No it isn't. I asked to go with you. You didn't want me to come, remember?"

"But - "

"Lucas, shut up," Brick interjected. "This is my fault, and no one else's. I was an idiot because I wanted to be like you, have your powers. But it's clear that this is no picnic for you, either. We're both victims here."

Lucas was baffled, though he kept his face still. This new Brick was *smarter*. Definitely more articulate. The bully Lucas known back in school could barely put two sentences together. Did the nanomachines do this? He wondered if they might have damaged some parts of his brain, but somehow improved others. *Maybe*, he thought, *this is similar to the way blind people develop sharper senses of smell and hearing.* Brick was crippled, but his mind was stronger.

"Had I known... I would have stayed far, far away from that warehouse," Brick continued darkly. "I would have burned it to the ground."

Lucas moved closer, taking one small, careful step.

"Have they been taking care of you?" he asked.

"More or less. They treat me alright, and Dr. Gill is nice enough. It's been really boring when they aren't doing tests."

"Do you ever see anyone? Besides the doctors, I mean."

"No. You're the first."

Lucas felt sick to his stomach with guilt. At least he had been asleep for all that time.

"That sucks," he said.

Brick looked at him. His expression seemed to brighten slightly.

"So does being in a forced coma," he said. "What are they keeping you here for?"

"Same as you, basically: observation. But I also see the agents. They want me to do work for them."

"Like what?"

Lucas hesitated again. But, he reasoned, who was Brick going to tell? He was trapped here just like he was.

"The CIA is catching terrorists; they want me to help track them."

"How?"

"With my powers… I can monitor them, remotely."

"What happens if you say no?"

"They kill me."

Brick raised one eyebrow.

"What makes you so dangerous?"

"I don't know," Lucas said slowly. "Kowalski said it's because I'm unpredictable. If I wanted to, I could see all their government secrets. That makes me a threat, I guess."

Brick nodded pensively. This new, intelligent Brick intrigued Lucas.

"They must be real scared of you."

"Maybe," Lucas shrugged, but he liked the idea. He pointed to the bookshelf.

"I didn't know you read books."

"Don't have anything else to do," Brick shrugged. "Do you have anything in your room?"

"No."

"You can borrow some, if you want."

"Thanks," he said. He stepped around the foot of the bed to the shelf, and squatted down to examine the titles. Among them were *Dracula*, *The Adventures of Sherlock Holmes*, and *Moby Dick*. He also had a dozen Stephen King novels and collections of the works of H.P. Lovecraft, Lord Byron, and John Keats. Being so close to Brick's wheelchair, Lucas began to feel uncomfortable again. He quickly picked out two Stephen King books and retreated. Then he felt awkward holding the books, so he set them down on the table and pulled up a chair to Brick's bedside.

"You like horror?" Brick asked.

"Not really."

"I like it. The creepier, the better. They bring me the books I want. I've also been reading a bit of philosophy and mythology--Greek, Norse, and Hindu. It's very interesting and… well, it passes the time."

Lucas nodded, then pressed his lips together, trying to find the right words. He didn't want to upset Brick now that things were going so well, but he was dying to know.

"Um, Brick," he said. "What did the blue stuff do to you?"

Brick didn't answer right away. Lucas feared he would get angry, but then he sighed and spoke very quietly.

"I can't walk anymore," he said. "It damaged my spine pretty bad. The docs said it ate through parts of it, and that I'm lucky to be alive. If anything else had been damaged, I'd have been completely paralyzed from the neck down, even unable to breathe on my own. But I can still use my right arm."

"I'm really sorry," Lucas said, and he meant it.

"You can quit saying that. It was my fault. You and the other guys tried to tell me not to do it, but I didn't listen. If you hadn't done what you did, I know I'd be dead."

"You remember that?"

"Some parts. Mostly, I just remember hurting a lot."

He looked at Lucas. In his hollow eyes, Lucas could see pain and fear. He could remember well the terror that he had felt watching Brick writhe on the ground, the blue liquid pouring from his eyes and mouth.

"My name isn't Brick," Brick said suddenly.

"What?" Lucas replied, surprised.

"Well, technically it is, but I don't want it to be. It says 'Brick Daniel Wallach' on my birth certificate, and that's what my mom wanted everyone to call me. She thought it sounded tough or something. But my dad had always wanted me to be called Bernard."

"Why are you telling me this?"

"Because you're the closest I've got to a friend now. And, let's face it, I'm not very tough anymore."

"Which do you like better?" Lucas asked.

He seemed to think for a few seconds.

"Bernard."

"Bernard," Lucas repeated. "Okay. But you're still the toughest person I know."

He gave a weak smile.

"Promise you'll come back to see me?" he asked. "I don't want to be alone here again."

Lucas nodded. "I promise. Whatever it takes."

Hours passed, during which time Lucas told Bernard how he'd helped the CIA find the bomb in Los Angeles, and described in detail the building above them, because Bernard had never seen it. Lunch was brought in for them, and two nurses lifted Bernard out of the bed and into his wheelchair. Lucas saw clearly then that he was truly a shell of his former self, physically at least. He was thin, and his shoulders hunched. His knees were knobby, and his left arm hung limp until it was placed in his lap. The nurse steered his chair to the table, while Lucas brought his chair over and sat down.

They ate pizza, and Lucas did his best to keep the conversation lighthearted. Fortunately, Bernard asked a lot of questions, so it wasn't that much work. He was obviously grateful for the company, and Lucas was, too. It was also clear that they didn't know much about each other, since they'd never spent time together in school, but Bernard seemed eager to share. He asked Lucas about his family, and then told him all about his own. Then he told Lucas what movies he liked, and his favorite subject in school, and his favorite books, admitting that he had never liked reading before coming here. To Lucas, the experience was a bit bizarre, but he listened and enjoyed himself.

"Can I ask you a question?" he asked, when he could get a word in.

Bernard gave a one-shoulder shrug.

"There's nothing else to do," he said.

"Why did you pick on me so much?" Lucas asked quietly. "I mean, I know it wasn't just you - it was also Val, Darren, and Howard - but why did you do it?"

Bernard didn't answer right away. His eyes were distant, like he was thinking.

"Are you sure you want to know?" he asked.

"Yes," Lucas said. He was worried now.

"Because it was easy," Bernard said. "Really, I felt almost like I *had* to do it. There was something about you that was... what's the word? ... off-putting?"

"Off-putting?" Lucas repeated, surprised.

"Yeah, like, weird... it made me uncomfortable. Not just me, other people, too--"

"Val and the other guys, I know."

"No, I mean everybody. Not very many people liked you, Lucas - except those those two nerds you hung around with."

Lucas was baffled. He opened his mouth to defend himself, but he didn't know what to say.

"They weren't nerds," he said lamely.

"You weird people out," Bernard continued as if he hadn't heard. "Sorry, but it's true. Everyone felt it. And I think I know now what 'it' is."

"What?"

"It's whatever it is that made that blue stuff attack me, but not you. It's what gave you powers, and not me. There's something inside you that's different, and it - whatever it is - was always there. You were always destined to be *this*."

Lucas lowered his head. He didn't want to admit it, but he had a horrible feeling that Bernard was right. What if it was true? What if he was always meant to be this way? What if it really was destiny?

No, it's the Rising's fault, he thought. *They made me like this. That's not destiny; it was their plan all along.*

"That was difficult to hear, wasn't it?" Bernard asked.

Lucas pressed his lips together.

"What happened to your stuff?" he asked, changing the subject. "Your clothes and your phone?"

"They're over there," Bernard replied, pointing to a cabinet across the room.

Lucas got up from the table and walked over. The cabinet wasn't locked, but there wasn't a need for it to be. It wasn't as if Bernard could get up and open it on his own. The clothes were unmistakably too big for him now, and the phone's battery was long dead. He picked it up and brought it back to the table. It was his own phone, his birthday present over a year ago, and the same one that Bernard had stolen. He held it flat in his open hand, and concentrated. Warmth spread through his palm and fingers, and with it came a gentle, crackling sound. He focused the energy, and breathed slowly.

A few seconds later, the screen lit up. In his head, a small spot of light blossomed as his brain connected to the phone's wireless.

"How did you do that" Bernard gasped.

"I can control energy," Lucas replied. "It's called fulgurkinesis."

The slice of pizza dropped from Bernard's hand as he leaned closer. Lucas showed him the phone, which was now booting up.

"It won't get any signal down here, but I had a lot of games stored on the phone that we could play, if you're up for it."

Bernard was too excited to speak. Lucas let him choose a game which they took turns playing for the next hour. Bernard lost, but didn't seem upset about it. Lucas kept the battery charged while they passed the phone back and forth until the door opened and Dr. Gill stepped inside. Bernard wordlessly hid the phone under his thigh, but Lucas knew they were being watched on the cameras. There were no secrets here.

"Time to go--Kowalski wants you," Dr. Gill said.

Lucas nodded, then pushed his chair back.

"Bye, Lucas," Bernard said quietly.

"See you later," Lucas replied.

He walked outside, and Dr. Gill closed the door.

Chapter 10

Aꜱ ᴛʜᴇʏ ʀᴏᴅᴇ ᴛʜᴇ ᴇʟᴇᴠᴀᴛᴏʀ up, accompanied by Lucas' security, he remembered that he had left the books on the table in Bernard's room. He was still close enough that he could feel the phone's signal, so he quickly typed out a text in his head, saying, *Forgot the books, but I'll be back for them,* and sent it to the phone. A few seconds later, the signal was gone.

"Did you have fun?" Dr. Gill.

"As much fun as two kids held captive by a government agency," Lucas said flatly.

Dr. Gill tilted his head.

"Do his parents know that he's here?" Lucas asked.

"Of course they do."

"You're just saying that. You don't know for sure."

"Look, I just do what I'm told," Dr. Gill replied, sounding hurt. "I don't know everything."

The elevator dinged, and the doors opened to a floor that Lucas' hadn't been on before. Kowalski and Iweala stood waiting with three other burly-looking men with sidearms. Iweala was dressed in slacks and a blouse, and her hair was done up in a neat bun; Kowalski wore track pants, a t-shirt, and running shoes, and was sweating as if he had just been working out; his blond hair stuck up wildly. He grinned when he saw Lucas.

"How are you, Lucas?" he asked. "Did you rest well?"

"Yes."

"Great. We have something special planned for you today. Walk with me."

He turned and strode up the hallway, and Lucas followed. Behind them came Iweala, then the full security team.

"What's going on?" Lucas asked warily.

"Have you ever worked out?" Kowalski asked.

"I took P.E," he replied. "Why?"

"We're going to test your fitness today."

"We're going to work out?"

"Sort of. You're going to do some activities that will test your mental fitness. They've been specially designed just for you."

He walked with Kowalski to a small room with a one-way glass window. In the middle of the room was a table and chair, and on the table sat a laptop computer. Cameras hung from the ceiling in every corner of the room.

"Go ahead and take a seat," Kowalski told him, and Lucas obeyed. The laptop was open, and the screen was black.

Iweala entered the room and stopped in front of the table, her arms folded. She looked down at Lucas with pursed lips.

"We will be testing the parameters of your abilities," she said. "There are some experts on the other side of that glass who are here to document everything that happens in here today. All you have to do is follow their instructions. Okay?"

"What do they want me to do?"

"I don't know," she admitted coolly. "But, trust me, no one is here to hurt you. We only want to learn more about what you can do."

Lucas nodded. Iweala and Kowalski left, and Lucas was alone. He sensed several desktop computers on the other side of the glass; displayed on them were documentations of his height, weight, and birthday. All the documents referred to him as "Subject 5." He could also see himself in the room, being recorded over the cameras. He felt nervous, and his palms were sweating.

Suddenly, the laptop came to life. The screen turned blue, and a three-dimensional shape appeared on it. There were a dozen stacked boxes forming a pyramid.

"Lucas," a voice suddenly came over the intercom. It was a voice that Lucas had never heard. "Can you manipulate the shape?"

"What do you want me to do?" Lucas asked. He couldn't see anyone, so he addressed the window.

"Move it, if you can."

He assumed that he wasn't supposed to use the mouse; they wanted him to do it with his mind. His hands stayed by his sides, his fists tightly clenched, as he concentrated on the pyramid. He studied the shape, and the pyramid appeared in his mind's eye. He rotated it, spinning it on an axis like a top. Then he found that it could turn sideways, so he turned it over and let it spin again. Everything that he did appeared on other computers' screens, behind the glass.

"Very good," the voice said. "Now solve the problem."

The pyramid disappeared, and Lucas was shown seven letters and one blank box. Text scrolled across the bottom of the screen that read, *Find the missing letter.* The letters were scrambled, but he saw quickly that all the letters present could spell out the word *Christmas,* except for the r, so that had to be the missing letter. He typed it into the box, and instantly more letters appeared to spell out a much longer word. He found the missing one, and then was told to find the pattern in a series of numbers. With each puzzle he solved, he was given a much more complicated one. He knew that the researchers were documenting each puzzle and how quickly he solved it. He also knew that each puzzle was generated randomly by the computer. After twenty minutes had gone by, he wondered if he could predict which puzzle would come next, if he dug deeply enough.

There has to be an end, right? he thought. *Eventually, they'll start repeating.*

Before he could test this theory, the game changed. He was given an avatar that he was told to guide through a dark forest. Shapes moved through the trees, and things shifted in the shadows. He moved his avatar forward over roots and boulders, feeling out his environment. His avatar was a cat that loped easily over the grass, paws padding silently. Leaves fluttered overhead, and insects hummed. Lucas watched a computer-generated beetle crawl over a moss-covered log. There was light ahead, and twigs snapped in the darkness behind him. The trees were moving, closing in and cutting off the way back. He began to run, his cat avatar leaping and over the shrubs and streams that got in the way, making for the light. He sprang over a boulder, and mid-jump, the ground below opened up to reveal a well of water that he plunged into, yowling with surprise. He tried to swim, but an invisible force kept pulled him ever downward under the dark water.

Lucas gasped for air, his chest tight. He was back in the blank, white room, not underwater in a dark forest. He breathed deeply, astounded at how real it felt. On the other side of the glass, people were typing rapidly away at their computers:

S5 displays advanced cognitive skill…

Subject fully immerses himself in the games. Impressive imagination but lack of awareness of bigger picture…

Complete synchronization between S5 and the program.

"Thank you, Lucas," the voice said. "You are done for today."

The door opened, and Brad was there, waiting. Lucas stood shakily and walked out of the room. Brad took him back to his cell where dinner was already on the table. He didn't feel very hungry, but he ate anyway. Then he showered, changed his clothes, and lay in bed. It was 9:04PM.

Lucas was tired, and his mind was still reeling from the games. What did the CIA hope to learn from them? That he was good at puzzles? He supposed that could be useful, but had little to do with his real powers. Iweala had said specifically that they were going to be testing the parameters of his abilities.

He felt a buzz, then saw a message from Bernard waiting for him in his mind. He had reconnected with the phone's wireless, unaware.

what are you doing?

Nothing, Lucas replied. *Just got back to my room.*

are you seeing this in your head?

Yes. Weird, huh?

very. working on the case?

No. They made me take some tests… it was really weird.

No response. Several seconds passed. Finally, a reply came.

can you come over?

Let me try.

Lucas got up from the bed and went to the door. Tim and Kenny stood guard outside, and no one else could be seen. Lucas tapped on the glass, and both turned to look. He waved, and Kenny pushed an intercom button by the door.

What?

"I want to see Bernard--I mean, Brick," Lucas answered.

I don't think you can do that, Kenny said.

"Yes, I can--come on, it's right there. You can walk me over."

Kenny got on his radio and asked Kowalski if Lucas could visit with Subject 4. Lucas waited for the reply, and was relieved when Kowalski came back with a "why not?" Tim and Kenny exchanged a look, then Kenny pushed the intercom.

Alright, step back.

Lucas moved away from the door, and it opened with a hiss. Tim and Kenny waited for Lucas to step out into the hallway, then followed him down the hall to Bernard's door. Bernard was sitting up in bed, waiting, with the phone in his hand and a thick book on his lap.

"Hey," he said, once the door closed and they were left alone.

"Hey," Lucas replied. He picked up the books he had left on the table, then pulled up a chair, placing them on his lap.

"What kind of tests did they do on you?"

"Computer-based ones. They were puzzles that I had to figure out, and they timed me."

"That's it?" Bernard said with a frown.

"Well, yeah, pretty much. I thought it was weird, too. Anyway, how are you doing?"

Bernard gave a one-shoulder shrug.

"Fine, I guess," he said slowly. "I wanted you to come over here because… well, I don't know who else to talk to about this."

"Whatever you want to talk about, I'll listen," Lucas said. "I don't have anyone else to talk to about stuff, either."

Bernard paused, and Lucas waited. He looked so frail, and his expression was weary.

"I've been getting these nightmares… like, really bad ones… and it was scary, but I could deal with it. I thought it was PTSD or something. But then I got one during the day."

"What do you mean? Like a hallucination?"

"I don't know--I don't think so. It was… different."

"Have you talked to the doctors about it?"

"Of course, but they said it's a normal symptom of my condition."

"What did you see?" Lucas asked seriously.

"Darkness, mostly. And I think there were trees. But what I saw wasn't so scary as what I felt. I felt like I was drowning."

Lucas furrowed his brow.

"When did this happen?" he asked.

"A couple hours ago. Before that, I kept seeing words and shapes floating in my head. I told the doctors about that, too, because surely that couldn't be normal. They couldn't explain it--or wouldn't."

Lucas's stomach dropped. He stood up and paced, his heart beating fast. He couldn't believe what he had heard. *It's impossible; there's no way,* he thought.

"Lucas?" Bernard said with uncertainty. "What are you doing? Did that mean something?"

He hurried back and sat down, his heart beating fast. He knew that they were being watched; he could feel the security camera in the upper corner behind him. He angled himself so that no one watching could read his lips, and he was blocking the direct view of Brick's face. Then he spoke in a whisper.

"Listen--this is going to sound weird, but those were the games they made me play when they were testing me. It was a video game, and in one of them, my character died because I fell into some water. I felt like I was drowning, because my brain connected to the computer. It became so real, and it happened the same way you saw it."

"How?" Brick gasped incredulously.

Lucas knew he was going to sound crazy, but he plunged on.

"What if we were connected somehow, like, telepathically?"

"But that's impossible. There's no such thing."

"Bernard, look who you're talking to. We should both be dead right now. We *are* impossible."

Bernard shook his head.

"No, listen--I know it's crazy," Lucas said. "But there's no other explanation."

"Of course there is. There has to be."

"Look, what were your other nightmares about?"

"A lot of pain. Being hit with lightning once; being burned alive; feeling trapped, with needles sticking into me."

"That's all stuff that happened to me," Lucas said.

Bernard lowered his brows.

"Seriously, I've experienced all of that--except that I made the lightning. And having needles sticking into you, that's how I feel all the time."

"Damn… when were you burned alive?"

"In an MRI machine; it's a bad idea to get inside one of those when your body's full of metal---oh!"

Lucas gasped and stood up.

"What?" Brick asked.

"That's it! It's the nanomachines! We both had them. That must be the connection!"

"But… those are gone now, right?" Bernard said, his face suddenly pale. "I don't have them anymore because you took them all out, didn't you?"

"Maybe not all of them… maybe some got left behind. That has to be why this is happening. It's how I communicate with other computers. Maybe my brain can still communicate with yours."

"What do you mean?"

Lucas pointed at the phone on the bed.

"Look," he said. "When I turned that phone on, I could feel it in my head. There was another presence there that I could sense, different from my own thoughts. I'll try to connect to your brain, and if I can feel the same thing in your head, then that would mean that some of the nanomachines are still in there. And if they are, maybe I can take them out."

Bernard looked sick. "I-I don't want them, Lucas," he stammered. "I don't want them in me."

Lucas understood completely. His heart ached for the terror Bernard must be feeling.

"Do you trust me?" he asked seriously.

Bernard nodded.

Lucas breathed deeply and focused. Bernard sat very still, his left hand lying limp on the bed, his right balled tightly into a fist, knuckles white. He looked pleadingly at Lucas, who closed his eyes. He concentrated, searching for a trace of any electrical energy. His senses were wide open, and he tuned out the surrounding noise. The room became quiet - so quiet, he heard Bernard's anxious pulse. Then he found it. Inside Bernard's brain, there was a small cluster of busily humming nanomachines, centered in the base of his skull. Lucas felt a flicker of recognition, the same that he had felt long ago at the warehouse. Then came the sharp tug in his chest. This time, he leaned into it and began to pull back with his consciousness, intent on drawing them out. Slowly and carefully he pulled, like removing a roundworm.

Bernard let out a shriek of pain, and Lucas froze. In that instant, he saw his own surprised face, as if he was lying down in Bernard's place, looking up at himself. Then the image was gone. He was standing over Bernard, who was clutching his forehead with his right hand.

"Bernard! Are you alright? Can you hear me?" Lucas asked.

To his horror, Bernard suddenly began to slam his own head against the wall with a loud *bang - bang - bang* as he wailed. Blood showed quickly on the white paint. Lucas began to panic. He threw himself on top of the bed and tackled him to the floor. Bernard flopped limply then lay still, like a corpse. Before Lucas could even process relief, he continued slamming his skull into the concrete.

"Bernard, stop! Please" Lucas begged. He felt helpless and overwhelmed with fear.

The door opened, and Brad, Tim and Kenny burst in. Dr. Gill entered behind them, and rushed straight to Bernard's side. He injected something into Bernard's thin, skeletal arm.

"What happened?" he demanded, glaring at Lucas.

Lucas couldn't speak. He stared at Bernard, who had become very still, staring blankly up at the ceiling.

"Get him out of here," Dr. Gill ordered the men.

Strong hands grabbed Lucas by the shoulders, and he didn't resist. But then, to his surprise, something sharp stung him in the neck, and his body went numb. He was picked up and carried, unconscious before he even reached the door.

Chapter 11

HE WOKE UP IN HIS bed. His head was clouded, but he could still move his arms and legs. Breathing out a sigh of relief, he rubbed his eyes, then struggled to sit up. With his mind, he searched for a signal from Bernard's phone. It was still in the room up the hall. He began to type out a text, but how could he know if Bernard was able to answer it?

"Hello?" he called out to the faceless people watching him.

No one responded.

"Hello?" he said more earnestly.

The door opened, and Dr. Gill entered the room with Brad, Tim and Kenny close behind. He looked tired, but bore a sympathetic expression on his face.

"Good morning," he said with a smile. "How are we doing today?"

"Where's Brick?" Lucas asked desperately. "Is he alright?"

"He's fine, just resting."

"What happened?"

"Brick still has a long way to go in his recovery," he replied gently. "He had a seizure, and won't be able to see anyone for a while."

Lucas glanced at the security team.

"That's it?" he asked incredulously. "That's all you can say?"

Dr. Gill only looked at him.

"Is he worse?" Lucas probed.

Again, Dr. Gill said nothing.

Lucas studied his face. Why were they keeping this from him? Why wouldn't they just tell him the truth?

"Was it my fault?" Lucas asked quietly.

"Why would it be your fault?" Dr. Gill asked.

"Because you had me knocked out."

Dr. Gill tilted his head. "You were upset. I was worried that you would put up a struggle when I requested to have you removed from the room."

"When can I see him?"

"I'm afraid you can't. Like I said, he still has a long way to go in his recovery."

"Yeah, but he's going to get better eventually, right? How long will that be?"

"Lucas," Dr. Gill said slowly. He sat down on the bed, his small eyes showing sympathy. "It's become clear that Brick still has some nanomachines in his system. We didn't know they were there before, but it seems your presence my have triggered some sort of response from them - waking them up, so to speak. Brick's body did not handle this response well, and we think that's what caused his seizure. Until we know that it won't happen again, it's not a good idea for you to go near him."

Lucas swallowed hard. *So it is my fault,* he thought.

"How will you know that it won't happen again?"

"This is still a new science, and we're still learning as we go. I'm sorry, but it's impossible to say anything for sure."

Lucas nodded, gritting his teeth in frustration. Dr. Gill gave him another sympathetic smile, then got up to leave. Lucas remained very still, though his heart pounded in his chest with shame and anger. The security team escorted Dr. Gill wordlessly from the room. When the door was closed, Lucas got up and paced the floor. He felt like a pit had opened up in his stomach. Bernard had trusted him, and he had only managed to make everything worse. Bernard could very well be paralyzed from the neck down now, or worse - a vegetable. He could be close to death. How could this have happened? Who could make something so evil and destructive?

Lucas screamed in rage. He kicked the table over, and lightning blasted from his hands, generating a loud boom that shook the walls, cracked the plaster, and burst the bulbs overhead. He dropped to his knees, exhausted, burns coating his arms. He attacked the cameras, shut off the power to his room, then rolled over in the darkness and cried.

Hours dragged by. When he couldn't cry anymore, and he had no more desire to destroy the things in his room, he began to study his hands.

Something nagged at him through his anger. He was changing; that was clear. He had more control over his abilities. If he had been made with a purpose, it followed that everything he could do also had a purpose; that was a matter of logic. What he couldn't figure was the intention behind *all* of his abilities. What could they want with a thing like him? What could all of this possibly be for? They made him to survive the nanomachines, but that couldn't be all he was made to do. Surely they planned for everything else that followed, right? This couldn't all be an accident… could it?

He sat up on the floor and speculated. The burns on his arms had already healed, the skin closed up as if they had never been there at all. That's a pretty good ability to have, he thought. His power of remote surveillance, too, was very useful. He couldn't control his ability to throw lightning, but that would be a good power to have in a fight, if he could learn to control it. That just left his apparent link to Bernard.

His anger returned quickly. This psychic connection, or whatever it was, just seemed like a sick joke. Infection with the nanomachines had nearly killed Bernard, and now what was left of him had to be tormented every day by the residue they left behind. What could the Rising gain from that?

The panicked look on Bernard's face returned to his mind, as real as if it was right in front of him. He could hear his tortured screams, and remembered the fear he felt as Bernard slammed his head onto the floor over and over again. Squeezing his eyes shut, he stretched himself out on the ground and cried himself to sleep.

Sometime during the night, he climbed back into the bed. The next morning, the door opened. Iweala entered the room, followed by some men carrying a long table, and two more pushing large carts.

"Good morning," she said. "We've got a special job for you today."

Lucas said nothing, but turned away and pulled the blanket up over his shoulders. His face felt warm and puffy.

Iweala came to the side of the bed and stood with her arms folded sternly.

"I don't want to work today," Lucas said.

"You don't have a choice," Iweala replied.

"What are you going to do?" he snapped. "What is *anyone* going to do? Kill me? Go ahead. I don't want to do this anymore."

"Lucas," Iweala said. Her voice was suddenly soft and gentle.

"What?"

"You want to get better, don't you?"

"What do you mean?"

"Don't you want to be able to use your gifts without hurting people? Don't you want to see your friends and your mother again?"

He turned to look up at her.

"Of course I do," he answered quietly.

"Lucas, I want to help you. We all do. That's why we're here."

"What are you talking about?"

"It's not just about stopping the Rising. It would be unfair to put all of that on you. These games and tests that we do are about understanding your abilities, so that we can help you."

"And then what?"

"I hope that eventually you'll be able to go home and live your life again," she said gently. "Once all of this is over, you would be free to do whatever you wanted."

"But I thought I was the government's property, or whatever."

"You wouldn't be, not forever. They only said that to make you cooperate. Truthfully, when your job was done, you would be free to go if it was safe to let you."

"What do I have to do?"

"Complete these tests," she answered. "And learn to control your abilities. No more throwing lightning when you're angry. Can you do that?"

Lucas nodded. "I think so."

"I think so, too," Iweala said with a soft smile.

"What about Brick?"

"He's going to be okay," she told him. "He's recovering now. The Rising wants him almost as badly as they want you. So, once they're out of the way, he can go home, too."

Lucas nodded. *I owe it to Bernard*, he thought bitterly.

"Then let's get to work," he said.

He was allowed to shower and change his clothes, then eat. He had pancakes and bacon, and a glass of orange juice. While he ate, the men set up the table and unloaded the carts with dozens of black metal boxes. They set them up in stacks of three, and plugged them in with long extension cords. Iweala stood off to the side, supervising. After Lucas finished eating, she motioned for him to come over.

"These are servers recovered months ago from the warehouse in Austin where you had your accident," she explained. "They might have important information stored in them. I would like you to retrieve what you can, then send it to that marked hard drive for your colleagues in the bullpen to review. Can you do that?"

Lucas looked at the large black boxes. They all appeared identical, and hummed softly, waiting.

"Yeah, I think I can," he replied.

"Good," she said. "I'll come back to check on you in an hour."

Lucas nodded.

Iweala squeezed his shoulder and walked off, leaving him alone in the room. He walked around the table, studying the servers. He knew, conceptually, what they were, thanks to his past research, but in practice he wasn't sure how he would break into one. He began to feel them out; with each probe of his mind, he saw thousands of dancing pinpricks of light. Then he dove in.

He found himself swimming through massive amounts of information, all of it encrypted. *No problem*, he thought. He spent roughly ten minutes finding the pattern amid the words and symbols before he cracked it, then everything was laid bare before him. This server seemed to contain thousands upon thousands of emails. The next server had hundreds of stored documents; the rest were all Web servers, networked together.

Lucas scanned through the emails for anything important. The addresses didn't work anymore, and the communiques used first names only: Dorian, Vlad, Mary, Igor, Mina, and Lucy; and two last names: Poe and Lovecraft. Lucas guessed that these were nicknames, or aliases. The contents of the emails were brief and composed of nothing but nonsense phrases:

Mina---

> *El Dorado. Blue sun.*
> *--Lovecraft*

Poe---
>   *Southern belle. Glorious morning copy back.*
>   *--Dorian*

Lovecraft---
>   *Red River. Lost.*
>   *--Victor*

It had to be some kind of code. He scanned through the remainder of the emails, then compiled a list of all the names and aliases used and forwarded it upstairs. He searched through the rest of the servers, combing through each of the saved documents, and found designs for bombs containing vials of nanomachines. *Definitely from the Rising*, he thought. He sent the information to other drive.

After exactly one hour, Iweala returned. She brought lunch with her: chicken sandwiches and small bags of potato chips. As he sat down at the table to eat, the men carted away the servers and the table and Iweala took the seat across from Lucas.

"How are you?" she asked as she opened one of the bags of chips.

"Better," Lucas answered.

"Productive work always helps me feel better when I'm sad," she said.

"Why would you feel sad?"

"I have a family, too," she replied. "It's been nearly ten months since I last saw them. I have a seven-year-old son, and a three-year-old daughter."

Lucas looked at her with surprise. Her dark features were solemn.

"Most of the people here have families and friends that they miss," Iweala continued. "It's too dangerous for anyone to travel and risk exposing this place. No one goes home until this is all over."

"What about Kowalski?"

"He's divorced, no kids. It's hard to maintain a healthy marriage with a job like this."

Lucas knew she was trying to make a point.

"Why do you do it?" he asked.

"Because we believe in the cause - protecting the country, you know, keeping everyone in it safe. We sacrifice so everyone else doesn't have to."

"I get what you're saying, but there's a difference here. You chose this; I didn't. I'm just a kid."

"And it's terrible that you've been forced to make these sacrifices," Iweala nodded. "But I want you to know that you're not alone."

Lucas leaned forward.

"The sooner we defeat the Rising, the sooner everyone gets to go home right? I'd be able to see my mom again?"

"That's right."

"You promise?"

"I give you my word," she said. "You will see her again."

Before the next test, they shaved his head. Then small plastic discs were stuck all over his smooth scalp with a glue-like adhesive. He could feel a tiny hum of power, like the wingbeats of a gnat, emanating from each one. Three computer monitors were set up in his room, and a group of scientists gathered outside, watching through the one-way glass. A puzzle was displayed on the middle monitor, and he was told to solve it. It looked like traditional jigsaw puzzle married to a game of Tetris. Pieces drifted down the screen and he had to find where they fit in the puzzle while a clock timed him. If he took too long to put them together, the pieces disappeared, so he had to work quickly. The pieces didn't arrive one at a time either; three, sometimes four pieces came drifting down at once, and he had to find a place for all of them. Before the clock reached five minutes, he had finished the puzzle. It formed a 3D picture of the Notre Dame cathedral.

"Very good, Lucas," Dr. Gill's voice came over the intercom. "How do you feel?"

"Fine," he said, wiping the sweat from his brow. "That was fun."

"We're going to kick it up a notch, then. I want you to solve two different puzzles, on two different monitors. Are you ready?"

Lucas rolled his neck and took a deep breath. He couldn't imagine this working out, but might as well give it a shot.

"Ready," he answered.

Puzzle pieces began to drift down the screens of two of the computers, three on one, and four on the other. The computers sat about three feet apart, so it was impossible for him to look at both at the same time. Once he opened up his mind, however, images of the screens appeared inside his consciousness. He found that it was not very difficult after all to divide his attention between the two games. One game had been hard; two games was now like juggling - after a while, he wasn't really thinking about it anymore. It was like different compartments of his brain had opened up: one to tackle the problem at hand, and others to monitor everything else that was going on around him. He stood with his arms at his sides, eyes closed as sweat beaded on his forehead and dripped down his face, yet fully aware of the electrical energy powering the laptops and the lights overhead, and the conversations taking place in the room next door.

His observers were typing away at their notes as scans were produced, displaying his brain activity; he felt a tickle over his scalp as the sensors did their work. A three-dimensional image of his brain appeared on one of the monitors in the next room, and someone began to draw digital markers all over the scan, highlighting areas in the front, sides, and back of the brain. Then a phone call was made.

Yes? Iweala's voice answered.

Get down here, Dr. Gill's voice said. *You'll want to see this.*

"Very good, Lucas, thank you," Dr. Gill's voice came over the intercom a second later. "Take a breather for a minute. Can we get you anything?"

"Water," he answered. His shirt was soaked with sweat, and his limbs were shaking. He wandered to a chair and sat down while an orderly brought him a bottle of water. Thankfully, the man also supported his hand while he drank, because Lucas was sure he would have dropped it.

Dr. Gill strode into the room, a broad smile on his face.

"Very impressive," he said jovially. "How are you feeling?"

Lucas was beginning to hate that question.

"Exhausted," he replied.

"Understandable. Clearly, you have been exerting yourself. I appreciate your effort in these tests."

"Sure. So Iweala's coming?"

"How do you know that?"

"I heard your phone call in my head," Lucas answered. "Same as I always do."

Dr. Gill's smile disappeared. His expression was something between disappointment and fear.

"You were supposed to be paying attention to the games."

Lucas stared at him, confused.

"Well... I mean, sure, they're hard work, but they don't actually take all my concentration. Besides, I can't really help it. It just kind of... happens."

"You mean, you go wandering?" Dr. Gill asked.

"Um, yes?" Lucas said. He wasn't sure what the question meant.

Dr. Gill's expression was definitely fearful now. He turned away and scratched his head.

"What difference does it make?" Lucas asked, standing up. "So what if I saw your reports? I don't understand them."

Just then, the door opened and Iweala stepped inside. Dr. Gill rushed to meet her at the door, and grabbed her elbow.

"Shelley, we need to talk outside," he sputtered.

She glanced at Lucas, but followed Dr. Gill out into the hall. The door closed behind them, and Lucas was left alone. He sat back down and drank more water.

The room was quiet. The door was well sealed, so he couldn't hear what they talked about. Dr. Gill was spooked, and Lucas still wondered what "wandering" meant. It was clear they didn't want him to see or hear whatever they said about him in the reports. But why did it matter? What would he have done with information anyway? Share it with Bernard? Neither of them had anywhere to go, or anyone to divulge information to.

After a few minutes, Iweala returned, closely followed by Dr. Gill, who looked much calmer now. Iweala smiled sweetly and pulled up a chair.

"Hello, Lucas," she said. "Sorry about earlier."

"What's going on?" he asked warily.

"Everything is alright. Dr. Gill just got a little upset."

"Why?" Lucas asked, looking over her shoulder to Dr. Gill, who smiled apologetically.

"I was upset because I felt that you weren't doing your best on our tests," he said, folding his hands together. "Lucas, if you don't do your best, then we can't get the best results and it will take much longer for us to determine how to help you. Do you understand?"

"Why didn't you just say that?" Lucas asked.

"This work is very important to me," Dr. Gill said solemnly. "We've been here a very long time, and we all want to help you and the rest of the

United States by stopping the Rising. I shouldn't have taken my frustration out on you. So, I'm sorry."

"See, Lucas?" Iweala jumped in. "We're all on the same side. Now, how do you think that you can help Dr. Gill?"

"By working harder, I guess," he said, but his inflection made the statement sound like a question.

"That's right," Iweala nodded. "Try not to get distracted again, okay? We all want to do our best here."

"Sure," Lucas nodded.

"Do you forgive me?" Dr. Gill asked.

"Yeah. I forgive you."

Chapter 12

He watched Iweala and Dr. Gill leave, and felt more confused than ever. A new game began and over the intercom, he was told to stand in the middle of the room while the puzzle game appeared on all three monitors. His mind was split three ways, each part fixed on one of the games in front of him, constructing three very different and exceptionally complicated images. He could visualize them all in his head as the pieces came tumbling down. It was challenging, but still not all that much work. He had a handle on juggling his attention, and was certainly tempted to let his mind wander. He could feel the observing scientists typing away, recording his brain's movements.

Sweat beaded on his forehead and he clenched his fists, hungry to unleash his full power.

Fine. You want me to focus? he thought. *Then I'll focus.*

He took a deep breath, and his mind searched until he found the source code of the games. Like a raging fire, his consciousness ripped each piece of code apart until it was unrecognizable. The screens flickered, then turned blue. Then, as his anger swelled, he attacked the laptop's batteries. He overloaded them with energy until they grew hotter and hotter, and then burst in a shower of sparks and flood of smoke. Meanwhile, he quietly invaded the computers in the next room and downloaded every bit of data he could find, squirreling it away in the back of his mind.

The door opened, and a couple of orderlies rushed in with fire extinguishers, with Dr. Gill on their heels. Dr. Gill hooked Lucas around the waist and jerked him out of the way while they sprayed the smoldering laptops, coating them with white foam. An alarm rang out as smoke filled the air.

"Are you alright?" Dr. Gill asked, bending low to look at his face.

Lucas pretended to be surprised.

"What happened?" he said groggily.

"We might have to get computers with faster processors," Dr. Gill replied, almost laughing. "You're much stronger than we anticipated."

Iweala entered, taking in the scene with wide eyes.

"What happened here?" she said to Dr. Gill.

"He overloaded the computers," he replied with glee. "They couldn't handle him."

She raised her eyebrows as Dr. Gill smacked him on the back. Lucas wobbled; his back was sticky with sweat.

"I knew you were holding out on us," he chuckled.

"Yes, very impressive," Iweala said, nodding. She beckoned for an orderly to come over. "Take him back to his room; he'll need some food, then a shower."

"Good job, Lucas," she said with a smile, turning back to him. "I am very proud of your progress."

Lucas looked at the pile of melted plastic and smoldering metal.

"But I broke the computers," he said.

"That's okay," Iweala insisted. "Now that we have a better understanding of how powerful you are, we can get better computers to withstand it."

Lucas was confused, but Dr. Gill and Iweala seemed too overjoyed to notice. Well, 'overjoyed' was probably an overstatement for Iweala's attitude.

"Maybe we should install some kind of buffer," Dr. Gill mused, rubbing his chin.

"Yes, get to work on that," Iweala told him. "Lucas, you can go rest now."

The orderly put a hand on his shoulder and began to guide him toward the door. Lucas went obediently, his head spinning. He couldn't understand what they were so excited about.

I haven't done anything... not really, he thought. *I've played a bunch of games that didn't mean anything. This has all been a huge waste of time.*

Back in his room, he was given a plate of chicken parmesan, diced vegetables that looked like they came from a can, and a bottle of water. He ate while his security team stood silently by the door. The orderly left and then returned moments later with a set of clothes, which he placed on Lucas' bed.

It's like a fancy prison, he thought distractedly. *Round-the-clock service.*

But something else was going on, and he was certain of it. Those games were a distraction… but from what? What didn't they want him to see?

He continued to eat, slowly, but inside his head he opened up the information he had stolen from his observers. He scrolled through hundreds of data tables filled with numbers and Greek letters, none of which made any sense to him. He set part of his consciousness to work cracking the code. A separate file contained reports, all mentioning his name and "Subject 5" in the heading, and authored by Dr. Gill. He hid those away to read through later. He then paused to study the images of his brain, which had been embedded within the reports. Each had various sections labeled and highlighted. In the upper left corner of the scan read, "Subject 5--Lucas," and a timestamp in the bottom left corner. According to the time, each photograph had been taken during one of his "tests," while he had been playing one of Dr. Gill's games. The scans were brightly colored, but each part of his brain was highlighted a different color, so the entire image was illuminated with like a rainbow. There were scribbles and labels dotting the image; most seemed to center on the red and yellow parts, which were in a different location depending on the image. Sometimes the back part of his brain was colored this way, and sometimes it was the front, or the middle, or only one side. He supposed that this might be interesting, but didn't understand why.

"Are you finished?" the orderly asked.

Lucas blinked, his mind rushing back to the real world.

"Yes," he nodded, pushing his plate back.

"Then I will take you to the bathroom, so you can shower if you'd like."

"Thanks."

Lucas stood and picked up his clothes from the bed. They were the same white pants and shirt, and a clean pair of socks. He saw that the orderly carried a small metal tray as he stepped close to Lucas.

"Hold still," he said.

His hands reached up to Lucas' head, and Lucas fought the urge to pull away. The orderly began removing each of the tiny metal disks that were adhered to Lucas' scalp. It was like peeling off a scab, and it stung. He couldn't help but flinch as each one was picked away. He counted twelve as they were dropped one by one onto the tray. By the time the man finished, Lucas imagined that his newly shaven head was quite inflamed.

He was walked down the hall to the bathroom. As he went past Bernard's room, Lucas felt a shiver down his spine. His mind went searching for the phone, to see if it was turned on, but he felt nothing. The battery must have died days ago. He wondered if Bernard was awake, and if so, was he upset that Lucas hadn't come to see him? Was there anything left of him to *be* upset?

The orderly left him alone, closing the door. Lucas turned on the water and steam filled the shower as he stripped down. In the fogging mirror, he saw that his bald head was indeed patched with angry red spots that were quickly fading as his skin healed. He was astounded at how much he looked like a different person, and it wasn't just because of his missing hair. Dark circles hung under his eyes, which seemed wider and more… he searched for the word, but couldn't put his finger on it. His eyes were different… somehow.

He stepped under the water and called up the files. He flipped through until he found a scan that was completely different. This brain was almost entirely dark, with some small spots of light scattered here and there. There were several more like these, all nearly black, except for a few light spots and one near-perfect circular section of the brain in the back that was rimmed in pale blue. Lucas glanced at the time stamp. Perhaps these scans were taken during the seven months while he slept? But no - these were only days old, and it wasn't his brain at all. In the upper-left corner, he read, "Subject 4--Brick."

This was Bernard's brain. Lucas studied the dark, hollow images and felt sick. This was what the nanomachines had done to him, his life ripped apart and devoured. Then what was that small, circular part?

Lucas. Lucas.

A tingle shot up the back of his skull, and Lucas jumped. He nearly slipped on the smooth tile, and turned off the water to listen. He had heard a whisper, but the room was completely silent except for the drip, drip of the faucet. He waited, then turned on the water again.

He placed one of his own brain scans next to Bernard's. His looked especially bright next to Bernard's dismally empty scan, but there was one

Spark

similarity. He saw that his brain, too, contained that strange, dark circle rimmed with pale blue, located in the lower section of his brain. What on earth could that be? He pondered over the other scans and each of the reports, searching for an answer. Maybe, he surmised, it was where the nanomachines nested. Both he and Bernard had it. He remembered finding them concentrated there, near the base of his skull. His hand rose shakily until his fingers touched the back of his head. There was nothing to be felt, no scar or mark of any kind. Looking from the outside, no one would never know they were there.

He shut off the water and stepped out onto the cold tile. He angrily ripped his towel off its rack and dried himself, then got dressed. As he brushed his teeth, a cold tingle ran down his skull once more.

Lucas... Lucas!

He gripped the sides of the counter, his toothbrush clattering into the sink. There it was again, that whisper.

What? he thought, panicked. *What is it?*

Lucas, it's me... I've been trying for days... this is so difficult... can't keep it up forever...

Chills overtook his body. The voice was *inside* his head, and it was reedy, like someone speaking through a straw. A foreign, sort of magnetic, force brushed up against his consciousness.

Who are you? he asked fearfully.

It's me... Bernard.

What!? You're alright? That seemed like a stupid question. *How are you talking to me? How are you inside my head?*

You were right all along... we are connected. I could feel it when you went inside my mind, looking for the nanomachines, but it's been there all along... I've been trying ever since to reach you...

Bernard's voice faded. Lucas couldn't believe what was happening; it was impossible. But he felt the connection, and it was not unlike what he felt when his mind connected to a computer.

As Bernard's presence in his mind slipped away, Lucas reached out. Taking a breath, his mind went searching for Bernard's mind. He had plenty of practice finding signals and formulating messages in his head; this was simply a matter of finding the right signal again, the one that he knew came from the nanomachines residing in the back of Bernard's head. Once he located them, he thought, *Are you okay?*

He waited for a response, but none came. He pressed, but was afraid to focus too hard and hurt Bernard's already fragile mind. As he looked deeper, he could feel... something. It was different from a computer, more haphazard and noisy. Bernard's mind was chaotic; lights, sounds, and pictures were tossed everywhere, strongly resembling the agitated surface of a lake. Lucas ventured even farther in, treading gently, and the pictures became clearer, but still made no sense. He saw leaves, then water, then faces of people that he didn't know, then white nothingness, then leaves again. He heard a rapid succession of voices that often chased each other and overlapped so badly that his head hurt. Finally, he saw pages of text: literal pages of a book, lying open on Bernard's lap. Beyond it, he saw white walls, a bookshelf, and wheelchair. He was looking through Bernard's eyes.

Lucas? Bernard's voice came.

Yes? he answered tentatively.

You're here! This is amazing! Bernard exulted, and Lucas felt a thrill of joy emanating from his thoughts. *I finally reached you!*

Yeah, I can't believe it, Lucas replied. *I can see your room.*

You can? How?

I see what you're seeing.

Wow! I wonder if it can go both ways?

Maybe, but I don't know how to try it, Lucas said. *Listen-- there's something strange going on here. I think I'm being manipulated.*

What do you mean?

All the games and the tests-- I think it's all just a distraction to keep me from seeing what's really going on here. Something bad.

How do you know?

I don't, I just--

I mean, they could just be regular government secrets, you know?

Yes, but I don't think that's it. I think there's something else going on.

You think the agents are dirty?

Maybe not all of them, but they seem really concerned with keeping me occupied and looking the other way. I downloaded some of the reports they had on you and me, and I'm going to read them and see what I can find out.

Okay, Bernard said slowly. *What can I do?*

I don't know, Lucas replied. *I guess I'll just keep you in the loop. How are you?*

I'm fine… or not worse, anyway. I woke up a few hours after you left that day. No permanent damage done.

Good, that's a relief.

A knock sounded on the door. Then came the orderly's muffled voice. "Lucas?"

I have to go, Lucas said. *Thank you… thank you for talking to me.*

Yeah, you too… good luck.

Lucas opened the door and stepped out. The orderly kept a hand on his back, and he allowed himself to be led back to his room. He could feel Bernard's presence in his head all the way there, and was so happy to know he was alive. Then the orderly and his security team departed, and closed the door. He was the only one in the room, but he didn't feel alone. He lay down on the bed and read through the reports from start to finish until he was overtaken by sleep.

Chapter 13

THE NEXT DAY, LUCAS WAS invited back upstairs. Brad, Tim and Kenny escorted him up to the ground floor, then drove him in the golf cart to an open, undeveloped part of the bunker. It was large and windowless, and Lucas suspected that it was part of the original warehouse. Kowalski stood waiting, wearing his track pants and athletic shirt. He strode over to a large, black trash bag and dumped it on the ground. With a loud clatter, dozens of aluminum cans spilled out.

"What are those for?" Lucas asked.

"Target practice," Kowalski replied. "Help me set them up."

"Am I going to learn to shoot?"

"Sort of."

He gave Lucas three cans and took three more himself, then walked about twenty yards out into the warehouse. He told Lucas to set them about five yards apart, and soon they were all lined up on the ground.

"Alright, so we're going to test your lightning-producing abilities," Kowalski said. He pointed at the first can in the line. "I want you to try to hit that can."

"Are you sure that's a good idea?" Lucas asked. "I can't aim it, and besides, I've never done it on purpose before."

"Because you don't control it; it controls you," Kowalski said firmly. "You do it when you're angry because the adrenaline lets you, but you can recreate those feelings if you try. Just look at your target and focus."

Lucas glanced over his shoulder at his security detail. Besides them, he and Kowalski were alone.

"Kowalski, I don't want to do this," Lucas protested.

"What's wrong?" Kowalski said, folding his arms.

Lucas hesitated. "Where's Iweala?"

"Downstairs," he replied. "Why?"

"All these tests, what are they really for?" Lucas asked. "Shouldn't I be in the Bullpen right now, looking for the Rising?"

"Believe me, Lucas, I want the same thing," Kowalski said. "But the higher-ups said you weren't ready. They see you as a liability, and if something were to go wrong, it'd be on us. So, we're training you."

Lucas narrowed his eyes.

"That's all this is about?" he asked. "Training me so I don't hurt anybody?"

"Yes," Kowalski answered. "We want you to to better control your powers. Then you can join the team and help us like I know you want to."

Lucas looked at the ground. The information he held was burning up in his head.

"What about the coded messages I found? Has anyone learned anything from those?"

"What coded messages?"

"Was that just another test?" Lucas said, heart sinking with disappointment.

"What are you talking about?"

"How much do you know about what they're doing down there?" he asked. "Do you get a say in what they do to us? Me and Brick?"

"Iweala is in charge of that," Kowalski replied. "That's her division."

"Well, I hate it; it's pointless," Lucas said bitterly.

"Everything is fine, Lucas," Kowalski assured him. "Tell you what--let's get this over with, and then we can do something useful. How's that sound?"

"What do you want me to do?"

"Shoot the can. Channel that anger you have building up inside of you; use it, instead of letting it take over."

Lucas looked at the can. He could clearly remember the anger that he had felt on that day, nine months ago, and the pain of his mother being taken from him; the fear of being captured, handcuffed and of fighting for his life. Guns were pointed at him, the men in white suits attempted to overpower him before his own body reacted.

Heat filled his chest, then spread down to his hands. There was a crackling, popping sound that echoed through the warehouse. Lucas looked down at his arms and saw sparks dancing across his skin. He gasped with amazement.

"Alright--you're doing great," Kowalski said gently. "Now, direct it where you want it to go."

Lucas raised his hands slowly. He visualized the target and took a deep breath, but nothing happened. The electricity crackled loudly, then suddenly faded. It fizzled, then there was only silence. Lucas dropped his arms, panting.

"What happened?" he asked.

"It's alright," Kowalski reassured him. "Just start again. You've got to focus; hold those feelings there and then let it all out."

"How do you know how to do this?"

"I know a few things about anger."

Lucas wanted to ask what he meant, but he let it go. He raised his hands again and focused. His anger rose, and the heat came more quickly this time. There was a sound like wood snapping as the electrical energy flew across his fingers.

"Now! Do it before it's gone!" Kowalski shouted.

Lucas tried throwing or pushing the energy, but nothing happened. The heat faded and the sparks vanished, and he was growing frustrated. The immense heat had caused raw, red blisters to appear along his arms.

"I can't do it," he said through gritted teeth.

"You're just not trying hard enough," Kowalski replied.

"It hurts!" Lucas shot back. "I don't want to do this anymore!"

Kowalski glared at him coldly. Lucas looked away, rubbing his now-healed arms.

"You're one of them," Lucas growled.

"What are you talking about now?"

"You're with *them*," Lucas said, the words tumbling out of his mouth. "You're with Iweala and Dr. Gill. I know what you're doing: you're torturing me and Bernard to study us. Like lab rats."

Kowalski blinked with confusion, then shook his head.

"Lucas, stop it. Nobody's torturing anybody; you're making no sense."

In less than a second, Lucas closed the distance between them. His fist collided with Kowalski's jaw with considerable force. His fingers broke on the impact, but Kowalski stumbled backward, then dropped to the ground. Brad, Tim and Kenny immediately responded, rushing forward with their guns raised.

"Wait!" Kowalski yelled, raising a hand. "Stand down!"

He staggered back to his feet. Lucas stood ready, lightning crackling in his good hand. Kowalski extended both hands toward him, palms out.

"Lucas, you have to stay calm," he said in a low, gentle voice. "If you don't cooperate, you're going to be locked up in your room again. Is that what you want?"

"I want to go home," Lucas said, his voice breaking. "I want to stop being used and studied. And I want to see my mom."

"And you will," Kowalski said evenly. "But first you have to do what we want, okay?"

"No!" Lucas shouted. Hot tears streamed down his face. He knew he should stop, but he couldn't. "No more! You're the monsters! I'd bet the Rising's not even real! I want to go home!"

All at once, four guns were cocked. Brad, Tim and Kenny had moved closer, their guns raised, and another agent who had appeared in the doorway. Lucas heard other voices approaching; the commotion had been overheard.

Maybe I can make a break for it, Lucas thought. *I may never get another chance; it's now or never.*

"Lucas, don't do this," Kowalski said clearly. "You're making a mistake. Just stand down."

Lucas took a deep breath. *Goodbye, Bernard,* he thought.

He lunged forward with a yell. Swinging his arm, he hurled the lightning as a deafening *pop-pop-pop* sounded in succession. Lucas felt like he'd been smashed in the chest with a sledgehammer. His legs gave way and he landed on his back; the lightning scattered in every direction in shimmering, snaky tendrils. He stared up at the ceiling, which seemed to be rapidly expanding outward, and wondered why he could no longer breathe.

He woke up on a gurney, hearing voices all around him. The wheels squeaked, and he was being rolled very quickly. His chest felt like it was on fire.

"He's healing," a voice said. "Give him another injection."

"Hurry," a breathless voice chimed in. "Or he'll be fully recovered before we get him back in his room."

"I can't believe you had him shot," a third voice, which he recognized as Kowalski's, said.

"If I didn't, you'd be dead, and he'd be escaping across the desert," a woman replied. "God, you're so naive. What were you thinking, bringing him up here?"

"I had the situation handled," the man snapped. "You didn't need to do that."

"He could've killed you."

"He needs help, not to be menaced!"

Lucas realized that his hands and feet were tied to the gurney. Three spots of blood had blossomed across his chest. That explained why it was so difficult to breathe. He felt groggy, and his powers were completely out of his reach. Through half-open eyes, he saw four people guiding the gurney, while two others ran alongside it, arguing.

"This thing is dangerous, Seth," Iweala said. "I don't think you realize that."

"That's just it--you keep calling him a 'thing,' or 'it.' He's a kid, not an animal."

"Yeah, and you're so great with kids," Iweala spat sarcastically. "This is not a child; it's an *android*. And your recklessness---"

"Hey, don't make me pull rank on you, alright?" Kowalski said sharply. "I know what I'm doing. You do this your way, and I'll do it mine. I've let you have your little science fair downstairs, but if you get in my way again, I can have you back in a cubicle before you can blink. Are we clear?"

Iweala made no reply. Then Lucas found that he was in an elevator, and the voices were gone. The next thing he knew, he was in his bed.

He woke up, but couldn't remember falling asleep. Breathing was easier, and he could move freely, so he sat up. Lifting up his new, clean shirt, he examined his chest. There was no more blood; the gunshot wounds had healed completely, without leaving any sign of a scar. He stood up shakily and bewildered.

Lucas? Bernard's voice whispered.

What time is it? Lucas groaned, holding his head.

I don't know. I don't have a clock in here, remember? What happened? I felt pain.

They shot me... god, it feels like there's a rock band in my head.

Why?

Because they drugged me, too.

No--I meant, why did they shoot you?

I attacked Kowalski. He brought me upstairs, and I got mad and tried to escape. They shot me three times to take me out.

Who's Kowalski? And why were you mad?

I thought he was one of them, one of the dirty agents... it was stupid. The whole thing.

Bernard was quiet. Lucas reached out inquisitively with his mind, wondering if he was still there. He got a stinging sensation in return.

Bernard?

Bernard's anxiety hit him suddenly, like a strong odor.

I felt it, his voice returned. *All of it. The gunshots, the lightning, even the weakness from the drugs.*

I'm sorry, Lucas said, his stomach sinking. He had forgotten that whatever he did would affect Bernard, too.

Why is this happening? Bernard said.

I don't know. Dr. Gill said that the nanomachines in your head were responding to me, but he didn't know how or why.

Why does it only go one way, though? Bernard inquired desperately. *You don't feel the stuff that happens to me, do you?*

No, I don't.

And why do they hurt me, but not you? You got powers, and I got... I'm broken... it's not fair...

Lucas sighed, rubbing his eyes.

It's because, he said slowly. *I'm not human. Not one like you, anyway.*

What? What does that mean?

The terrorists that we're hunting... they're called the Rising. They're a huge organization and they've been around for a long time. They made me. I'm an artificial human... an android. I'm the only one that can't be killed by these things; instead, I can control them, and talk to them, like we're doing right now.

I'm really confused... Bernard said, and a flood of fear washed across their link. *You're like... what, a robot? That's what you've been this whole time?*

145

I'm not a robot, but I was created. When I first touched the nanomachines, they became apart of me. I think that's what they were meant to do.

So you belong to them, Bernard said fearfully. *You're one of the Rising, too?*

No, Lucas answered firmly. *They made me, but that's all. They gave me these powers, but I make my own choices. I'm going to use my powers to find them, wherever they are, and stop them.*

Bernard was quiet again, and Lucas waited. He tried to be patient, but he had a headache and felt very uncomfortable.

What did they make you for?

I don't know. I've wondered about that a lot.

Us being able to talk like this… you think that was on purpose?

I don't know.

Lucas folded his hands over his chest, feeling defeated.

At that moment, an alarm began to blare loudly, screeching through the halls. Lucas jumped and threw his hands over his ears.

What is that? Bernard exclaimed. *Did you do that?*

No, Lucas replied. *Something's wrong.*

He tried to send his consciousness outward to investigate, but his mind was still fragile from the drugs. After several failed attempts, he managed to get a glimpse of the hallway through the cameras. Brad, Tim, and Kenny stood in the hall, backs to each other, their guns raised. Far overhead, a loud *boom* shook the walls.

Lucas slid off the bed. His legs were weak, and he stumbled as he ran to the door. The alarms continued to blare, and lights flashed in the hallway, winking through the small peephole on the door. Another explosion echoed like distant thunder.

We're under attack, Lucas thought. *Someone is attacking the bunker.*

A third explosion reverberated seven hundred feet overhead. Fear gripped his chest. What would happen if the bunker above him was destroyed? He would be trapped under half a mile of rubble. Worse, there would no chance of escape or discovery if everyone who knew about his location was killed. He began to pound on the door with his fist.

"Hey!" he shouted to his guards. "Hey! Open the door!"

No answer came. Lucas pounded again. The door was enormous and several feet thick. He wondered if they could even hear him knocking on the other side. He closed his eyes and breathed, trying to feel the lock, but of course it was purely mechanical. There was nothing for him to control.

"Hey!" he shouted again.

He stepped back a few feet, summoned lightning into his hands and blasted it at the door. The thunderous sound made his ears ring. The metal front of the door was completely blackened now. Brad's eye appeared in the peephole a second later, glaring at Lucas.

"Let me out!" Lucas yelled at him. His mind raced for an excuse. "I can help you!"

Brad's voice came over the intercom.

"What do you want?" he said harshly.

"I can fight! Let me out of here!"

"Fat chance!"

"I'm serious, I can help!"

"There is no way on earth I am letting you out of there. You don't want to fight; you want a chance to escape. And who do you think shot you last time you tried that?"

Lucas wanted to glare back at him, but he kept his face calm.

"No, I get it. That was my fault. But please… I'm begging you."

Brad's eye disappeared. Lucas roared with anger and fired another blast of lightning. He didn't know how much time passed while he paced the floor. A battle raged overhead, many stories above him. Between who? And which side was winning? All he knew was that his chance of escape would soon be gone.

Suddenly, he felt a buzz across his skin. The three guards outside had switched on their radios. Empty static filled his head; no signal could reach them so far underground.

Lucas ran to the door again. This time he spoke through their radios.

"Guys! You have to let me out!"

The three began swearing.

"Somebody needs to put this kid back to sleep," Kenny grumbled.

"Get off our radios!" Brad yelled. "If you don't shut up, I *will* shoot you again."

"Go ahead," Lucas replied. "But you'll have to open the door."

They ignored him, and began flipping through channels, at each one calling out for a status update from someone, anyone.

Lucas began to feel desperate. He stepped back from the door, rage boiling in his chest. He kicked the table over, then picked up the chair and hurled it at the wall; shards of wood flew everywhere. Then he fired another bolt of lightning at the door. His scream was followed by an echoing boom, and he dropped to his knees, shivers wracking his weakened body. Sheetrock dust snowed down from the ceiling, and hot blood pounded in his ears.

Then he saw it: small, spider-web cracks in the wall, just beside the steel frame of the door.

He stood up and staggered over, running his fingers along the crack. A flicker of determination ignited inside him. Electricity crackled across his fingers; the air hummed, charged with the power culminating in his hands. He raised his arms as the energy built, then flung it with all his might at the door. Blinding light flashed, and thunder clapped as he blasted the door again. And again. The force shook the walls, and the paint cracked. His breath came in quick gasps and his legs grew weak, but he continued throwing bolt after bolt that pounded like a battering ram against the door. Then the stone crumbled and gave way, and the heavy metal door fell outward with a crash and a cloud of dust.

Chapter 14

Dazed, Lucas was greeted with shouts and gunfire. He threw his arms over his head and dropped to the ground.

As the dust began to clear, he raised his eyes. His three guards had taken cover around the corner, behind a set of overturned desks. To Lucas' left, a squad of men in black tactical gear were attempting to come down the stairwell. They wore gas masks over their faces, and each man had a red sash tied around his upper arm. The gunfire paused, and two or three of the intruders suddenly tossed cans into the air that hissed, releasing clouds of white mist.

Lucas rose to his feet and stumbled back into his room; the mist stung the inside of his mouth and throat, and burned his eyes.

"It's him! He's loose!" one of the masked men shouted.

"Subject 5 is free! The door is open!" Brad yelled into his useless radio. "If anyone can hear me, I repeat, the door is open and Subject 5 is free!"

Bullets peppered the wall just above Lucas' head. He set his jaw as heat filled his body, and electricity crackled across his arms and chest. He stormed into the hallway, yelling with rage, his attention laser-focused on the masked men. He raised his hands and released the lightning, knocking them all off their feet. The stairwell was flooded with screams of pain, flashes of light, and the crash of thunder. Then silence descended, and all of the men in black lay still.

Something stirred behind him, and Lucas turned. Brad, Tim, and Kenny stood up, holding their firearms ready. They all gaped, eyes wide.

"Told you I could help you," Lucas said, panting.

"They're here for you," Brad said gruffly, once he'd recovered his voice.

"What do you mean?" Lucas asked. "Who are they?"

"It's the Rising. They found us."

He felt a chill which quickly grew into icy hatred. This was his chance - not just to escape, but to unleash upon the Rising the punishment that they deserved. They had made him, and he was going to make sure they deeply regretted it. He was determined that not a single one of their people made it out of this building alive.

"I'd bet that all that racket upstairs was just a distraction to get a team down here to fetch you," Brad was saying, interrupting Lucas' thoughts.

"Well, I'm not going with them," he replied. "I'd rather die. If I help you get out of here alive, will you let me go?"

"I can't do that," Brad answered stiffly. "You're too valuable, to them and to us."

"You'll die down here without me."

"With all due respect," Kenny cut in. "What exactly do you think you're gonna do against them? They have an army, and you're just a kid."

"Seriously?" Lucas exclaimed. "You saw what I just did, right? You think any of them stand a chance against me?"

"If there's enough of them, yes," Brad replied. "You can't take them all on, and if you get shot enough times, you're out of the game."

"I can heal."

"They don't need to kill you, only slow you down. Then they'll trap you, lock you up, and take you anywhere they want. We've done it, and they can do it, too. And, most likely, they know how you work better than you do; they made you, after all."

"Then *help* me," Lucas pleaded. "I have to get back at these people. Besides, we'll die anyway if we get trapped down here."

The men's faces were inscrutable, which only added to their menacing appearance. They did, however, finally lower their weapons.

"It's our job to keep you out of their hands," Kenny said. "We're certainly not going to risk that for revenge."

"No, but he does have a point," Tim said ruefully. "We will die if we stay here, one way or another. Either they'll come for us and beat us with sheer numbers, or they'll starve us out. Our best chance is to take the fight to them."

"Won't we still be outnumbered?" Brad countered.

"Yes, probably. But up there, we'd have a unique advantage. Wouldn't we, Lucas?"

Lucas nodded. "I'd be able to feel their radios, and hear any conversations they have. I could tell you where they are."

"And he does pack quite a punch."

Brad rubbed his chin. He looked at Kenny, who closed his eyes and shook his head, then sighed heavily.

"Alright. But we are duty-bound to save as many of our own agents as we can."

"Sure," Lucas replied impatiently. "And there's one other thing we need."

He turned and strode toward Bernard's room. This door didn't have the failsafe locks; probably because Bernard had no chance of getting anywhere on his own. Lucas commanded the door to open and walked cautiously inside. Bernard lay on the bed; a heavy bandage was taped to the side of his head, covering one eyebrow and shadowing one of his eyes. His eye was swollen shut, and the flesh around it was purple and green, pounded into a pulp during his seizure. He was clutching a book like he was ready to throw it, and gasped when he saw Lucas.

"Come on," Lucas said quickly. "We're getting out of here."

"What's going on?" Bernard asked weakly.

"The Rising is here, attacking the bunker," Lucas answered. He looked over his shoulder. Brad and Tim stood in the doorway.

"One of you has to carry him," Lucas said.

"He'll slow us down," Tim said flatly.

"We're not leaving him."

"He's right," Brad nodded. "The Rising won't turn up their noses if they find him."

Tim rolled his eyes, but stepped forward and scooped Bernard up from the bed. Long ago, Bernard would have been far too heavy to carry, even for a man Tim's size, but now he was so thin and frail that Tim lifted him easily. They left the room behind and hurried for the stairs. The elevator was out of the question.

Brad, Tim and Kenny surrounded Lucas on all sides, with Tim carrying Bernard. The group traveled at a run, taking the stairs swiftly while pausing every few seconds to listen for anyone coming the other way. Lucas was soon panting and sweating; he had pushed his body nearly to its limits. Hunger gnawed at his stomach. He had not eaten anything since breakfast, and it was now early afternoon. Since then, he had healed from gunshots, then spent far too much energy breaking out of his room and taking out a squad of Rising operatives. Not that he had had much physical power to spare; the many months he'd spent lying in stasis had completely ruined any athletic fitness he had before. When he slowed, Brad or Tim put a hand on his back to guide him forward. The group stopped halfway up to rest.

"I can hear them," Lucas said, panting.

"What's our status?" Tim asked.

Lucas listened to the cacophony of voices rushing through his head.

"Kowalski's down, and the rest are dead or captured," he reported. "And they are real pissed that I haven't been taken yet; that squad was supposed to incapacitate me. Apparently, they weren't expecting me to fight back."

"I don't think anyone was," Brad said. "Has Austin been alerted?"

"Yes, and they're sending choppers."

"Alright, how many do we have waiting for us when we get up there?"

"I don't know for sure, but I can feel sixteen radios just above us, right outside the door."

In his mind's eye, he saw them fanned out in front of the doorway.

"I don't suppose you can tell us what kind of weapons they're packing?" Brad asked.

"No," Lucas replied. "It doesn't work like that. I can only sense things that use EMF. But they're getting closer."

"So, we're trapped," Kenny said acidly. "We can't take them all out, and they'll shoot us once we open the door, anyway. It would make more sense for us to wait here until help comes."

"I'm not sitting and waiting," Lucas replied. "I'm going to fight. I've been waiting almost a year to dish out some payback."

"You can barely stand."

"I'm fine," Lucas snapped.

"Even if you were--and you're not--how would we get past these guys?"

"Let's get to the top, and I'll handle them."

They continued on. After five more flights, Lucas had to be carried. The men exchanged uneasy looks, but said nothing. The explosions had stopped, and Lucas sensed the presence of one hundred more men total, gathering in the bunker. Brad asked about their formation, and Lucas reported that they seemed be moving in groups of twenty or fewer, moving in on the bunker from different entry points. There also seemed to be a sort of radio system set up about twenty yards outside the bunker that all the Rising were reporting to.

"Probably a mobile command center," Kenny surmised. "Can you take it out?"

"That would cut off whoever's in charge from the action," Brad nodded. "Start some chaos. Good idea."

Lucas shook his head, then sank down onto one of the stairs.

"It's really far away," he said weakly. "And... I need to eat."

"Here," Brad replied, reaching into a zipped pouch on his belt. He handed him a protein bar and a packet of nuts. Tim followed suit, and gave Lucas half a sandwich. He ate the sandwich first and felt better almost immediately.

"Well?" Tim said after a moment.

Lucas reached a tendril of thought outward, feeling for the comm center he had brushed up against earlier. It was like creeping along the perimeter of a spider web, searching for its center. Like piano wires, the radio signals were all tuned to the same note, and he was determined to find it. He wormed his consciousness through the chorus of voices, until one in particular froze him.

"It's Kowalski!" he said with a start.

"What?" Brad asked incredulously.

The voice was unmistakable. *This is Seth Kowalski... is anyone on our side alive? I'm down... over...*

"Kowalski is calling for help," Lucas relayed. "He's hurt."

"Where is he?"

"I don't know yet, and he didn't say."

"Is anyone close by?" Brad asked. "Any of ours responding?"

Lucas expanded his reach, listening.

"I don't sense anyone," he answered.

Tim responded by scooping up Bernard.

"Well, let's go find him," he said. "Then we can all get the hell out of here."

"Alright," Brad replied. "We'll go, then figure out a plan for getting to the helicopters, or hijacking one of theirs."

They began to climb once more, but froze when the door at the top suddenly opened with a *bang*. The Rising stormed the stairwell; their footsteps pounded like hammers above. The group cowered down, pressing themselves against the wall. Lucas felt a trickle of courage as he met Brad's eyes.

"Watch," Lucas mouthed.

He closed his eyes and focused. It took some effort to reach for his power; it was like digging down into a deep well that was now mostly dry. Once he found it, he craved the energy, but sent it instead at the enemy's radios. At his command, the batteries inside them were filled with energy to the point of bursting, then well beyond that. A series of popping noises signified the devices exploding, and they were quickly followed by screams of pain and frightened shouts. One by one, bodies dropped to the ground with loud thuds. Some rolled down the stairs, and one tumbled to a stop directly at his feet. He opened his eyes. The body in front of him bore a massive, gaping hole in his stomach that smoldered with the smell of cooked meat. Through his mask, an expression of terror was frozen in his eyes.

"Okay," Lucas said shakily. "I'm going to open the door; you can come or not, but one of you has to stay with Bernard. I'll be coming back for him."

If I survive, he thought to himself. Some sensible part of him insisted that this was madness, but he was too revenge-hungry to care. His mind and body were on fire; each beat of his heart pumped white-hot energy to through his veins.

"I'll come," Brad said grimly.

"Count me in," Tim said.

Kenny shook his head. Lucas looked at Bernard. His head leaned against the wall, but his eyes were sharp.

I will come back for you, Lucas thought to him.

Give 'em hell for me, came Bernard's grim reply.

He reached for the doorknob and gave Brad a short nod, and he raised his gun. After silently counting to three, Lucas opened the door. He burst forward with impossible speed, as if he was shot from a cannon. A group of the Rising rounded the corner, and Lucas was ready. Heat and sparks rushed to his hands; he raised them, but instead of a lightning bolt, a flickering wall of light rushed at the men, flattening them to the ground.

Lucas started in surprise. *That's not what I was expecting... what the hell was that?*

He stared down at his hands, bewildered. He was changing; his powers were evolving. He wondered where they would stop, but there was no time to think about that now.

Brad and Tim appeared beside him. They gestured silently to each other, then at the hallway, then appeared to reach some sort of an agreement. With guns raised, the two men took up position on either side of the opening. Brad motioned for Lucas to follow him. Lucas nodded, then they began to move slowly and stealthily down the hallway. The lights were out, but emergency bulbs embedded in the walls glowed red, providing enough light to see just a few steps ahead. Lucas walked like someone in a dream. His head was fogged, his body enervated, and the edges of his vision were blurred. Fear was beginning to creep into him; he was evolving, and he had killed at least sixteen men, probably more. It ate into him. He couldn't deny that he was beginning to second-guess himself. Revenge had been his desire, but was it really his right to kill? Clearly, he was willing to go all the way to obtain his freedom, and that scared him. What would he become, when this was all over?

Suddenly, gunshots rang out. Brad and Tim dropped to the ground in the hall, and Tim dragged Lucas down with him and crouched protectively over him. Between Tim's arms, Lucas looked back. It was complete chaos in the Bullpen; people were running and ducking behind tables and chairs, and there were more than a few screams. Agents were returning fire, then ducking back down. They seemed to be firing at each other. Then Lucas spotted Kowalski on the ground, lying on his side. His hand was in his jacket, and his face twisted in pain. With his other hand, he held his phone and appeared to be trying to make a call. His radio sat on the ground beside him.

Brad had seen him, too.

"There he is," he said in a low voice. "I'll go for Kowalski--you two cover me."

"What's going on?" Lucas whispered. "Why are they shooting each other?"

"We seem to have moles in the agency," Tim replied. "Now come on, and stay low."

Tim pulled him up to his feet but kept a firm hand on his shoulder, and Brad guarded his other side. Lucas began to stumble forward, head down and shoulders hunched. He could hear Kowalski dialing, but nothing made it through. Then he quit trying. Lucas suddenly realized that there was no cellular signal anywhere; no calls or texts coming in or going out from anywhere in the building. He looked backward at Kowalski. One hand was staunching the blood from his wound, while the other clutched his gun. He had spotted Brad, and they made signs to each other. Then he began to crawl, very slowly, on his stomach while Brad inched toward him, his back to the wall. There was roughly ten feet of distance between them, with no means of cover.

"Get ready," Tim said in his ear. He raised his gun and cocked it. Lucas felt stiff; blood pounded in his ears, and his hands shook. He took a breath and reached for the power that seemed to be sinking farther and farther down, deep inside of him.

At that moment, Brad took a shot in the leg and went down. Another bullet tore through his head, and he flopped lifelessly to the ground. Kowalski retreated under a table as gunfire racketed over his head. Lucas stared at Brad's body, his head burst open; dark blood and chunks of brain matter were sprayed across the hard floor. Ice gripped Lucas' heart, and he found his fists clenched. His nails dug into his palms and drew blood.

"Lucas! Lucas!"

Tim shook him by the shoulders. His voice sounded muffled through the ringing in his head.

"Lucas," he said firmly. "Snap out of it!"

"I can't--I can't do this," Lucas mumbled in response. Something hot trickled down his cheeks. *Am I crying?*

"Look, I need you!" Tim said. "We're committed now, there's no going back. We've got to get Kowalski. Can you help?"

Lucas nodded, swallowing hard. He couldn't shake the image of Brad's destroyed face from his mind.

"Alright, cover me," Tim said, beginning to edge past him.

"No, I'll go," he said. "I can heal; you can't. It would be worse for you, if you got shot."

"Alright, be careful."

Lucas' heart was racing. Though he knew he could heal, he didn't *want* to be shot again. He crept to the end of the hallway, just ahead of the Bullpen. Tim was just behind him. Heavy gunfire began outside, and then an explosion shook the walls. They both ducked at the sound. Lucas wondered what was going on outside.

Then the gunfire ceased, and the relative silence was deafening.

"Now, go *now*," Tim whispered.

Lucas looked at Kowalski, who met his eyes. He bore a grim, determined expression. His eyes flicked to his right, to a spot just around the corner. Lucas heard a breath and the smallest crunch of glass. Someone was approaching from his left side. He sprang, reaching almost blindly. The black barrel of a gun passed over his head, and a large man in a mask and bulletproof vest jumped in surprise. Lucas shot out with his hand, catching the man's knee, and lightning crackled as it coursed through his body. The man's muscles seized and his gun fired into the ceiling. He flew backward, and a second man behind him rushed forward. A bullet whizzed past Lucas' head, making his ears ring. Lightning leapt from his hands and blasted into the man, throwing him off his feet. Lucas rolled to Kowalski's side. Not a second later, bullets peppered the wall behind him, and Tim and Kowalski returned fire.

"Hey," Lucas gasped, ducking under the table.

"G-good job," Kowalski replied shakily. "That was some great w-work."

His face looked gray, and sweat beaded on his forehead. Blood soaked through his shirt and jacket. His breathing was ragged, and the hand that clutched his gun now shook uncontrollably. Shooting back seemed to have taken the last of his energy. His gun dropped to the ground beside him, next to his phone; Lucas picked up the phone and tucked it into his pocket.

"Are you shot?" Lucas asked.

"N-no, s-s-stabbed," he said. "Iweala... she's one of them. She was a mole."

Lucas gritted his teeth. He had held suspicions; now that they were confirmed, he felt his blood boil.

"She's been working for them this whole time," Kowalski said, straining. "Giving them intel. They're going to overrun this place. You've got to get out of here. It's no good; I'll just slow you down."

"I'm not leaving you here," Lucas said.

Kowalski lowered his brows.

"Why not?"

Lucas shook his head.

"Because it would be wrong. I can save you."

He said this firmly, but he had no clue how to move Kowalski. He didn't look capable of walking on his own. He glanced backward at Brad's body, lying face down with a cavernous hole in his head. Tim looked on from his hiding spot behind the corner.

"Do you have any idea how to get out of here?" Lucas asked.

"You've got to clear a path for us," Kowalski answered quickly. "More will come soon. I c-can walk; I just need a little help. We can head for the helipad."

He paused to breathe. Another explosion shook the walls, followed by gunfire.

"Lucas," Kowalski said seriously. "If it seems like I'm slowing you down, you've got to leave me here and run. Whatever happens, they must not get you. It would be over for everyone if they do. Do you understand?"

"I don't need convincing," Lucas replied.

"Didn't think so," Kowalski said. "Now, those computers need to be destroyed. We've got to prevent any of our data from from falling into their hands. That can also double as a distraction."

Lucas understood, and nodded slowly. Glass crunched about a dozen feet away, The enemy was drawing nearer.

"They're coming," Lucas said.

"It's got to be big… and we've only got one chance. I'll signal the others to go on your cue."

"My cue?"

"You can hear them."

With his free hand, Kowalski made a series of gestures to Tim. Lucas could hear the Rising operatives' breathing as they drew closer. He gave Kowalski a nod, then focused, summoning reservoirs of energy and allowing it to build in his hands. The bank of computers that lined the bullpen started a few feet away; he took control of the internal software and ordered the computers to begin scrambling themselves, ravaging the information they held. The hard drives began to overheat, then, with a loud *crack*, sparks began to fly. This caused the Rising hiding on the other side to take a step back; Lucas slid out from under the table and saw the top of one's head as he was briefly exposed. The man was quickly taken out by a shot from Tim. Lucas followed it with his lightning, blasting the bank of computers and causing several to burst into flames.

Tim ran across the gap during the diversion and pulled Kowalski free, then both began to hobble, with heads down, back to safety; Lucas watched for the response, and it came quickly. Roughly a dozen men flooded the bullpen, and Tim opened fire, dropping three of them. Lucas sent a bolt of lightning at the rest, flinging them away.

"Lucas, come on!" Tim called. He and Kowalski had made it across the gap, and only Lucas was left, ducking under the table. He summoned more lightning into his hands, jumped up, then released it. With a thunderous crash, more monitors and hard drives exploded and the lights overhead burst. Some men were flung backward, while others were dealing with flames that erupted on their clothing. The overhead sprinklers went off, beginning a steady rain. Lucas dashed across the gap to the hallway where Tim and Kowalski were waiting. Tim had torn off part of his shirt and stuffed it into the wound.

"The helipad is up ahead, down this hall," Kowalski said weakly. "Lucas, you go first."

"We can't go yet," Lucas protested. "Kenny and Bernard are waiting for us in the stairwell. We have to go get them."

"That's on the way," Tim urged. "Keep moving."

"Let's get going, quickly," Kowalski said. Tim set off, half-carrying him, while Lucas padded after them in bare feet. "Any luck calling out?"

"No, sir," Tim answered. "They must've taken out the cell tower."

"I'm not picking up any cell signals," Lucas added.

"They must have rehearsed this," Kowalski muttered. "They know what they're doing. It all went to shit so quickly."

They moved stealthily down the hall, Lucas in the lead with heart racing. His fists were tightly clenched with adrenaline. With half his attention on the immediate situation, the other half checked the bunker's cameras for any sign of the Rising. While the Bullpen blazed, a group appeared to be searching for a way around it. In another area, they had gathered some CIA hostages; there were a few dozen people handcuffed and on their knees in groups, surrounded by guards. Then the hallway was suddenly plunged into darkness and silence, except for the group's startled breathing.

"They've cut the power," Kowalski noted.

For Lucas, this was a strange sensation. The needle-like prickle that he had felt constantly across his skin for nearly a year had suddenly lessened. He felt like he'd unexpectedly lost his sense of taste. Tim holstered his gun and switched on a flashlight, and Lucas blinked in the brightness. The wide hallway now resembled a dark tunnel, but with no light at the end.

"Keep moving," Tim urged.

They came to the door of the stairwell. As they drew nearer, Lucas felt Bernard's consciousness brush against his. He opened his mind to it, bridging the connection, and said, *We're back, open up!* He tapped on the door and a second later it opened. Kenny's face appeared, illuminated by flashlight.

"Alright, let's go, quick!" Tim said.

"Where's Brad?" Kenny asked, his eyes flicking between them.

"Gone," Tim replied shortly.

Kenny's mouth twitched, but he gave his flashlight to Lucas and scooped Bernard up into his arms. Tim slung Kowalski across his back, and both men began to jog. Lucas pushed himself forward, running to keep up, with the light from Kenny's flashlight at his feet. The explosive booming began to fade into the distance. The hallway came to an end, with the option to go left or right. Kowalski said left, and Lucas went first, feeling his way along. By now, the air had become quite thick, and sweat soaked his shirt. Kowalski's breathing had also become more ragged, and the metallic stench of blood was strong. Lucas, who had fallen behind, noted several spots of blood dripped onto the paved floor.

Finally, the exit appeared, and it was unguarded. Tim called for everyone to stop. He lowered Kowalski to the ground and propped him up against the wall, and Kenny did the same with Bernard. They looked like a pair of cadavers, with heads lolling, skin drawn and sickeningly pale. Blood continued to seep from Kowalski's wound; the shirt that Tim had stuffed there was soaked, and leaked onto the floor. His face was ashen, and his breath shallow, almost inaudible. His head dropped forward so that his chin rested on his chest. Lucas stared blankly. It occurred to him that Kowalski didn't have long.

"Lucas," Tim said.

Tim beckoned to him from where he stood by the door. Kenny stood silently a few feet away, his gun raised and flashlight pointed up the hallway. Lucas walked over to Tim's side, his legs still burning from the run.

"Can you tell us what's out there?" Tim asked.

"There are some Rising about fifty yards away," Lucas answered, eyes closed. "Maybe twenty or thirty of them."

"Which direction?"

Lucas raised his hand, pointing east of their location.

"That way."

"Good," Tim said with a stiff nod. "We came the right way."

Suddenly, he knelt down so that he was eye-level with Lucas. His dark skin was streaked with sweat and grime; it gathered in the creases of his brow. He wiped his mouth and looked at Lucas, his eyes like bottomless pools.

"This is it," he said. "Before we go out there, I wanted to say thank you for what you've done getting us this far. And I want to apologize on the behalf of everyone here for the way you've been treated. Nobody deserves that."

Tim's gaze was piercing. Lucas met it, and said nothing.

"I'm going to have to ask more of you," he continued. "We're going to have to run, and we're most likely going to meet gunfire out there. That wall you made earlier--or force field… whatever it was. Can you do it again?"

"I don't know," Lucas admitted. "I've never done that before… it was an accident."

"You'll have to provide cover for all of us, because I'm going to be carrying Kowalski, and Kenny will have Bernard. Neither of us will be able to shoot."

Lucas gave a short nod that he understood.

"I'll… I'll try."

"I'm counting on you," Tim said firmly. "Our lives are in your hands. Are you ready?"

Lucas nodded again, a tight knot in his throat. Tim straightened and called Kenny over. They picked up Bernard and Kowalski, and lined up in front of the door. Lucas was first, his fingers shaking as he wrapped them around the door handle. His muscles strained as he pulled until the door cracked open. Bright sunlight flooded in, temporarily blinding him. He blinked, but all he could see was glaring white light. Heat barraged his face as if he'd opened an oven. His feet moved forward on hot, gravelly pavement. Gradually, his vision cleared, and he began to make out hazy shapes. One hundred yards ahead was a single parked helicopter, blurred by rising heat waves. A sidewalk met a long driveway that led to the helipad.

"Go, go, go!" Tim urged, and Lucas began to run. The soles of his feet were burned by the pavement; the heat thickened the air and slowed his movements so he felt as if he were swimming. He forced himself to keep going, and the helicopter drew nearer. He staggered, chest burning. Tim and Kenny charged on behind him.

He heard the roar of engines, and his heart sank. Two Jeeps, tops open, rounded the warehouse with clouds of dust trailing behind them. At least a dozen Rising rode inside, rifles ready. Lucas heard commands shouted over their radios. He paused in his run, his head snapped in their direction. Lightning surged into his hands and he released it with a single throwing motion. A bolt shot into the hood of the first Jeep with a sound like cannonfire, causing it to careen out of control. Smoke and flames erupted from the front of the car. The second Jeep pulled over and men jumped out, rifles cocked. Three dropped to their knees, and three stood upright. These weren't terrorists, Lucas realized. These were soldiers. They wore military fades with a red symbol on the sleeve, and seemed to be receiving orders from someone in the back of the formation who called:

"Hostile android located... on target. Kill shots only. Fire when ready!"

Lucas didn't wait. With a yell, he summoned more energy than he ever had before. It felt like jet fuel was running through his veins. The power built until he couldn't hold it anymore, and then the dam broke. With hands open, he released it at the same time that the soldiers opened fire. A wall of energy sprang from inside of him, soaring upward ten feet high and twenty feet across. It was shapeless, and fuzzy at the edges but transparent in the middle. It was also extremely difficult to control; it warped and bent regardless of Lucas' will. To his amazement, the bullets struck against it and bounced off, ricocheting in every direction. The soldiers dove for cover behind the vehicle, and were quickly joined by those that had recovered from the first Jeep's crash. Metal clanged as bullets punched through the doors and hood, and the tires hissed.

Lucas had expected the force field to vanish instantly as before, but, to his great surprise and relief, it held. He fed it with his concentration and what remained of his power. Seconds crawled by. The drain of energy on his body was immense, but he was determined to buy the others time. Through the corner of his eye, he saw Tim and Kenny reach the helicopter and heave both Bernard and Kowalski inside. Kenny climbed to the cockpit, while Tim drew his weapon. There were more shouts from the men, and Tim's voice somehow reached him over the din. It was time to go, but how could he release the force field and make it to the helicopter in time? There were twenty yards between him and the chopper. More soldiers were likely on the way.

Surely enough, another vehicle swerved around the corner, this one much bigger and with a large gun mounted on top. Tim was frantic now, screaming Lucas' name. Lucas released the force field and flung it in the direction of the oncoming vehicle. The field crackled half-heartedly, fizzling out and disappearing into the air before it reached the Jeep. Lucas ran, his feet dragging and fear pounding in his chest.

A clap of thunder reached his ears. It was followed by a second, much shorter, one.

A bullet clipped his skull, stopping him in his tracks. He fell to his knees. Immense, horrible pain shocked his senses.

Chapter 15

Lucas stared up at a white, hazy sky, ears ringing. The back of his head was wet with the blood that pooled around him.

Muffled voices spoke; he couldn't make any sense of them. People, silhouetted by the sun, approached him from all sides. A gun was jabbed in his face, and strong hands grabbed each arm. He felt a sharp sting in the inside of his elbow. His arm quickly grew numb.

"Pick him up," a woman's voice said.

Lucas' head lolled as he was lifted off the ground into a kneeling position. Blood trickled down his face and dripped onto his shirt. Standing before him was Iweala, Dr. Gill at her side. They were surrounded by armed soldiers. Helicopter blades throbbed in the distance.

"I-Iweala," Lucas mumbled.

She held a handgun pointed at him. Dr. Gill hugged a black briefcase. Both watched impassively as Lucas was handcuffed. His head wound was healing, but he felt his mind beginning to fog. He was drugged again, this time with something powerful.

"Iweala, why?" he croaked.

"Oh, Lucas," she said gently. Her eyes did not match the tone of her voice. "You must stop fighting. If you only knew what we were trying to accomplish, you would be on our side."

"You stabbed Kowalski," Lucas growled. "You betrayed everyone."

"Not you," she said sweetly. "All of this is for you. Don't you understand?"

"What? What do you want with me?"

Adrenaline fought to counteract the drugs, but to no avail. Soon, he couldn't hold his head up. Then he slumped into the soldier's arms. He couldn't catch his breath, and nausea rocked his stomach.

"You are an integral part of this movement. Everything I've done was to make you into what you were meant to be. You were the purpose of this venture from the very beginning, plans laid in place long before you were born. All of that was put on hold, until now. The Rising needs you; without you, we were nothing. Now, we are taking you home."

Lucas didn't understand what she was talking about. Maybe it was the drugs, but nothing she said registered inside of him. Her face swirled and shifted, like he was looking at it from underwater. She looked up. The soldiers parted to allow a group of men to approach, pushing a large cart bearing something that looked like a long coffin. Many tubes wove in and out of its steel frame, and the lid was reinforced glass. A large tank was attached to the end of it. The men grunted with considerable effort as they brought it to a stop a few feet away.

"What's going to happen to me?" he asked, the words slurring.

"Don't be afraid, Lucas," Iweala said. "You are with your family now."

He wasn't afraid, though he knew he should be. He should be screaming, but his mouth hung open dumbly.

She gave a nod to the nearby soldiers. They hefted Lucas up by his arms and legs, then carried him to the coffin. He couldn't kick, or thrash, or reach any of his power to fight back; he could only watch helplessly as they laid him inside. Once he was in the coffin, Dr. Gill passed the briefcase to a nearby soldier, then set to work. He attached one of the tubes to Lucas' neck by inserting a long needle, then added a few more into his forearms. A clear fluid immediately began to pump through it into his veins. He was uncuffed, then his arms were strapped down at the wrist, and his legs at the ankle. Last of all, Dr. Gill fitted a mask over his face, and Lucas found that his breathing was suddenly easier. He felt sleepy, and his eyelids drooped. The lid to the coffin closed, and he could see his reflection in the glass: a thin, ghoulish boy with bloodied clothes. His eyes closed as the coffin was rolled away.

Something heavy hit the lid with a *thud*, rocking him, and he opened his eyes. Dr. Gill lay across the coffin, his face against the glass, eyes and mouth wide open. It was difficult to feel surprise; his breath remained deep and steady, even as blood began to drip from Dr. Gill's open mouth in red streaks down the glass. Small, muffled explosions sounded, and his coffin was rocked again. Lucas closed his eyes and sank back into sleep.

"Lucas!"

A voice was pulling him roughly back into consciousness, but he didn't want to leave. He felt so warm and comfortable, and his mind was gently padded against the sharpness of reality.

"Lucas, wake up! Can you hear me? Wake up!"

He was dragged out of sleep once more. Someone was shouting and shaking him. Then he was lifted out of the coffin and placed on hot pavement. Wind whipped his face as someone pressed their fingers to the side of his throat. Strong hands picked him up again and carried him at a run. Bright sunlight shone, making him squint, but he could see brown earth, trees, and gray haze over the horizon. His head was flooded with the roar of a million voices, like distant applause.

"Are you with us, Lucas?" a man's voice asked.

"I can hear the sun," he answered drowsily.

He was lifted into a helicopter and laid across the floor on a stretcher. Across the cabin, Bernard was buckled into a seat, staring out the window. Beside him, Kowalski lay bandaged heavily with a mask on his face, and an oxygen tank on his other side. His face was white, and his lips were gray, almost blue. An IV bag swung from the roof of the chopper. Lucas looked up and saw that he had one, too. His head slowly became clearer, but he couldn't lift any of his limbs. He seemed to be sweating profusely, though he shivered with cold.

In the center of the helicopter's cabin, Tim sat wrapping one of his hands. Kenny stood forward by the pilot.

"Tim," Lucas said.

"Hey," he replied, scooting to his side. His knuckles were bleeding through the bandage. "How are you doing?"

"Can't move."

"They pumped you full of carfentanil, the monsters. That's elephant tranquilizer. How do you feel?"

"Like shit. What happened? H-how am I free?"

"The cavalry finally came from San Antonio," he answered. "It was a deadly battle, but we got you out. We're almost to Austin now."

"Austin?"

Home.

"You're safe now, Lucas," Tim said. "It's gonna be okay. We're going home."

Lucas suddenly pictured his mom's face. At long last, he really was going home. He longed to be held, to feel safe with her arms around him.

Then her face was gone, and he saw Brad's dead, blown-open face instead. He saw blood and brain matter splattered across the ground, and the scattered, burnt bodies of the people he himself had killed. He saw the looks of surprise and fear frozen on their faces. Uncontrollable emotion began to well up inside of him. He turned his head to the side as tears flowed from his eyes, wetting the pillow. Tim quietly left him, moving back to the front of the cabin.

The helicopter landed on the roof of St. David's Medical Center downtown. Lucas, Kowalski, and Bernard were all wheeled inside by an army of attendants. Kowalski was taken immediately into surgery, while Bernard and Lucas were met by a team of CIA agents in suits and escorted down to a room adjoining the ER. Guards were posted outside while the doctors checked them both over, scrutinizing every inch. Lucas' injuries had long since healed, but he was still unable to lift his arms or move his legs. He was also dangerously dehydrated. In the end, he was moved to a bed beside Bernard's with an IV to wait until the tranquilizer was flushed from his system.

"He should be dead," Lucas overheard a doctor speaking to one of the agents. "There is no possible way that someone his size could take a dose that large and live. He was given enough to kill three grown men. And how did he get it?"

"That's classified," the agent replied in a flat voice.

"What is he?" the doctor demanded.

"That's also classified."

"Well, how much *can* you tell me? I still need to do my job. I can't treat him if I don't know what he is. I need a frame of reference. Is he... is he even human?"

"We've given you his file, that should be enough. He is a very unique individual with unique gifts. You and your team will be briefed only on what is relevant to his treatment. Any questions will be addressed Mr. Dunn, when he arrives. And you'll all need to sign non-disclosure agreements."

Lucas and Bernard were left alone. He dozed off, and slept for hours, maybe even days, but it felt like minutes. He woke up ravenously hungry and groaned, clutching his abdomen. His insides felt like they were clamped in a vice.

"You can move," Bernard's voice said.

Lucas looked up. Bernard sat in a wheelchair, facing him. He looked healthier; his skin had some color.

"Yeah, it's a relief," Lucas replied sardonically. "I'm starving."

"I know," Bernard said, tapping the side of his head with his good hand. "I feel everything."

"Then you should know that I need some food, *now*," Lucas said testily.

"Your powers are back. Call for someone."

Lucas glanced over his shoulder at the call button on the wall. He didn't reach for it, opting instead to signal the nurse's station directly with his mind. Then he turned on the television and flipped through the channels until he found the news. Then he did a full mental sweep of the hospital. The place was abuzz with activity, and he could see and hear it all. He skimmed through every cell phone, iPod, and TV. His mind was flooded with phone calls, TV shows, music, and text alerts. At first, it was overwhelming; his head swam and he felt the jabbing pain of a migraine. The pain soon passed, and he found the white noise comforting. It was a symptom of the busyness of the city he grew up in. He was back among civilization, and familiarity. People were connecting with other people and with the world around them, and he was spectator to it all.

"There are agents everywhere," Lucas noted.

"Yeah, we're VIP," Bernard said. "They're really freaked after the bunker went down."

"How long was I asleep?"

"Eleven hours."

With a dreary flicker, Lucas's brain told him that it was 9:31am on July 8th.

"Has my mom come?" he asked.

"No. I don't think our parents even know we're here."

"This is bull," Lucas complained. "I'm fine; we should be going home!"

The lights flickered as his anger flared. The curtains parted and a nurse appeared on the other side of the sliding glass door. She caught one look at Lucas, then immediately disappeared. A few seconds later, Lucas felt a tickle inside his skull as an agent just outside made a phone call.

Sir, he's awake.

Very good. No one goes in there until I talk to him.

"Who's that?" Lucas asked, sitting up.

Bernard shrugged with one shoulder.

A minute later, a tall man who looked to be in his fifties, with graying hair, entered the room. He wore a wrinkled, pinstripe suit and his tie was loosened. Bags hung under his eyes. He was accompanied by a middle-aged, pudgy woman in a pink dress and cardigan. Her feet were squeezed into a tiny pair of heels, and she carried a clipboard clasped in front of her. She smiled cheerily at Lucas, pearl earrings bouncing. The man managed a smile, but it looked painful. He smoothed his hair absent-mindedly. Lucas sensed that both carried cell phones, and that Mr. Dunn was wearing a listening device and an earpiece. He immediately tensed, clenching his jaw.

"Good morning, Lucas," he said. "My name is Jensen Dunn. I'm a special agent with the CIA, and I'm in charge of your case now. This is Ms. Heidi Rinehart; she's a social worker, here to make sure you get taken care of. May we talk to you?"

"I guess so," Lucas answered. "How is Agent Kowalski?"

"He's doing just fine. He's in recovery now. That's in part thanks to you; you're a hero in our book."

"When can I see my mom?"

"That's not possible yet," Mr. Dunn answered. "There's a lot we need to clear up first. First, how are you feeling?"

"Hungry."

"I'll have someone bring you something," Mr. Dunn said quickly. "What would you like to eat?"

"Anything, I'm starving," Lucas replied, his stomach growling.

"Alright then," Mr. Dunn said, and poked his head outside the door. He spoke to one of perhaps a dozen agents outside, who then trotted off.

"You seem to be recovering well," he remarked once he returned.

Lucas gave no reply.

"Are there any books or movies we could get for you?"

"Why? Will I be here long?"

"No longer than necessary."

Lucas chewed his lip, growing more and more impatient and frustrated.

"I can tell that you're suspicious of us," Mr. Dunn said with another of his painful smiles, straightening his tie. "And that's very understandable, but you must believe us when we say that no one is here to hurt you. We're all on your side."

"Everyone says that," Lucas said. "But nobody really is. Iweala was on my side, too, til she got what she wanted."

Mr. Dunn's face fell.

"Yes, well… that was very unfortunate," he said, scrambling. "That's what we wanted to talk to you about…"

"Where is she?" Lucas asked. "Where's Iweala?"

"She killed herself," Mr. Dunn replied. "Before we could take her into custody. Shot herself in the head. As did all the Rising operatives that remained alive after the battle."

Lucas was stunned. *She had kids.*

"Lucas, I know that must have been difficult," Ms. Rinehart cut in. "Was her betrayal hard on you?"

"No," he answered hoarsely. "I had suspected it."

"What made you suspect her?"

"I overheard a phone conversation she had with Dr. Gill."

"What did she say?" Mr. Dunn asked, surreptitiously touching his earpiece. The gesture was smooth, like he was merely scratching his ear.

"Nothing, really. They were doing some tests, and Dr. Gill called her to say that she should come down and look, and she said yes. But when they found out I listened in, they got really freaked, like they were worried about what else I might have heard."

"*Had* you heard anything else?"

"No."

Mr. Dunn frowned.

"Is there anything that you can tell us about Ms. Iweala, or Dr. Gill?"

"I want to eat," Lucas said, folding his arms. "I'm hungry."

"Of course, once the nurse comes back."

"She *is* back. She's right outside, and she's been there for two and a half minutes."

Mr. Dunn blinked at Lucas, who glared back at him. Grudgingly, he opened the door for the nurse to enter. She came bearing a tray with two sandwiches, a bag of chips, cup of fruit, and a chocolate milkshake in a styrofoam cup. She set it on Lucas' lap, then left. Lucas started on the first sandwich, snatching it up from the tray.

"I don't think you read my file properly, *sir*," he said acidly. "If you had, you'd know that you don't screw with me. You would know what I'm capable of."

"Lucas, you misunderstand--"

Lucas cut him off, pointing at Ms. Rinehart.

"I don't want to talk in front of her," he said, mouth full. "She can leave. She's not doing her job, anyway."

"Lucas--" Mr. Dunn objected.

"If you want to talk to me, you'll get rid of her, and bring Tim instead. He was on my security team. I'll talk in front of him. Maybe I'll even turn your recording device back on."

Mr. Dunn's mouth dropped open. He reached into his jacket and briefly fiddled with the device. Lucas caught a glimpse of Bernard, who was grinning broadly. Ms. Rinehart looked embarrassed; she and Mr. Dunn exchanged an awkward glance. Without another word, Ms. Rinehart left. Lucas heard her calling for Tim Carter to be brought in.

"Alright, Lucas," Mr. Dunn said with a sigh. "Kid gloves are off. What do you want?"

"I want my mom brought here," Lucas answered. "Bernard's parents, too. Then I want to go home. I want nothing more to do with the Rising or the CIA. I'd like to be left alone. My family, too."

"And what do you have for us, so we can make that happen?"

"Files that I took from Iweala's and Dr. Gill's computers."

"Where are these files?"

Lucas answered by tapping the side of his head.

"I don't think there's any way you could take those forcefully," he said coolly. "But I will give them to you, if you do what I want."

Mr. Dunn's mouth twitched.

"You're in no position to bargain," he said acidly.

"Are you sure about that?" Lucas replied wryly. "You want to try me?"

A tense silence weighed upon the room. Finally, Mr. Dunn wilted.

"Very well," he said.

He left the room. Lucas devoured his food as Bernard wheeled his chair up to the side of his bed.

"You sure showed them," he said.

Lucas offered a half-smile.

"I'm just tired of them pushing us around," he replied.

He finished eating in silence, then pushed back the tray. Bernard sat patiently, and Lucas regarded him with an ache in his chest. His hospital gown hung loosely over his bony frame. His red hair shaded his sunken eyes.

"You said you feel everything," Lucas said, lowering his voice. "Did you feel what happened to me yesterday?"

"You mean when you got shot in the head?" Bernard replied, tilting his head. "Yes."

Lucas scrutinized his calm demeanor. It baffled him.

"How can you stand it?" he asked. "It must be torture."

"It was," Bernard nodded. "And sometimes it still is. But you never seem to stop getting hurt, so I learned to compartmentalize it, I guess. I'm still aware of it, but it's not as much of a shock to my system. I keep it all kind of tucked away in the back. It does less damage that way."

"Do you think the CIA knows? About our connection?"

"I don't know," Bernard replied. "In the beginning, I had a really difficult time coping with it. There were a lot of painful episodes, and blacking out. But I don't think they've connected the dots; I didn't either, at first."

"I think we need to tell them," Lucas said quietly.

"Why?"

"When Iweala and Dr. Gill--well, when the Rising almost took me, Iweala said that all of this was for me. I'd been at the center of their plans from the very beginning, from before I was born. Dr. Gill said before that I wasn't an accident."

His voice quavered, and he paused to take a breath.

"What are you saying?"

"The Rising made me with a purpose," Lucas said. "I think that means that everything I can do was intentional; they know about it and fits in somewhere with their plans."

"So? They didn't get you. It's over; you're here, and safe. Why would you want to keep helping the CIA after everything they did to us?"

"You're not worried about what might happen?"

"What else can they do?" Bernard said. "I'm not afraid of them anymore. They can cripple me, imprison me, put you in my head, but it doesn't matter. I could have been hit by a car and ended up basically the same way. At least I still have my spirit; I'm still me. Nobody can take that away."

Bernard's blue eyes flashed with ice, and Lucas looked away. Bernard was wrong; he wasn't the same person. He certainly wasn't Brick anymore, anyway. Though Lucas was sure he didn't miss the old Brick, he was disturbed by how far removed Bernard was from his old personality. It was was gone, destroyed by the nanomachines when his body had been destroyed. The question was, how much of *Bernard* was owed to the nanomachines, and how much had been there, hidden, waiting for the chance to come out?

But more than anything, Lucas wanted to believe that it was finally over, and that he was free. When the door opened and his mother entered the room, he began to really believe it. Leah's face was drawn with worry, and she had more gray hairs than he remembered, but he had never been happier to see her. Her hand flew to her mouth when she saw him, and tears ran down her cheeks. She came straight to his bedside and embraced him tightly. He buried his face into her shoulder and cried, his body shaking with sobs. Bernard's parents were brought in as well. His mother, a large, ruddy-faced woman with short hair, collapsed to her knees and wept, then hugged his neck and kissed him over and over. His father, a tall, thin man with a shaved head and tattoos, stood off to the side. He wore heavy, stained jeans and boots, and there were dark sweat stains under his arms. Lucas recalled hearing once that he was a road worker. The man hugged himself and looked emotionally overcome.

When neither of them could cry anymore, Leah sat on the edge of his bed and they talked. The thing that no one wanted to talk about, and she didn't ask, was what had happened to Lucas during his eight months at the Bunker. He could sense her pain and desire to know, though she tried to mask it. Instead, she told him about everything that had happened to her since he had been gone. She had been given a new job, as a clerk at a library, and was making much better money than she had been before. The CIA had moved her and Maria to a house on the northwestern side of town. It was much larger than the old apartment, with three bedrooms and an upstairs loft, and a spacious backyard.

"I can't wait for you to see it," she said with a smile. "And we'll buy you a bike, so you can ride around the neighborhood."

"Does this mean I'll be going to a different school?" Lucas asked, crestfallen.

Leah looked taken aback; she tucked away a stray lock of hair.

"We haven't talked about you going back yet, or whether it's the best thing for you to go at all."

"Let's talk about it then! I don't want to go to a different school."

"Lucas, one thing at a time!" she pleaded. "I just got you back!"

"What about Nate and Ty?"

Leah sighed with exasperation.

"I haven't seen them since you were taken," she answered.

Lucas fell silent, pressing his lips together. His eyes wandered to the other side of the room, where a doctor spoke quietly to Bernard's father. The more he said, the more agitated Mr. Wallach became. He shifted between his left and right foot, and rubbed his arms. Every so often, he glanced in the direction of Bernard and Mrs. Wallach, who clasped Bernard's good hand tightly. His left hand was laid across his chest.

Lucas wondered what the doctor could be telling them; he couldn't possibly know the truth. Would the CIA ever allow Bernard's parents to know the truth behind his paralysis? He could imagine what kind of agony they must be in.

Suddenly, Mr. Dunn returned with Tim closely behind. Tim wore a black t-shirt with the CIA's logo inscribed over the left breast, and grey sweatpants. His right hand bore a clean bandage, and he looked rested. He smiled at Lucas as he entered, then stood upright with his hands clasped behind his back.

"We're very sorry to interrupt, but we'll need you to take this outside," Mr. Dunn said brusquely to the doctor and Bernard's parents. They gave him shocked glances, but the doctor recovered quickly.

"It's alright," he said gently. "There's a room down the hall we can use."

He stepped behind Bernard's wheelchair and began to roll it out the door, Mr. and Mrs. Wallach in tow. Bernard gave Lucas a sideways look. His consciousness brushed Lucas' gently.

Good luck, he said.

Lucas nodded, then sat up straighter. The door closed behind them. Leah squeezed Lucas' hand. She was given a chair to sit at his bedside.

"It's good to see you feeling better," Tim said. "You're a hero, to all of us."

"I killed people," Lucas replied quietly, and Leah stiffened.

"You did what was necessary," Tim countered. "You saved Kowalski's life, and none of us would have made it out without you. You showed more bravery than most grown men I know."

Lucas flushed, but lowered his eyes.

"Well, Lucas, how shall we begin?" Mr. Dunn asked, not kindly.

"What else do you want to know?"

"Anything that you can remember."

"Just before we left the Bunker, you were captured by the Rising," Tim broke in, speaking in casual tones. "They had you only briefly, but Iweala said something to you before you were put into that pod. Can you talk about that?"

Lucas looked at him, and he gave a small nod, which strengthened his resolve. He took a shuddering breath, then reached back into his memory.

"I was trying to get to the helicopter, after stopping the Rising from shooting at you and the others. I had waited too long, and more Rising came in a big truck. Someone shot me. The bullet only grazed my head, I think, but it still knocked me out for a second. When I opened my eyes, Iweala, Dr. Gill, and some other Rising soldiers were standing over me. They handcuffed and drugged me, then Iweala told me that I should stop fighting. She said that I would be on their side if I knew what they were doing, and that it was all for me... I was the most important part of it."

"What did she mean by that?"

"I don't know," Lucas said. "She didn't say."

"Did she say anything else?"

"No."

"Did Dr. Gill say anything?"

"No," Lucas replied. "But he was carrying a black briefcase."

"I saw that, too," Tim said. "What was in it?"

"Capsules of nanomachines," Mr. Dunn answered.

"What? Where did he get them?"

"From the Bunker's storerooms," he answered sheepishly.

Lucas tensed. An image of the sickly blue liquid flashed through his mind.

"Nanomachines?" he exclaimed. "They kept nanomachines in the Bunker?"

"Of course. Everything related to you or Dr. Lytton's work was kept there, for research purposes. You must understand--we had vetted Iweala and Dr. Gill. We had no reason to doubt their allegiance. Kowalski was in charge of your case from the beginning, but it was Iweala who first suggested moving everything to the Bunker in Goliad. She brought Dr. Benjamin Gill on to the project about a month after you were put under. She's been playing this entire organization from the start. We had no way of knowing where her true allegiance lay."

"She said you were the object of their plans all along," Tim said, shaking his head. "But what exactly are they planning to do?"

"How many capsules of the nanomachines were kept in the Bunker?" Lucas interrupted.

"All that was recovered from the warehouse where your accident happened," Mr. Dunn replied.

"What's gonna happen to those?"

"Right now, they're still at the Bunker under heavy guard until we can find a more secure place for them. We believe that the Rising wants to use them in their bombs, as they have before, or launch some other kind of biological warfare. And based on what we've learned from Brick, it would be devastating for everyone if they succeeded."

"If they can cause so much damage with those, what do they need me for?"

"We wish we knew."

Lucas located Bernard's mind.

They kept nanomachines in the Bunker, he said.

What!?

His anger fired across their connection.

They say it was to keep them safe from the Rising.

Obviously they knew about them. Iweala would have told them.

Yeah, probably.

How are they going to keep it from getting into their hands again?

Lucas repeated the question aloud.

"We have added every reinforcement we have on hand, and done our best to keep this out of the media," Mr. Dunn answered. "No one will be allowed within miles of that place without the highest security clearance. Perhaps you can help us by keeping an eye out, and if you see anything about the incident in the news or social media, you'll let us know?"

"Sure," Lucas said. He relayed Mr. Dunn's answer back to Bernard.

Assholes, came the reply.

Mr. Dunn pulled Tim aside and whispered something to him. They conversed quietly for several seconds, and Lucas couldn't hear what was said because Mr. Dunn covered up his listening device. Then the two came back, and Tim was rubbing his chin pensively.

"For now, you'll both be sent home," Mr. Dunn said. "When we need you again, we'll call you."

"I'm going home?" Lucas asked, his heart skipping a beat. "For real?"

"Yes. We've discussed it with the administration, and Agent Kowalski insisted that you should be allowed to return to your mother's house and recuperate there. But first, those files please?"

Lucas couldn't believe what he was hearing. Tears stung his eyes, though he fought to hold them back and maintain his composure. Leah squeezed his hand tightly.

"Hold out your phone," Lucas told Mr. Dunn, and he complied. Lucas took it with trembling fingers, then closed his eyes and located the files he had stored away deep in the recesses of his mind, like plucking a fish from a still, dark pond. He tapped the surface of his memories to stir the waters and see what surfaced. Through the ripples, he located what he wanted, and drew it out. Then, with a breath, the electrical current flowed through his fingers into the device. The currents oriented themselves into code, then digits and letters and images. Finished, he returned the phone.

Mr. Dunn looked at it suspiciously, then scrolled through a few pages of the file. His eyebrows rose, then he looked up at Lucas.

"Very good," he said. "When the doctor clears you, you'll be free to go."

We're going home, Bernard!

Lucas sensed apathy, even fear at the news.

What's wrong? he asked.

Home is not going to be the same for me. My parents are not taking any of this well.

They're happy to have you back, right?

Of course, but we were barely getting by as it is, and now this, Bernard said bitterly. *I can't walk, or cook for myself, or even get to the bathroom on my own. I'm going to be a burden to them.*

I'm sorry. I didn't think of that.

It's fine. Don't worry about it.

But Lucas did worry about it. Though he knew it wasn't, he still felt that all of this was somehow his fault. The Rising made him, didn't they? And the nanomachines, too. They existed, and he existed, and both had damaged Bernard beyond repair. The guilt was a hole inside of him.

Later that night, while Bernard slept, he found himself examining a banking website. Bernard's family needed money to take care of him. He knew what would happen if they couldn't. Bernard would end up in the care of the state, separated from his family again. He deserved more than that.

Lucas moved on to learning banking software. Everything was online now, even money. It was just a bunch of ones and zeros, pushed around from one account to another. His consciousness tested the barriers; all the latest security measures were built in to online banking. It took a few minutes, but his mind broke through. A few minutes later, he found the Wallach's account. Then he compiled a list of the two hundred wealthiest people that banked where they did, subtracted one hundred dollars from each of them, and dumped it all in the Wallach's account. That done, he retreated, fastidiously covering up his tracks. Odds were, few of them would notice the loss. If they did, no one could prove that it was anything more than a computer glitch.

He smiled to himself.

Chapter 16

LUCAS SPENT THE ENTIRETY OF the next day with his mother in the hospital room. Bernard's parents returned that afternoon, and kept to themselves on their side of the room. A nurse brought dinner, and Lucas and Leah ate together in silence. Though Lucas had eaten a large meal only hours before, he dug in hungrily. Leah had changed the channel on the television to a sitcom to lighten the mood, and even chuckled a handful of times at the character's antics. Lucas half-watched it with her, but found the other part of his attention wandering. He surfed other channels in the privacy of his own mind, skimmed through social media out of boredom and, slightly, out of obligation to Mr. Dunn. Quickly, he learned that the media had indeed caught wind of the attack on the Bunker. The report said that the United States government had followed up on a tip they had received about human traffickers in the area. A standoff between government agents and the traffickers led to a shootout, resulting in casualties on both sides. All was not lost, the report read that two children were rescued. Neither he nor Bernard were named, nor did the report discuss anything about the CIA, the mole, the experiments done in the Bunker, or the Rising. Lucas decided that these reports were safe, but directed part of his attention to stay alert, constantly panning for anything more.

In his search, Lucas realized that the Rising wasn't named anywhere, in any news reports. He scoured the internet, but couldn't find a single mention of them. Kowalski had called them an international terrorist organization bent on mass destruction and overthrowing the government; if that was true, why weren't people talking about it?

He read through the reports on the bombings of last year, and the ones this year he had helped to prevent. The news labeled them "random terroristic events," or "unrelated attempts at mass violence," and encouraged the American people to "carry on as usual." There were only a few outlets that covered them at all, and, within a day, the events seemed all but forgotten about on social media. Lucas was baffled.

"What's wrong?" Leah said, noticing his pensive expression.

"Mom, do you know what the Rising is?" Lucas asked her seriously.

"No, I've never heard of it," she replied. "Is it important?"

"I don't know," he lied, but inside he was reeling. *They're the ones who began all this*, he wanted to scream. *They ruined your life when they tortured you and then created me!*

"I need to go talk to Kowalski," he said aloud.

"I don't think they'll let you."

"It's important."

He climbed out of bed, then swayed when his bare feet hit the cold floor. His powers had fully returned, but it seemed that his body hadn't yet caught up. Sliding open the door, he was met by two guards in bulletproof vests, bearing sidearms. They were posted on either side of the door, while three more stood in a semicircle. Lucas was relieved to see that two of them were Tim and Kenny, who in turn gave him surprised looks. His appearance had interrupted a hushed conversation.

"Lucas, do you need something?" Tim asked, leaving Kenny's side.

"I want to see Kowalski," Lucas answered.

"Okay. Let's go see if he's awake."

He turned to walk up the hallway, then paused for Lucas to follow. Lucas looked back at his mom, who nodded.

"I'll be here," she said kindly.

Lucas followed after Tim, pleased that he didn't protest. As they walked, he cast his mind around the ER, morbidly curious of the frenetic commotion nearby.

"Are you excited to go home?" Tim asked, interrupting his thoughts.

"Yes."

"Still in shock about it?"

"Yeah," Lucas admitted with a half-smile.

"That's alright. You deserve some rest."

"Why are they letting me go?"

"I'm not sure they are," Tim answered with a bemused tone. "I think they've finally realized the insanity in trying to keep you contained. You showed everyone that you're on the right side yesterday, so they don't have anything to worry about. Not to mention that you can obviously take care of yourself."

They reached Kowalski's room up the hall, which also had armed guards posted. They appraised Lucas with narrowed eyes as he approached, and both were fierce and formidable-looking. They stepped aside at a gesture from Tim, allowing him and Lucas to enter.

"Knock, knock," Tim said cheerily as the door closed behind them.

Kowalski lay with his head and shoulders propped up on a pillow, his chest bared with a thick, white bandage adhered to his abdomen. His face still looked deathly pale, and dark circles hung under his eyes. An IV tube fed into his arm and an ECG lead was fastened to his index finger. His head turned as Lucas entered the room behind Tim. Lucas felt hollow inside, and tried not to stare at the bandage.

"How are you feeling, Seth?" Tim asked.

"Not dead yet," Kowalski replied hoarsely. His mouth turned slightly upward in a weak attempt at a smile. His heavy-lidded eyes moved slowly to Lucas. "What are you doing here?"

"I wanted to ask you a question," Lucas answered, shifting uncomfortably.

"Go ahead."

"Why aren't there any reports in the news about the Rising?"

"Because we buried them. The government didn't allow any reports to get out, to prevent frightening the public."

Lucas was baffled. He hadn't expected an answer at all, and Kowalski's bluntness caught him off guard.

"But doesn't everyone have a right now about the danger? Don't the people of LA have a right to know how close they were to dying if the Rising had succeeded in bombing the city with the nanomachines?"

"There's always some sort of catastrophe on the brink of happening," Kowalski said tiredly. "If everyone was aware of it, the mass panic alone would destroy the economy and everyone's way of life."

"But they have a right to know!"

"No, they don't," Kowalski snapped. "We have a duty to stop it and make sure that they *never* know. Civilians can't handle that kind of awareness. Can you imagine what the world would be like if the public found out about *you?*"

Lucas blinked, taken aback.

"What do you mean?" he asked.

"You're an artificial, super-powered human," Kowalski said. "A child with more firepower than an RPG. The power you hold in your head alone is enough make internet security laughable. No one's private information is safe. Think about it."

Lucas said nothing. He knew what Kowalski was getting at; he had just done exactly what Kowalski was alluding to.

Kowalski rolled his eyes in exasperation, and sweat beaded on his forehead with the effort of talking.

"For a supercomputer, you're astoundingly slow," he remarked.

"Just say what you mean," Lucas said through clenched teeth.

"It would be an arms race," Kowalski rasped. "Every country in the world would want to take you, or try to build one of their own. The Rising knows that. If Iran, or China, or Russia got a hold of you, they would beat 'em to the job."

"Then why are you letting me go?"

"We're not. You're going home… that's all."

Lucas gave him a blank look, so he continued.

"You will always be watched; that's never going to change. You may live at your house, with your mother, but you're still the property of the U.S. government."

"So I'm still not free," Lucas said, a tight knot of understanding forming in his throat.

"Freedom is an illusion fed by ignorance," Kowalski replied coldly.

Tears stung Lucas' eyes, and he turned away to hide them. He hated Kowalski. Anger built inside of him and he didn't know what to do with it. Tim put a gentle hand on his shoulder, but he shrugged it off.

"Why did I save you?" he spat, turning back to face the bed.

Kowalski shrugged.

"I asked you that same question, remember? And do you remember what you said?"

"Well, I wish I hadn't done it," Lucas said through gritted teeth. "I wish I'd let Iweala kill you."

Kowalski showed no reaction. Tim took Lucas firmly by the shoulders and began to pull him away.

"Come on, Lucas," he said in a deep, kind voice. "Let's go now."

"That anger you feel," Kowalski said, his breath shallow. "It's going to save all of us."

Tim led Lucas toward the door, but Lucas stopped. He didn't know why. He looked back at Kowalski, whose eyes were closed and his gray face glistened with sweat. His lips were moving, but nothing came out. As the door began to close, he took another, gasping breath.

"Don't lose that anger," he said. "Don't lose it."

In the hall, Tim released Lucas and let him walk by himself. Lucas wiped the tears from his face and took a few breaths to stabilize himself.

"Are you alright?" Tim asked.

"I'm fine," Lucas answered.

"Hey, it's going to be okay. Don't worry; things will get better. Maybe even normal, eventually."

My life is never going to get back to normal, Lucas thought dismally. *I might as well accept that.*

"Lucas, wait," Tim said, catching his arm. They were only a few yards from Lucas' room.

Lucas looked up to meet Tim's dark eyes. They were kind, but frighteningly serious.

"You saved our lives," Tim said. "And I, for one, am never going to forget that. Do you understand?"

"I think so," Lucas answered.

"Whatever it takes, I'll make sure you're treated right."

"Thanks," Lucas said, because he didn't know what else to say.

They returned to the room, and Leah hugged Lucas. He knew that she could tell he was upset, but was thankful she didn't ask why. He telepathically related to Bernard what he had learned, and warm, pitying emotions traveled across their psychic connection in return. Lucas felt annoyed, but comforted. He guessed that Bernard would never be left alone either, since he was almost, but not quite, as valuable to the government and to the Rising. They were in a similar predicament. Neither of them could ever escape the accident in that warehouse eight months ago.

The next morning, Bernard was released. The U.S. government had arranged for him to be sent to a hospice care center on the east side of Austin. Lucas watched passively as he was wheeled out with his mother walking forlornly beside him; his father had already gone back to work.

Lucas and Leah left the hospital soon after that. The sun was high in the sky and baked the asphalt as the two of them walked with their bags to the parking garage. Lucas marveled at the hard, golden light that he had missed for so many months. It beat down on his neck and caused sweat to drip down his temples, but he felt nothing but gratitude. He squinted up at the clear blue sky between the alleys of skyscrapers; a gentle roar sounded in his ears: the muted noise of electromagnetic radiation shooting down from millions of miles away.

Their tiny Toyota was escorted by a squad of unmarked cars; they boarded the highway, and the group of SUVs remained close behind in a tight formation. He and Leah rode in tense silence. Lucas wore a t-shirt and pair of jeans that were nearly a size too large; one of the agents had brought him a new set of clothes and shoes. The sneakers pinched his feet at the sides and were an obnoxious neon yellow. He watched the glittering city pass by outside and let his mind absorb the noise, searching for his old friends, Ty and Nate. He wondered what they had been doing while he was away, and if they missed him at all. The memory of their cell phone signals were still stored away in his brain; he dug them up and sent his consciousness outward, looking for a match. Then he stopped, letting the signal fade, hanging his head. He didn't know what he would say or do if he found them, and he didn't want to think about it yet. He wasn't ready.

"Are you alright?" Leah asked.

"I don't know what to do," he answered quietly. "I thought this day would never come, and now that it has… I just don't know what I'm supposed to do now."

"Be a kid," Leah said. "And that's all. Stop bearing burdens that you never should have had, and live your life. This nightmare is over; let's just put it behind us and move on."

Lucas noted the tone of bitterness in her voice, and made no reply. They rode the rest of the way in silence. The highway swept around the perimeter of the city and swung north. Lucas admired the deep blue of the endless sky, stretching from horizon to horizon. They exited and drove into a neighborhood of eclectic-looking houses; twentieth-century homes sat cozily next to modern ones with sharp, geometric exteriors. Deep green leaves rustled overhead in the gentle breeze. Leah pulled up to a medium-sized house with a columned porch and a swing. It had bright pink siding, white trim, and small, curtained windows. A round window peeped from the second story, and a large magnolia tree with sweet-smelling blossoms stood in the front yard.

Their escort vehicles parked on either side of the street and idled while two agents stepped out of the nearest vehicle and walked casually up to the Toyota where Leah was unloading bags. One of them helped by picking up the large duffel, while Leah slung the backpack over her shoulder. She smiled at Lucas and nodded up at the house.

"Welcome home, Lucas."

Lucas looked at the house, but his attention was drawn away by the golden sunlight filtered through the trees, dappling the sidewalk. He loved its warmth. He tiredly followed his mother up the front walk, then the steps and inside the house. It was clean, of course. The door opened into living room where polished dark wood floors were accented by a cream-colored rug and a white sofa and chairs sat before a large flat-screen television. A watercolor of a mountain sunset hung on the wall, and a vase of orchids sat on the coffee table. A tall bookshelf in the corner bore a set of encyclopedias, the wooden turtle, and Lucas' baby album. The rest of the furniture and decor was simple, elegant, and matched perfectly. The CIA had set his mother up comfortably.

He wandered down the hall, passing more watercolor artwork that looked like it belonged in a doctor's office. He found the master bedroom, and a second bedroom that was filled with his grandmother's things. The third room appeared to be an office, with a writing desk and more books. Stymied, he made his way up the stairs. At the top of the stairs was a heavy curtain that he drew aside and found a bed with a greenish blue bedspread, a blond wooden dresser and bedside table, and floor length mirror. He examine his reflection briefly: thin, coffee-brown face with a long nose, shaved head, and too-big clothes that hung on his lanky frame, before turning away. The loft was well lit with warm sunlight through the round window, and was very spacious. A Superman poster hung on one wall, and a flag for the University of Texas football team was pinned to the opposite one, above the bed. He opened the dresser to find it filled clothes and socks, all folded neatly. A stereo clock sat atop the dresser, next to an army of dinosaur figurines; from the ceiling hung a two-foot-wide model of the *Millenium Falcon*. To Lucas, it all felt wrong.

A creak on the stairs caused him to turn. His mother crested the stairs, then stepped through the curtain.

"What do you think?" she said with a timid smile. She noticed his expression and frowned. "If you don't like it, we can move you downstairs and relocate the office--I just thought you'd like the space--"

"No, no, it's great," he replied quickly. "It's just, I don't like football, and none of this stuff is mine."

"Oh, yes," Leah winced. "I'm sorry, they sent someone to decorate. I didn't realize--well, I haven't come up here--I couldn't, you know. You can change it; we'll go shopping and get whatever you want."

He sat down on the bed and looked down at the green-and-brown checkered rug, then kicked off his shoes.

"I'm tired," he said. "I think I'll just sleep for a while."

"Sure, sweetheart," Leah nodded, squeezing his shoulder. "Just call downstairs if you need anything."

She drew the curtain, and Lucas pulled back the covers and lay down. The bed was new, and much softer than his old mattress had been. Even so, he hated it. He missed his old bed, and his old room, cramped as it was. This was not what he had hoped to come home to for so long.

Outside, except for the birds singing and cicadas buzzing, all was quiet. He could hear Leah moving about downstairs, pans and dishes clattering. Slowly, so slowly, he began to relax and his head sank into the pillow. Within minutes, he was fast asleep.

He woke up with a start to the sound of two voices conversing downstairs. Lucas recognized his grandmother's husky, accented voice. Streetlights shone outside the round window at the far end of the loft, and a steady buzz hummed inside his skull. It was peppered with spikes and tickles like rain on a tin roof. He crossed the room once more, pulled aside the curtain and padded down the stairs, drawn by the aromas of savory food and the clink of dishes. The conversation ceased as his footsteps creaked on the stairs. Leah and Maria both looked up from their seats at the table.

"Lucas," Leah said, standing. "I thought you'd sleep for a while. Are you hungry?"

"Yes," he answered, eyeing the food.

Maria stood slowly, then gained momentum as she covered the remaining distance to throw her arms around him. She ran her fingers over his stubbled scalp, then kissed his forehead.

"It's so good to see you again," she said softly.

"Thank you. It's good to see you too, Grandma."

She nodded forlornly, avoiding his eyes. He pulled out a chair next to Leah and sat down. She scooped pasta and vegetables onto a plate and handed it to Lucas. He stabbed at the garlic-laiden asparagus.

"You saw the office, right?" Leah asked. "That's for you to do your schoolwork in. I finally settled on a homeschooling curriculum that should arrive in a couple of days. That whole library is full of history books, poetry-
-everything you need for an education."

"So, we're really not even going to talk about this?" Lucas said incredulously.

"No, it's already been decided," Leah replied firmly. "I'm your mother, and I think that this is the best thing for you. Maybe in a year or two, once things have gotten back to normal, we can talk about you going back to school."

"I don't even *need* school anymore," Lucas said, his temper flaring. "Anything I ever wanted to know, I can find out instantly. I just want to see my friends."

"We can talk about that, too," Leah answered. "After everything settles down."

"*Tu madre* said we can't ask you about where you've been," Maria said suddenly.

Lucas froze with his fork halfway to his mouth.

"Mama!" Leah gasped. "*No podemos hablar de eso!*"

"Can you at least tell me if they hurt you?" Maria asked, ignoring her. Her voice broke and her lower lip trembled. "Did they hurt you?"

"Mama, stop!" Leah demanded.

"I need to know!" Maria protested. "I need to know what those monsters did to your baby!"

"Is there a problem here?" a man's voice said. A man in a black suit stood up from where he had been reclining in one of the large chairs, just out of Lucas' view. Lucas shot out of his chair, knocking it to the ground.

"Who are you?" he demanded.

"Agent Wharton," the man replied coolly.

"Lucas, it's fine," Leah said, reaching for his hand. "He's an agent assigned to watch the house. Everything is alright."

"He's assigned to watch *me*," Lucas growled. His blood pounded in his ears.

"Whatever," Leah said dismissively. "He doesn't matter; just sit down and eat."

She looked at him with pleading eyes. He picked up his chair and sat, back tense. Robotically, he lifted his fork and continued eating, but his mouth felt like sandpaper and his stomach was so tight it made him nauseous. He caught Agent Wharton still looking at him, and lowered his eyes. Then something brushed the back of his neck and he jumped, jarring the table and tipping his glass.

"Lucas!" Leah cried in shock, jerking her hand back. Lucas saw that she had attempted to reach her arm around him.

"I'm sorry," he said, shamefaced.

Her eyes glistened with tears until she covered her face with her hands.

"Mom, I'm sorry," Lucas said again, his voice catching. *What's wrong with me?*

"What happened to you, *mijo?*" Maria asked again. "Those monsters did hurt you, didn't they? You can tell us!"

Lucas picked up the chair.

"No, I can't," he said. "I'm going back to my room."

He climbed the stairs and drew the curtain behind him. Within minutes, Leah and Maria began arguing loudly, their voices carrying up the stairs. Maria insisted that they could sue the CIA for mistreatment and wrongful imprisonment, while Leah maintained that the whole ordeal would put too much stress on Lucas to be worth it. At long last, he tuned their voices out and sat cross-legged in the floor. He cast his mind outward, searching for a familiar signal. A galaxy of electrical signatures opened up before him, soaring through his head. The city danced with lights and halos in kaleidoscopes of colors that only he could see. He narrowed the signals down, bit by bit, until he found the one he was looking for.

Bernard?

He waited, receiving a long, empty silence. He stretched farther.

Bernard? Can you hear me?

Still nothing.

Lucas couldn't contain himself any longer. His fist flew out, striking the wall with a loud bang and the voices downstairs fell silent at the sound. Shaking, he stared at the round hole in the drywall, then down at his bruised knuckles.

Sinking to the floor, Lucas drew his knees into his chest and waited as the minutes dragged on. He found a playlist of heavy rock music on the internet and played it in his head to drown out the argument that carried on downstairs, then climbed into bed. Sleep found him quickly.

Chapter 17

SLEEP DID NOT COME SO well the next few nights. He spent most of each day outside, feeling the grass under his bare feet, watching the wind through the trees, and listening to the sun. When the summertime heat became unbearable, he retreated back into his room with a book from the downstairs library. He lay on his bed or the floor, pouring through book after book and absorbing the information into his endless memory stores. He found that he could remember every word he read and practiced calling up the pages from each book, even playing the whole volume back in his mind as if he was reading it all over again. He figured he could read the whole library and never forget any of it.

As each day passed, he began to feel more and more restless. He tried to ignore the fact that there was always an agent downstairs. He passed by him or her each time he went for another book, and never looked them in the eye, though from his room he tracked their movements. The agent on watch was relieved every six hours. Leah offered each one a meal and coffee, and, following that, ignored them as much as possible. Each of the home's residents seemed eager to pretend that they weren't there. To Lucas, it was further evidence that he had traded one prison for another.

By the third night, he slept only a couple of hours. He tossed and turned, then spent the rest of the night surfing the internet for distractions. He watched movies, listened to music, and spied on the neighbors. A week after his release from the hospital, he stopped sleeping altogether. He had read every book in the his mother's library, then began invading the public library's database for e-books. Between binges, he learned that two of his neighbors were having affairs with each other, that the family across the street had a new baby, and that four registered sex offenders lived within five blocks of his house.

He had still received no reply from Bernard, and hoped that it was only because he was out of range. He mined the CIA's communications for any information, but none were forthcoming. So the days dragged on.

"Lucas."

His consciousness was dragged back into his body, like an astronaut suddenly snapped back to earth. He opened his eyes to see his mother poking her head in the doorway.

"Someone's here to see you," she said.

Lucas sat up. She stepped aside, and Agent Kowalski ducked through the curtain. Her footsteps retreated back down the stairs as Kowalski stepped inside the loft, looking around with a bemused expression. He stood tall; his head nearly brushed the ceiling. His blond hair was combed neatly back. He looked every bit like the old Kowalski, but his movements were slower, more careful.

"What were you doing?" he asked Lucas.

"Watching traffic patterns."

He raised an eyebrow. "Why?"

Lucas shrugged. "The other day, I heard the traffic guy on the radio telling listeners how much their commute would be delayed due to various traffic accidents around the city, so I wanted to see how those numbers were determined. I've been watching for hours."

Kowalski shook his head.

"Jesus, kid. You're bored out of your mind being cooped up in here, aren't you?"

"Yeah, I am."

Kowalski sighed and sat down on the bed, running a hand over his smoothed hair.

"Look, I know you'd rather be out there, doing something useful. Believe me, I want the same thing, but you need to move past this. It's time for you to be a kid again."

"I can't move past it. I'm not even the same person that I was."

"Sure, some things are different, but you can go back--"

"Everything is different!" Lucas interrupted. "I missed eight months of my life!"

"I know," Kowalski said evenly. "I didn't say it wasn't going to be difficult to adjust. But you have to try."

"What are you doing here anyway?" Lucas asked.

"Your mother called me. She's worried; she said all you do is lay around all day, staring off into space. We both know what you're really doing."

"Why do you care?"

Kowalski's brow furrowed.

"I was kind of dick to you, after you saved my life," Kowalski replied. "I'd be the first to admit that I'm not great with kids. Believe it or not, I do care about you, though I might have a hard time showing it. I know what it's like to experience things that you can't talk to anyone about, because they can't understand it; and I know what's like to feel alone. I don't want that to keep you from living again."

"You don't know what this is like."

"I've been in charge of your case for the past thirteen years," Kowalski replied sardonically. "I know better than most. And your mom--remember that this all started with her. She probably gets it more than anyone."

"She'd rather pretend like none of this ever happened."

"Of course she would. All I'm saying is, everyone's got issues."

"I don't sleep; I haven't for days," Lucas said, picking at the bedspread. "When I do, all I see is the inside of that pod. And I can't keep everything that's inside my head contained. It's like my brain's on a rocket, moving thousands of miles an hour, but I'm stuck here. I can't stop it; eventually, it just goes on without me."

Lucas fell quiet; he rolled a piece of lint between his fingers, eyes on the window. Kowalski was quiet for a moment, too.

"I can't promise that everything's going to be okay, but I do know that you can't stay in here forever," he said finally.

He stood up, smoothing his suit.

"Let's go," he said.

"What?" Lucas looked up in surprise.

"You have to go out sooner or later."

"Where?"

"To get some ice cream. Or burgers, or tacos--whatever you want. We're getting out of here either way."

"I thought I couldn't leave," Lucas said, standing.

"You can with me. Put on some shoes."

Lucas pulled on a pair of sneakers, then followed Kowalski down the stairs. Leah and Maria sat at the table, drinking tea.

"We're going out," Kowalski said.

"What?" Leah said, jumping up.

"Don't worry; I'm just taking him to get some fresh air."

"Is it safe?"

Kowalski leaned in close to her and spoke in low tones. She nodded slowly, her lips tight. Maria watched with narrow eyes, her teacup hovering. Finally, Leah sat down.

"Just bring him back safely, alright?"

"Of course," Kowalski said jovially. "You can count on me. Come on, Lucas, time to go."

Bewildered, Lucas followed him out the door, then down the sidewalk to a black BMW. It was just after noon, and the sunlight baked the front yard. Lucas began sweating immediately. It became worse once they got inside the car; the air was thick, and the leather seats hot. Kowalski started the car and selected a button on the dashboard, and air from the vents blasted Lucas' face. Within a minute of pulling away from the curb, the climate inside the car had reached a comfortable temperature.

"Where are we going?" Lucas asked.

"What do you feel like eating?" Kowalski replied.

"What did you tell my mom?"

"Oh, we're back to being hostile now, are we?" he said, giving him a sideways glance. "I told her not to worry; we were just going out for a bite, then coming straight back."

"Is that true?"

"Of course it is," he answered. "You really should learn to relax."

"I would if I could tell whether or not you're lying."

"I'm not lying."

"What would happen if I jumped out of the car right now?"

"Nothing right away," Kowalski replied. "It definitely wouldn't be a good idea. Geez, kid, we aren't even a block away and you're already thinking about escaping? Just calm down; nobody's trying to hurt you. There are no secrets here. We're doing exactly what I said: just going to get a bite to eat. Just chill out, alright?"

Lucas became still, but did not relax. His back was straight and his shoulders tense as he watched the passing houses and trees outside. They turned onto a main avenue and proceeded toward downtown. Skyscrapers towered over them, and the air became busier with advertisements, transmissions, and conversations all tickling Lucas' senses. Nearly everyone passing by on the sidewalks had their phones out in front of them or held to their ears; most were multitasking, texting or surfing the internet while listening to music.

They pulled up to a restaurant a few blocks south of the city's center. The front was red brick, with tall rod iron windows. The name of the restaurant was graffitied onto a reclaimed barnwood sign.

"Hey," Kowalski said. "Remember something for me, okay?"

Lucas looked at him. Kowalski rested his left arm on the window, and his right hand on the back of Lucas' seat.

"Your mom and I are probably the two people in the world that care about you the most," he said. "I know you didn't know me before, but I've been looking out for you since you were born. I watched you grow up, though it was from a distance. I wish it had been under better circumstances, but it's been a privilege getting to know you over the past few months."

His blue eyes were fixed on Lucas' face, and were deep with sincerity.

"I guess what I'm trying to say is that you're a good kid," he said. "Don't let everything that's happened over the past few months change that."

"Okay," Lucas said with surprise.

"You ever eat tacos here?" he asked, nodding at the restaurant.

"No, never," Lucas replied.

"Then you're in for a treat."

They stepped out of the car and Kowalski led the way. Lucas felt very exposed walking around without his usual escort. Kowalski held the door open for him and he ducked in, taking in his surroundings with vigilance. The place was mostly empty, because the lunch rush had just ended. A family of five was seated toward the front of the restaurant, the young mom spooning baby food into an infant's mouth while the father was attempting to explain to the older two children why this place had no pizza. Kowalski told Lucas to sit while he went up to the counter to order. Lucas selected a table in the corner and sat with his back to the wall. He watched Kowalski interact with the girl at the counter and nervously tore the corners off a napkin.

A flicker of a familiar sensation lit up the back of his brain. The door opened while Kowalski filled their drinks from the soda fountain, and a blond boy with a familiar face and a startled expression walked in.

"Lucas?" Nate asked.

His eyes were wide as he moved, slowly drawing closer to the table. Lucas couldn't believe what he was seeing. He stood up cautiously.

"What are you doing here?"

"I saw you through the window," Nate answered. He looked like he was talking to a ghost. "My mom is shopping next door."

"Well, you want to sit down?" Lucas asked awkwardly.

Nate was still staring at him when Kowalski walked up, carrying two cups filled with ice and soda. Nate looked up at him and jumped.

"You're the guy from the warehouse!" he said accusingly.

"Nate Wissen," Kowalski replied. "Would you like to join us? Are you hungry?"

Nate looked between Kowalski and Lucas with confusion and fear.

"What are you do---" he began, but Kowalski interrupted in a low, urgent voice.

"You're welcome to ask any questions you like, as long as you don't make a scene," he said. "Sit down quietly, and we'll talk."

He motioned to the table, and Nate sat, almost robotically. His mouth was still partly open. Lucas sat, too, while Kowalski slid into the booth on Nate's other side. He set the drinks down, then interlaced his fingers.

"Nate, what would you like to know?"

"Wh-where have you been?" he stammered, his eyes on Lucas. "It's been, like, a year."

Lucas felt a pang in his heart. He had missed his friends so much, but could never imagine what he would say when he saw either of them again.

Nate looked different. He had a different haircut; it was shorter, and darker. He had grown an inch, maybe more, and there was a hollow look in his eyes.

"I was taken to a CIA facility," Lucas answered, his eyes flicking to Kowalski, who gave a subtle nod. "For research."

Nate's eyes widened with horror, and Lucas turned to Kowalski again.

"Can we talk alone?" he asked.

"I'll be close by," Kowalski replied. He got up and moved to a booth about six feet away. Once he sat down, Nate leaned close, his forearms on the table.

"They *experimented* on you?" he whispered hoarsely.

Lucas nodded.

"To find out what really happened to me in that warehouse," he said. "And how my powers worked."

"How did you get out?" Nate blurted. "Did you escape? And what's that guy doing here--he's one of them, isn't he?"

"They let me go. He's just supposed to watch me."

"They let you go? Just like that?"

"Sort of," Lucas said, scratching his head. "It's complicated."

Nate sat back in his chair, giving Lucas a look of disbelief.

"It *is*," Lucas insisted. "And I don't know how much I should tell you."

"Are you going to be around?"

"I don't know."

"Is anything going to get back to normal?"

"Probably not," Lucas answered heavily. "It's not that I don't want them to, I just don't know how they could. I'm not the same person I was back then; I'm not even the same *thing* that I was."

"I don't understand," Nate said.

"I know, I'm sorry," Lucas replied, and he meant it. Suddenly, he felt like crying, but he wasn't sure that Nate would forgive him for it. Once upon a time, they could shed tears in front of each other and knew that neither of them would breathe a word about it to anyone. Now, he felt that he just didn't know Nate that well anymore.

"I should probably go," Nate said, sliding off the bench. "My mom's probably looking for me."

Lucas watched him get up, feeling helpless. He didn't want Nate to leave, but had no clue how to persuade him to stay. He felt a tickle down the back of his skull, and his consciousness opened outward. Hundreds of thousands of messages zoomed through his mind at a blinding speed, until one rushed into view. It was a social media post: white lettering on a black background that read, *For the Rising.*

Lucas leapt to his feet, his heart pounding.

"What's wrong?" Nate said nervously, taking a small step backward.

"Kowalski," Lucas gasped. He sent an image of the post to his phone, and Kowalski's mouth tightened into a thin line.

"Do you know where this came from?" he asked, standing up.

"I--I could find out," Lucas stammered. "Give me a second."

He sat back down and closed his eyes, zeroing his focus onto the post. He searched for the timestamp and GPS coordinates. This led him on a trail that danced all over the state, an electronic signature that jumped away each time he drew close to it. There seemed to be hundreds of different phones passing it on like a game of hot potato. He concentrated harder, pain beginning to blossom in his skull, until he locked in. A shimmering bright glow hovered in his mind.

"Found it," he said, opening his eyes.

"What happened?" Nate asked loudly. "Will one of you tell me what's going on?"

"Where?" Kowalski asked.

"Here in the city, getting closer," Lucas replied, jumping up. He raced to the door and out onto the sidewalk. Kowalski and Nate ran out on his heels.

"What do you mean?" Kowalski demanded. "Is it a bomb?"

"I don't know," Lucas said. "The signal is moving very quickly, and headed this way."

He saw the shimmering glow rushing like a falling star across the digital map of the city he had formed in his mind.

"It's four blocks away, moving 45 miles an hour."

"So it's in a car?" Kowalski guessed. He began to dial the agency.

Lucas took over the nearby traffic cameras, his mind leaping from intersection to intersection until he saw it: a commuter bus, barreling through an intersection while pedestrians ran and screamed in terror.

"It's a bus," Lucas reported as dread crept through him like ice.

Kowalski's face paled, his phone hovering by his ear.

"Does it have a bomb on it?"

"I don't know--probably. That's what they do, isn't it?"

Nate looked between the two of them with an expression of confusion mixed with fear. The bus drew closer, accelerating to fifty miles an hour. It charged through red lights as terrified drivers careened out of the way. Lucas looked around at the street and the surrounding buildings. He stood at the edge of the financial part of town. To his left, the city center and block after block of glittering towers. To his right, the main avenue led to the shopping district. Traffic became busier and pedestrians more frequent. Lucas could see the bus now. It's headlights were on, despite the blazing sun overhead. It rushed through another intersection as a man and a woman barely dodged out of its path.

"I have to stop it," Lucas said.

"What?" Nate cried. "Why?"

"Because I can. I have to, before more people get hurt."

"Lucas, wait," Kowalski warned.

"There's no time!"

He stepped off the curb. The bus was now a hundred yards away. Lucas walked to the middle of the street, his blood pounding in his ears. He took a deep breath to steady himself, and electrical energy began to crackle across his arms and chest.

Fifty yards.

Through the windshield, he saw the driver.

Twenty yards.

It was a young man with scruffy, light brown hair and a goatee. He was wearing a black shirt and had a smudge on his face.

Ten yards.

The smudge was a tattoo of a coiled snake. His look of fierce determination turned into a look of surprise as his eyes met Lucas'.

Five yards.

Lucas breathed again. He wasn't sure it would even work again. White-hot energy spread from his hands and bubbled outward. It popped and snapped like lightning, but instead of branching outward, it formed a wall. It was transparent, but bent the light like glass. It shot up, fifty feet into the air, spanning the width of the street. A woman screamed somewhere nearby. Lucas braced himself.

The bus slammed into the invisible wall. The front of the bus crumpled beneath the weight of the back as momentum continued to carry it forward. Metal twisted and bent with a horrible screech. Lucas felt a shudder through the force field and fought to hold it in place. Then, with a thunderous roar, the bus exploded into flames. The top of the bus blew off and folded backward onto itself. Shrapnel peppered the force field like bullets from a gatling gun, followed by a shockwave that shattered the windows of every building in a two-block radius. Lucas' muscles screamed, and his skull felt like it was being split open. He could barely see through the pain. With a final shudder, the force field vanished, and heat from the blast hit Lucas all at once. The hairs on his arms were singed instantly, and his face burned raw. He felt himself falling backward, and something struck him in the back of the head.

Chapter 18

THE NEXT THING HE KNEW, he was picked up and cradled in someone's strong arms. His head rocked back and forth as the person carried him at a run. The wind hurt the raw, exposed skin on his face. His ears were ringing. Then the wind stopped; he was placed into a car, laid across someone's lap.

"Hold him steady," Kowalski said from the driver's seat. "Don't let him roll."

"My mom's going to be pissed," Nate's voice muttered from somewhere above him. It was Nate's lap he was lying on.

"You didn't have to come," Kowalski snapped.

"What was I gonna do--just go home like nothing happened? He's my friend. I had to do *something*."

A second later, Nate jerked in surprise, jarring Lucas.

"The burns are healing already! He can do that?"

"Yeah, he heals quickly. He'll be fine in an hour or two."

"So, we're not going the hospital?"

"No, we're taking him home. That was an attack by a terrorist organization called the Rising. They're after Lucas, and will do anything to take him. We need to get back to the house and regroup."

"He feels really cold," Nate said shakily. "Are you sure he's all right?"

"What happened?" Lucas managed to force out. His lips cracked and bled.

"Jesus Christ! He's awake!"

"Welcome back," Kowalski said, looking at him in the rearview mirror. "That was quick. How are you feeling?"

"Got a massive headache, but I'm fine, I think," Lucas groaned. "What happened?"

"You went out in front of that bus and put up a force field."

"Did it work?"

"Yeah, but there was a bomb on the bus," Nate said. "It blew up."

"Was anyone hurt?" Lucas asked, pulling himself up to a sitting position. He put on his seatbelt as Nate began to answer, then hesitated. He looked off into the distance, and Lucas' heart sank.

"Don't worry about that," Kowalski interjected. "The main thing here is that the Rising clearly isn't done bombing innocent people, and they've changed their M.O. There was no wait time after the message was sent."

"Why are they after Lucas?" Nate said.

"Because of his powers. They made him, probably for spying. Lucas can monitor anyone with a wireless signal and is impossible to trace."

"They *made* you?" Nate asked.

Lucas nodded. "It's a long story."

He noticed Kowalski leaned in his seat, his right hand pressed to his side.

"You're bleeding," he said.

"Yeah," Kowalski winced. "I tore my stitches, carrying you. Forget about it; I'm alright. When you can, check in with your mother. My phone must be broken, I can't call out."

Lucas sent part of his consciousness to examine the phone that sat in the center console, its screen cracked. The other part he used to connect to his mother's phone. He sent a text, then called when he got no response. The car raced through the neighborhood, closing the distance quickly. When they were two blocks away, Lucas spotted a strange line on the road. Before he could tell what it was, the car rumbled over it and the tires blew. The vehicle slammed to a stop, Kowalski's face colliding with the airbag that deployed with a hiss. Lucas's seatbelt felt like a baseball bat hitting him in the chest as it locked, and his head snapped forward. The world spun.

When he could lift his head, he turned to look at Nate. He slumped in his seat, blood dripping from his nose. Kowalski groaned in the front seat. Suddenly, the doors opened and big men reached inside. One of them dragged Kowalski out of the car and dropped him face-down onto the pavement.

"Hey!" Lucas shouted, outraged.

The man responded by aiming a gun at the back of Kowalski's head.

"Cooperate, or he dies," he said with an English accent.

Lucas silently raised his hands. They quavered in the air. Another man reached across him and cut the seatbelt, then clamped a hand the size of a boxing glove around his upper arm. Lucas was practically lifted out of the car, his legs dragging. At the same time, Nate was removed from his seat and leaned across the hood with his hands behind his back as he was cuffed with zip-ties. His head lolled, and blood continued to drip from his nose. His eyes were partly open.

"Are you alright?" Lucas asked.

"No talking," the Englishman said.

The boys walked side by side with the big men close behind. There were four men in total; two remained with Kowalski while the boys were guided away. They stepped over the spike strip, then up the sidewalk toward Lucas' house. Lucas began to feel increasingly terrified. They were being abducted, in broad daylight; these men didn't seem to care who saw them. He wondered who they were, and why Nate's hands were tied, but his were not. And did these guys know about his powers? Adrenaline pumping, he searched for a cell phone or any kind of device on the men. He found none, not even a radio. He tried again to reach his mother's phone, but found only a kind of white noise surrounding the house. It sounded like a swarm of bees in his head. He was perturbed; he had never felt anything like that before.

They reached the house. The front door had two more men in dark suits on either side. The bee-like humming of white noise grew stronger. The door opened, and Lucas stopped cold. His mother and grandmother were bound and gagged in chairs, with men holding guns to their heads. Leah's cheeks were streaked with makeup that ran with her tears. Her muffled screams had begun as soon as Lucas had walked in the door. In the loveseat, Bernard lay like a crumpled rag doll. His eyes were closed, and his forehead beaded with sweat. The bandage over his eye was missing, leaving the bruised flesh and stitches exposed.

Lucas saw all of this in a second, and his anger burned. His fists clenched when he saw Agent Wharton lying behind the couch, a bullet wound in his head. Nate was dropped against the wall, now awake and gazing around, bleary-eyed. Then a tall man stood up from where he had been reclining in a big chair. He wore grey pants and a white shirt with a blue tie, and an embroidered vest. He had a dark complexion, and wavy black hair cut short and groomed neatly. He looked middle-aged, and a gold earring flashed in one ear.

"Lucas Tavera, I presume?" he said with a smile. His accent sounded European, maybe French.

"Let them go," Lucas growled.

"No, I think not. I must ensure your peaceful cooperation. My name is Gabriel Petra. You've never heard of me, but I have heard a great deal about you, and I am very happy to finally meet you. My people have been searching for you for a very long time."

"*Your* people," Lucas repeated. "The Rising."

"Yes, that's right," Petra nodded. He spoke to Lucas like he was speaking to a small child. "You are a part of my people as well, and we've come to bring you home."

"Maybe you missed the message I gave Agent Iweala," Lucas replied acidly. "I'm not coming with you."

"I did receive that message," Petra said, bemused. "That's why we will be taking your family with us. You are free to choose, but if the answer is no, your mother and grandmother will die. Quite painfully, too."

Lucas shook with rage. The deep hum inside his mind grated on his nerves. *What is that?* Part of him wondered if they had a device hidden somewhere, something meant to keep him trapped inside his own head, because each time his consciousness ventured out, a stabbing pain came in return.

Tears stung his eyes as he looked into his mother's terrified eyes. She whimpered behind the duct tape that covered her mouth.

"What do you want with me?" Lucas choked out. "Why do you keep coming after me?"

"I am so glad you asked," Petra responded. "I believe firmly that if you only understood what we were about, you would agree with us wholeheartedly. You have been told that we are a group of terrorists and criminals, out to destroy for the sake of fear. That is simply not true; our aim is good. We want to end the many injustices that occur in this country and so many others. With your help, the Rising could end this nation and rebuild a new one completely free of crime and every kind of oppression. We could guarantee equality for everyone."

"What would I do?" Lucas asked quietly.

"With your gifts--that perfect combination of genetic ingenuity and the nanomachines working throughout your body. You are our greatest tool in this venture; you can locate our enemies, monitor them, then help us put a stop to them. They don't stand a chance against your powers; you've seen this yourself."

"You're killers," Lucas snapped. "I'm not going to help murderers."

Petra's eyes grew cold, and his smile vanished. He folded his eyes behind his back and took a few slow, easy steps toward the sofa were Bernard lay curled.

"Your friend, Brick--he prefers to be called Bernard, yes? He has experienced the vicious effects of the nanomachines. They are constructed to interact only with a person of your particular genetic code. For everyone else, they have another purpose: they get very hungry. The spinal cord is the first to go, followed by the brain. It's slow, and it's painful. Now, who could fight against a weapon like that? Once the world knows we have this in our arsenal, they will surrender, and no one has to die. Peace will be achieved quickly."

"That's not fair," Lucas protested, but Petra pressed on.

"True peace does not come without a price. Now, you say you will not help us. What if I told you that you could save anyone you wanted, like you saved your friend Bernard? I would not stop you. Only our common enemies would be destroyed. You can keep your mother and grandmother alive, if you work for me. Do we have a deal, Lucas?"

"No," he answered, his fists clenched so tightly that his nails dug into his palm. "This is wrong."

"To the people out there, you're an abomination, but you were made to be a prince among us," Petra replied forcefully. "You will never belong to them. But I will never mistreat you. You will be given the respect owed to a god."

"Do it, Lucas," Bernard said suddenly. His eyes flew open. "Do it. He's right; take the deal."

"What?" Lucas gasped.

Bernard pushed himself up onto his elbow. His eyes were blank and hollow.

"Take the deal," he said in a quavering voice. "You can't fight them. If you try, they'll take you anyway, or kill you. Either way, you can't win. Just take the deal, and at least then you can live, and so can we."

"But, Bernard--" Lucas stammered. "You said you'd never stop fighting. You said they could never take your spirit. What happened to all that?"

"Listen to your friend," Petra said calmly. "He knows what he's talking about."

"It's over, Lucas," Bernard said. "It's time to let this go. I'm done fighting. I can't do it anymore."

As he spoke, the bee-like humming assailed Lucas' mind. It rose and fell with Bernard's words, then began to echo them, like someone talking through the static on an old radio. Lucas' realized that the hum centered around Bernard; to his extra senses, Bernard was a flare of foreign energy. It emanated from him.

Lucas, help! came Bernard's mental voice, shocking Lucas' mind.

He's trapped, Lucas realized. *Something else is in there.*

"Listen to me, Lucas," Bernard continued aloud. His eyes were completely flat and dead, but his voice was full of emotion. It shook with the effort it took to speak. "You can't fight this. This is going to happen with or without you."

"That's not true; as long as I resist, your plans won't work," Lucas said, his eyes on Petra. "Without me, you've got nothing."

Surreptitiously, he probed closer, trying to reach Bernard's mind while betraying nothing on his face. A thick cloud of energy surrounded him like a swarm of locusts. Lucas sent strands of his own thoughts to surround the barrier, testing it for weaknesses. Immediately, the foreign presence stabbed back, worse than ever before. Searing pain filled Lucas' head, and he dropped to his knees, crying out.

It's alive, he realized.

His mother screamed and twisted in her binds, and Nate yelled.

It's alive, the energy is alive.

"Stop! Stop it! What's happening to him?" Nate was shouting from the floor.

"Someone shut that one up," Petra spat.

The nearby guard bent down, his hand raised to backhand Nate. Lucas, eyes blurred with tears, reached out and released a small bolt of electricity into the man's leg before his hand fell. The guard yelped, his knees buckling. Then he rose up and struck Nate in the face anyway. Petra laughed a shrill, piercing laugh.

"Ever the fighter, aren't you?" he said, still chuckling. "You can't protect everyone, Lucas. Come now, give this up. You must see how futile all of this is. You're fighting your maker, after all."

"You didn't make me," Lucas said, standing. "Dr. Lytton did."

Petra's eyes flashed. The guard seized Lucas by his shirt collar and pulled him to his feet.

"I *own* you," Petra spat. "There is nowhere you can go where I will not find you, and take what is rightfully mine."

"Then I guess I'll just have to kill you," Lucas said calmly.

Heat crackled into his hands. The man's gaunt face was twisted in a smile; his eyes looked black, like a shark's. As heat gathered into Lucas' hand once more, he slammed his palm into the guard's chest. With a bang, the man was thrown backward into the wall, releasing Lucas. He lunged at Petra, leaping over the couch with a yell.

Bernard fell silent, then collapsed into the sofa as something moved in the shadows. A girl, quick as a leopard, sprang at him. Her auburn hair flew as she tackled Lucas to the ground, catching him mid-jump, then rolled to her feet. She wore a black and grey bodysuit, like a scuba diver's. Lucas could only stare up at her as her green eyes stabbed into him, the bee-like humming now a piercing shriek.

It's you, he thought, stunned. The energy was her. Her mind.

He had little time to react before the girl's mind attacked him once more. The room shifted, as if gravity had suddenly flipped, and his stomach lurched; his brain was enveloped in a shroud of humming fog as she reached toward him with a slender hand. The air shimmered with heat; ions sparked and bent the light. A rippling wave shot from her hand and slammed into Lucas' chest, flattening him into the ground. His ribcage was crushed against the floor and his bones groaned to the point of snapping. He couldn't speak or breathe, and the fog slowed his thoughts.

Footsteps creaked over the floor. Petra stood over him, then casually tapped the girl on the shoulder. She immediately released Lucas, straightened, and folded her hands behind her back like a soldier. Lucas lay gasping on the floor.

"You see, Lucas," Petra began. "Your friend was right: indeed, I don't need you. I have had others willing to take up your mantle and do what I ask. You really are quite special, just not as special as you think."

He pressed his lips together, and shook his head with a sigh.

"But I can't have you running free and causing me more trouble. I really don't like messes."

He looked at the girl again, and she turned to face Bernard. Her slim face blanked with concentration, and Lucas felt the energy in the room shift again. Bernard lifted his head, his eyes flying open. Lucas heard the humming, static-filled voice in his mind before the words left Bernard's mouth:

"I am Romana. You are done. You are obsolete. You are unnecessary. There is nothing left for you to do but surrender."

The room became completely silent, except for the sound of Bernard's ragged breathing. Blood dripped slowly from his nose, and his eyes rolled back in his head.

"L-l-lucas," he choked out, as Lucas gaped in horror. He couldn't move. He couldn't do anything to stop it.

The girl's mind invaded every part of Bernard's brain, silencing his panicked thoughts. His mind was ravaged, then wiped blank. She released him, and his head dropped against the sofa, then lolled to one side as blood poured from his nose and into his slack, open mouth.

"NO!" Lucas screamed.

He struggled to his feet, then rushed at her, head down and arms out. He intended to barrel her to the floor, but Romana sidestepped him easily. An invisible wave of energy lifted Lucas into the air and tossed him onto the dining room table. He slid, then crashed to the ground as plates clattered on top of him and shattered on the ground. Filled with rage, he got up and sprang over the table. Lightning shot from his hands, illuminating her pale face with a sickly glow. Her eyes were enormous, and her nose and jaw pointed. Her face showed no emotion at all, even as she absorbed the lightning into her strange, invisible field and redirected it back at him. Heat and pain covered his body, and his muscles seized uncontrollably.

Suddenly she was directly in front of him, her hand raised, palm out.

Romana's huge eyes bored into his. Lucas froze on his knees, unable to move; he was trapped by that same, crushing force.

Petra sidled up beside Romana, looking down at Lucas. He straightened his jacket and sniffed.

"I am very sorry that it had to end this way," he said. There was a hint of actual emotion in his voice. Lucas glared up at him, his teeth clenched. It was nearly impossible to breathe; his lungs were collapsing.

"All of this was quite useless," Petra continued. "I hope you realize this. When you awake, you will be in a new place, and a new state of mind. Maybe, after a few months of re-education, you will be open to reason. Goodbye, Lucas."

He nodded to one of the nearby guards, who stepped forward and drew his sidearm. He cocked the weapon, then placed the muzzle against Lucas' head.

"Remember to avoid the base of the skull, please," Petra said.

Tears streamed down Lucas face, and his heart hammered in his aching chest. His ribs snapped, and his arms felt like they would soon to follow. Across the room, his mother thrashed. Her chair tipped onto its side as she fought against her bonds. Maria lowered her head and turned it away, hiding her face. A second guard had Nate locked in a bear hug as he kicked and squirmed, yelling in outrage.

This is it, Lucas thought. *This is how I finally die.* He held his breath, waiting for the bullet to rip through his skull.

An explosion shook the walls, and light flooded the room. Lucas fell to the ground, suddenly released from the constricting force. He wondered if the light he saw was it... the end of everything. *No, I can breathe. I'm still alive... somehow.* He gasped like a fish, lying on his side. More gunshots sounded, and bodies dropped. One fell directly in front of him; it was the guard that had held the gun to his head. Blood oozed from a hole in his face.

Chapter 19

Lucas lifted his head as a SWAT team dressed in black tactical gear charged into the room, guns raised. Bullets were fired in every direction. The team was followed by Tim and Kenny, and, finally, Kowalski. They moved about the room, checking the dead guards. Kowalski bent down over him, his face badly bruised, and lifted him to his feet.

"Are you alright?" he asked Lucas. "Are you hurt?"

Lucas was numb. He couldn't find the energy to speak. His ribs healed, yet he still felt indescribable pain in his chest.

Petra and Romana were nowhere to be seen.

Lucas stood in the middle of the room. He swayed, hollow inside. Someone cut his mother free from her bonds, and she ran to him. She embraced him tightly, tears falling, but Lucas couldn't react. He couldn't hug her back; he could only stare at the sheet draped over the crumpled form on the couch.

Lights flashed outside. He watched as Bernard's body was lifted onto a stretcher and carried outside. An EMT told Lucas to sit in a chair as he was examined. To his left, Nate was seated on the floor with a blanket around his shoulders, also being looked over by an emergency technician. A dark bruise showed on his jaw, and one eye was swollen shut. Tears dripped off his chin. Cops were everywhere: stepping around broken glass, pushing aside the furniture, coming and going from the bedrooms and the dining room. Many spoke to Lucas, but no words came out of his mouth in answer.

His hands felt cold.

He found himself in a car, and now he had a blanket, too. The car took him and his mother to a hotel. Kowalski rode in the front seat; he kept looking over his shoulder at Lucas, saying,

"It's going to be okay. It's going to be okay."

At the hotel, Lucas was offered food that he didn't eat. He stood in the doorway of the bedroom, staring at the walls, the bed, then the floor trying to summon a coherent thought. Only one came to mind: *Bernard is gone.* He reached out with his mind, but found only emptiness, a hungry hole where Bernard's mind had been. He had been eaten away by the poison that had taken so much from him already.

And that girl... she killed him with no feelings at all in those huge, cold eyes. She was like a demon, arriving out of the darkness and disappearing just as suddenly, leaving no trace.

"Lucas," Kowalski said, appearing beside him. "Are you ready to talk?"

"About what?" Lucas said. His voice sounded small, and empty. As if the tiny hallway they stood in was really a cavern.

"About you," Kowalski replied. "Come on, take a seat."

He beckoned for Lucas to sit on the bed, and he did. Kowalski took the chair. His hair was a mess, and he had white tape over his broken nose. He moved stiffly, wincing as he sat down. His shirt still had blood on it from his torn stitches.

"What about me?" Lucas asked.

"I know that what just happened back there must have had an impact on you," Kowalski replied. "Brick was close to you, wasn't he?"

Lucas nodded, his jaw tight.

"I'm very sorry," Kowalski said gently. "But the girl... Lucas, there's no evidence that she, or that man--Gabriel Petra-- were ever there."

"But they were!" Lucas shouted.

"I believe you," Kowalski said gently. "What I mean is, there must be something else going on here. They just... vanished. No one saw them leave, and we had the place surrounded."

Lucas narrowed his eyes. What kind of powers could this girl have?

"Her name is Romana," he said. "And she's like me."

"How? What do you mean?"

"She has powers. I felt her in my head as she controlled Bernard. She spoke through him, forcing him to talk, before she... she..."

Lucas trailed off, a knot forming in his throat.

"She entered his mind?" Kowalski asked, disturbed. "How could she do that?"

Lucas hesitated. He'd forgotten that he never told Kowalski about his psychic connection with Bernard.

"Yes. She destroyed it. I watched her do it. I felt it, too. She was stronger than me; I tried to fight her, but her powers were different than mine. She knew what to do; she was so fast. She attacked my body and mind at the same time; I couldn't do anything about it."

"She's had training," Kowalski interjected, his eyes flinty. "This changes everything. You're right, she must be an android, like you, which means what we feared most has come true: they made more than one. That may explain why they were so difficult to track--if they had someone like you on their side. And if they made more than one, it's likely they made more than two. They could have a whole army for all we know. Lucas, you may be our only hope."

"You didn't see the fight; they nearly killed me. They would have, if you hadn't shown up when you did. I don't stand a chance against her. What can I do?"

"We'll train you, of course--as best we can, anyway. We still don't know what they're up to, but we'll be ready for anything. And it's more important than ever that we keep you safe; that will be our first priority."

"I'm not a soldier."

"You are now. You don't have a choice; you're the only chance we have."

Lucas stared, mouth agape. He had begun to believe that Kowalski really understood him, that he cared for him. But it seemed that was all gone now; he was all business.

"Kowalski, there's something else," Lucas said. "When I mentioned Dr. Lytton, Petra reacted funny. He got angry, like I had struck a nerve. That has to mean something, right?"

Kowalski nodded.

"Maybe," he said. "Like what?"

"I don't know. Maybe he's bitter; maybe he and Dr. Lytton didn't get along. We should try to find him; maybe he could help us. If anyone knows how to stop someone like Romana, it would be him, right?"

"We've searched for him for fifteen years," Kowalski replied. "Either he's gone deep underground, or he's dead. But if you want to take a crack at it, be my guest."

He stood up cautiously, one hand on his tender side.

"Take a few days to rest and recuperate," he said grimly. "I'll call you when it's time to begin. In the meantime, you know what to do."

"I do?" Lucas queried.

Kowalski lowered his brows.

"Ensure that none of this reaches the public," he said. "They can't know about any of it. This war must be fought quietly and secretly. I'm counting on you."

"Of course," Lucas mumbled.

"Good."

He started toward the door, then paused. His face softened slightly as he looked back.

"You've done well," he said, then left.

Lucas sat by himself, staring at the floor. It had only been a few hours since Bernard had died, yet he felt that he was supposed to have already moved on, somehow. How could he? None of this was fair. He didn't ask for these powers, or to be the property of a bloodthirsty, cold-hearted terrorist like Gabriel Petra.

How am I supposed to stop him? He's got Romana, and I'm just me.

Discouraged, he closed his eyes and let his mind open. At least he could do his job. The bus bombing was obviously the biggest headline. It occurred to him that the Rising must have planned it that way. The media said that police had no leads as to who was responsible. Some reports said that a boy was seen in the street and stopped the bus with his bare hands, but these were limited to the tabloids. A few of them claimed that he floated up into the sky afterwards, vanishing into the clouds. There was only one mention of the tragedy at his apartment; it was labeled a robbery gone wrong, leading to a hostage situation and a standoff with the police. No names were given, not even Bernard's. Lucas imagined his family, torn apart with grief. No one would ever know the truth of how he died.

Lucas drifted off to sleep, his clothes still on. He awoke several hours later, cold and dehydrated. It was dark, and quiet outside his room. He sat up to undress and kick off his shoes, then felt a buzz inside his head - a humming sensation, like a swarm of bees inside his skull.

That was when he noticed the silhouette of the girl against the window: her slim form, and two pinpricks of light reflected in her eyes.

He brought his legs underneath him, coiled to spring. But he hesitated; he was dazed, and usure he was really seeing her.

We will come for you, Lucas, her voice hummed in his ear. *There is nowhere you can run where we won't find you.*

His senses shocked, he leapt off the bed, lightning crackling, but he was halted in the air by an invisible force.

I've come only to give you a message, she continued, unperturbed. *There is more at stake here than you know. The path you choose will affect the lives of countless others. If you choose to join us, people may die, but it will be a small price to pay for peace and harmony among nations. But a battle between you and me could lead to thousands of lives lost, and for what? Continued war, and more death. I am pleading with you to make your choice wisely, Lucas. Don't let your selfishness blind you to the possibilities. You could be apart of something truly great.*

Someone pounded on the door. Lucas heard his mother's voice calling his name. The door shook as the doorknob twisted, but Romana was holding it closed with her invisible field. Her pale hands were outstretched, almost glowing in the moonlight. Lucas tried to call out, but he couldn't speak. He hung motionless, five feet above the carpet.

I don't want to fight you, she said emphatically.

I don't know what you want, Lucas fired back. *But I'll never help you. You killed my friend. You and all the rest of the Rising are nothing more than monsters.*

Open your eyes, and you may feel differently, she said, and Lucas felt sympathy travel across their link. *When you are ready to make your choice, you know how to find me.*

Don't hold your breath, he hissed.

The air sparked and fizzled, and just like that, Romana was gone. Lucas didn't have time to blink before he dropped like deadweight to the floor, and the air was forced out of his lungs. The door opened, and his CIA security rushed in.

"Are you hurt? What happened?" they asked.

Lucas stared into the open air. He tasted something metallic, and felt the remnant of an electrical charge that made the hairs on his arms stand on end.

"I'm fine," he answered.

There's work to be done.

The End

CPSIA information can be obtained
at www.ICGtesting.com
Printed in the USA
FSHW02n1553110718
50295FS